RESCUE

JENNIFER A. NIELSEN

RESCUE

SCHOLASTIC INC.

Text copyright © 2021 by Jennifer A. Nielsen
Map by Jim McMahon, © 2021 Scholastic Inc.
Photo on page 384 courtesy of SWNS.

This book was originally published by Scholastic Press in 2021.

ISBN 978-1-338-62101-3

10 9 8 7 6 5 4 3 2 1   22 23 24 25 26

Printed in the U.S.A. 40
This edition first printing 2022

Book design by Christopher Stengel

To my grandfathers, Bernell and Lennart,
Veterans of World War II.
Heroes.

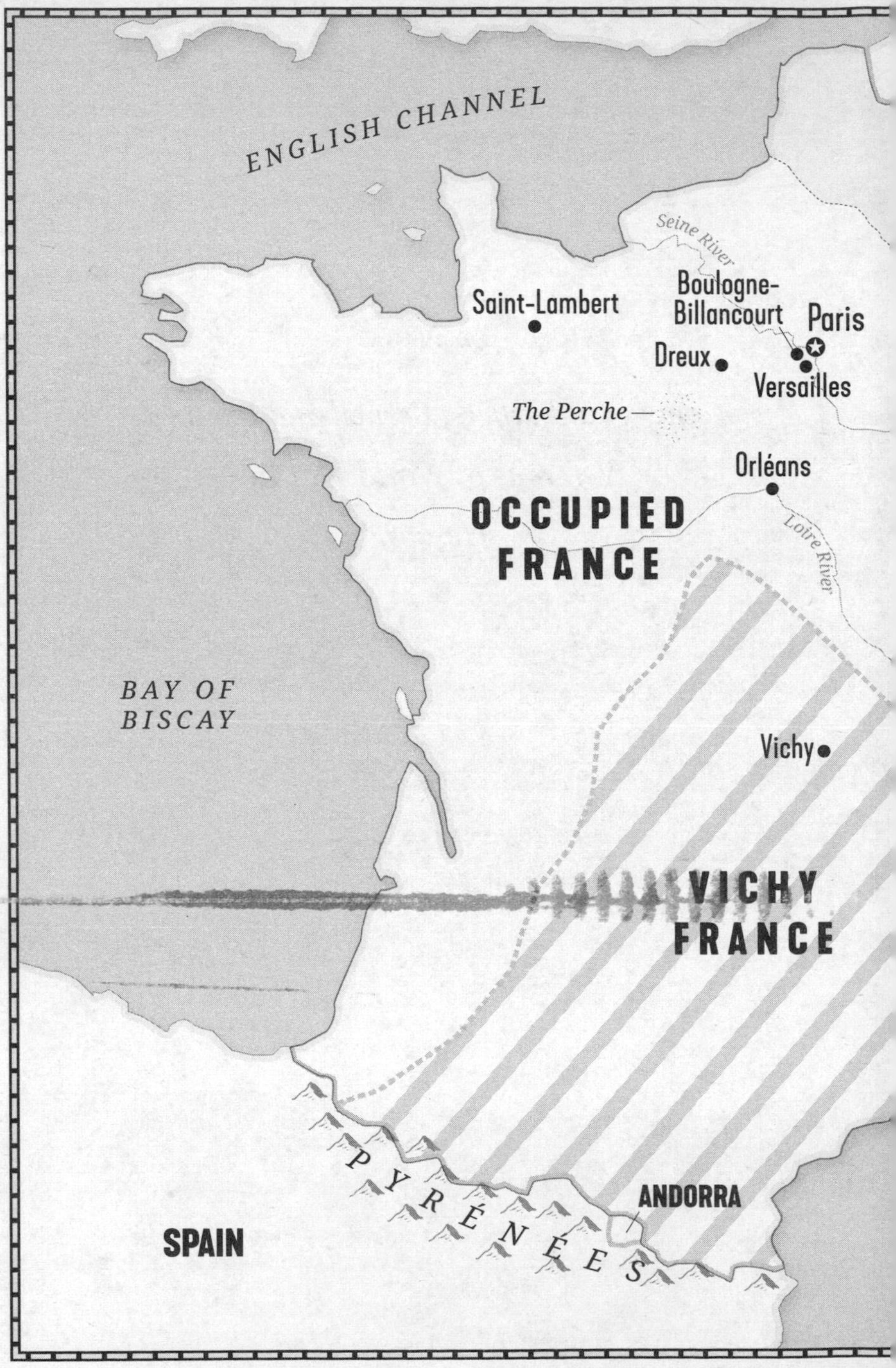
ENGLISH CHANNEL
Seine River
Saint-Lambert
Boulogne-
Billancourt
Paris
Dreux
Versailles
The Perche
Orléans
OCCUPIED
FRANCE
Loire River
BAY OF
BISCAY
Vichy
VICHY
FRANCE
PYRÉNÉES
ANDORRA
SPAIN

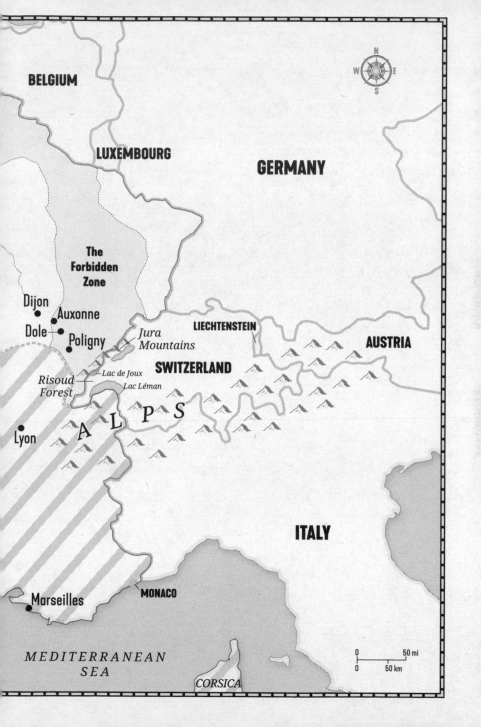

PROLOGUE

Papa stood at the gate by the road and waved goodbye.

He wanted me to wave back at him, but I didn't. I couldn't. Even if I tried, I couldn't make myself smile and send him off as if he were only going for a simple walk.

Not going to war.

Maman stood beside me, her arm tight around my shoulder. "One day you will understand this, Meggie. France needs him now."

No, *we* needed him! What if the war came deeper into France—what if it came to this same gate—and he wasn't here to protect us?

He wouldn't be here. I did understand that. If the Nazis came, we would have to defend ourselves.

All this had happened so fast. Four days ago, as German troops began lining our border, Papa received a telegram from London, one that had kept him and Maman awake all night in a whispered conversation I wasn't supposed to hear. I did catch a few words: resistance . . . sacrifice . . . secret.

Two days later, on the eve of the invasion, we abandoned our home near the German border and fled to an area known as the Perche to stay with Grandmère on her farm. She lived much farther from the border, and we hoped that would be safer.

I doubted anywhere was safe. Because only one day after the Germans stormed through our border, Papa was leaving us.

And no, I could not understand that. So I didn't wave.

It was something I would regret every single day that followed.

CHAPTER
ONE

Friday, February 27, 1942

I hadn't seen my father for 657 days. From this exact moment, that is one year, nine months, two weeks, four days, and one hour. That's how long it had been since I had not waved goodbye. In 657 days, we had not heard anything about him . . . or from him.

Maman believed that Papa was still alive, and so did Grandmère. I was beginning to have doubts.

But I never said that aloud. Life for our family was difficult enough without me bringing up the fact that if he could, Papa would have written us by now. Besides, we were hardly the only family wondering what had become of their loved ones.

On May 10, 1940, Germany invaded France. They bypassed our thin lines of defense on the border, then rolled through the country in a blitzkrieg—a lightning war. Within two months, France surrendered. Germany took possession of our land, our resources, and nearly two million French soldiers, who became prisoners of war, almost overnight. Maybe Papa had been taken too. Or maybe something worse had happened.

But I didn't want to think about that. I couldn't, because today I had a job to do. I entered it in my journal with the codename FEMALE LONG THROW. If the journal was ever found, most people would think I had spent my day practicing how far I could throw a ball, but that wasn't even close to the truth. The real message would only be found by unscrambling the letters.

Maman didn't know my real plans for the day. She'd be furious if she did, and for good reason. If I were caught by the Nazis, they wouldn't care that I was only twelve. An enemy was an enemy. And all enemies must be stopped.

That was how I thought of them too. An enemy that must be stopped.

Maman believed my only plan was going into town to sell our extra food. It was illegal and risky to sell on the black market, but also necessary. There wasn't enough food legally available in France for everyone who was hungry, especially in the cities. People here had to choose between hunger and breaking the law.

My family's choice was whether to supply that food. Our prices were higher than what a person could find in the stores, but that was the problem—too often, the store shelves were empty.

People were angry about the prices we charged, but they didn't understand how expensive it was to run a farm during wartime. Maman was saving every franc that she could in hopes of getting us out of France. These last two years of the German occupation had been difficult.

No, not difficult. That wasn't the right word at all.

They had been devastating.

When the war first broke out, Papa had wanted to get us out of France. He planned to bring us to England with him, but Maman worried that England wouldn't be any safer than France. Then the telegram came from London, and all the plans changed.

Papa left for the war.

He didn't go as a soldier, but I knew by the worry on Maman's face that he was in the battles somehow. The only thing I could think was that he must be part of the resistance.

That was why I helped the resistance. It felt like I was helping Papa too.

Thus, the Female Long Throw.

"Meggie, are you ready to go?" Maman called from the back door of the house. She's French, so it sounds like M'gee when she pronounces my name, but I loved that. Papa is British. In public, he called me Margaret, but when it was only him and me, he called me Daisy, because the French word for the daisy flower is *marguerite*. I especially loved that.

"Almost ready, Maman," I called back.

I finished my entry for the day and set the journal into the small hole Papa had dug out beneath the floor of Grandmère's barn before he left.

My pencil went on top of the journal, and then I returned the two pieces of barnwood flooring where they belonged. As always, I covered them with dust and straw to be sure that my hiding place looked the same as everywhere else.

In the distance, the church bells rang out the time, eight in the morning. I was late today. Some customers would already have begun arriving from Paris. I needed to be there to greet those I knew, the people I trusted. And I wanted to sell all my food before any newcomers could find me. Most of them were safe, but there would also be those who stole food out of desperation, or those who might report us to the authorities if they didn't like what we had to offer.

I didn't blame them when they did, not much. From the reports we heard on the radio, we were better off here in the forests of the Perche than in the cities, where they faced a stronger Nazi presence, sharp questions of loyalties, and where hunger, even starvation, was a constant threat.

I wouldn't have much to sell today. It was still cold outside, and so far, this seemed to be the kind of winter that would linger, trying to stretch as far into spring as possible. Maman said that while we needed the money, we also needed food for ourselves until the first harvest came in. We wouldn't eat like the wealthy, or like the Germans did in our pubs and restaurants. But I held back enough food that we wouldn't starve either.

I tried not to think about my hunger as I chose several of the softer potatoes for today, those that wouldn't last much longer. Even if they were old and rubbery, they'd still sell. Some people had resorted to grinding acorns to make coffee and boiling pumpkins to create a sugar substitute. By comparison, a rubbery old potato was fine dining.

I finished packing my bag, covering our potatoes with a few schoolbooks, which was only for show. I didn't see the point in studying the German-approved books that we were now supposed to read. It was little more than propaganda, which I'd become numb to long ago. Pro-German stories flooded through the radio waves until my ears ached with them; their phony pictures and slogans were plastered on posters pasted up all over town, so that I saw them when I shut my eyes. The German propaganda was even drummed into our heads in newsreels on our rare trips to the movie theater.

But I put the books in my bag anyway. If a German tried to search my bag and found a book he approved of, then he'd send me on my way rather than hold me for further questioning. I had to be smart about these things. I'd had to grow up quickly over the last two years and learn to take care of myself. Most of the time, I felt older than my age.

I picked up my bag and slung it over one shoulder, then stood up straight, as Maman had taught me.

"Never look as though you're carrying anything heavy. Never make anyone curious about you." She had warned me of this so often, I never failed to hear her words in my head whenever I left to sell food.

Maman was waiting at the door as I left the barn, and I couldn't help but stare. Most people did. She was a beautiful woman—everyone said so. I doubted I'd ever grow up to be as beautiful as she was, but few people ever could be. My hair was brownish, without actually being brown, and my eyes changed with the light, or the colors I wore. I hoped that made it harder for people to identify me, or to remember my face. That was important, because I had my father's courage, and these days, courage mattered most to me.

As I came closer, Maman gave me one of her pretend smiles, and even that quickly faded.

"You will sell the food and come home quickly?"

"Yes, Maman, I promise." Maman and I used to sell together, but last summer, we decided it was less suspicious if I worked alone. So far, I had managed fine on my own.

"I have a few errands to do today. Be sure to do your afternoon chores."

My brow wrinkled. "What errands?" Maman hesitated

and I glanced behind her, spotting a brown suitcase on our tile floor. I'd seen it before, but Grandmère had told me not to be curious about something better left to adults. Since then, I'd been more curious than ever. I knew only one thing about it: The suitcase was heavy, but whenever Maman left the house with it, she'd stand straight and tall as if there were only feathers inside.

Just in case someone was watching.

"These errands are nothing to worry about." There was an edge to her voice that made my gut twist into knots. I wanted to believe her—I *needed* to believe her—but I was already worried, and she hadn't even left the house.

Maman must have seen my worry, for she brushed a hand over my hair and smiled. "There are things to be done, that's all."

Things to be done? What was that supposed to mean?

Maman often talked that way lately, in bundles of words that said nothing whatsoever, giving long explanations without a hint of information. She didn't want me to know her plans for the day.

As much as I didn't want her to know mine, I supposed.

Maman gave me a quick hug. "After I return, we'll plan a fun evening together. Perhaps you can solve the last of your father's codes."

My muscles tightened. "No, Maman, I'm saving that one until he comes home."

Maman nodded as if she understood more than I was willing to say. She kissed my cheek, then fastened the top button of my coat. "Be safe, come home quickly."

"You too," I replied.

I didn't know what Maman's errand would be: maybe buying supplies off the black market that we needed, or selling something bigger than a few potatoes. But I did know what my plans were, and I had to stay focused on them.

I had the Female Long Throw.

TWO

Rule: *Trust is earned, not given.*

One of our family's rules for the black market was not to sell to strangers, or *les inconnus*, as my grandmother called them: the unknowns.

"The Great War taught me more than I wished to know about human nature," Grandmère often said. "War makes people desperate. Good people will sometimes do bad things if it's the only way to survive. We only sell to those we know and trust. Not *les inconnus*."

So once I got into town, I didn't stay out in the open. Our usual customers knew I'd be waiting inside an abandoned little building that had been a flower shop before the war. I kept my bag beneath the counter, opened one of the schoolbooks, and pretended to read.

"*Bonjour,*" a woman said, poking her head inside the shop. I didn't know her name, and she didn't know mine—we were both safer that way—but I did know she was kind and had two young children. "What are you reading today?"

"Nothing too interesting," I replied. "Just information about potatoes."

She smiled. This was our usual code. "I'd find that very interesting." She passed me forty francs. "What can you share with me for that much money?"

"Nine things I've learned." It should be eight, but I thought of her young children. We could spare one extra potato.

Now the woman's smile faded into a frown. "Forty francs is good money. Give me twelve potatoes, at least."

I shook my head. "I'm sorry, but those are the prices."

"They're higher than when I last came here. This is robbery."

A pit formed in my stomach. This woman had shifted so suddenly to anger, and to making accusations that simply weren't true. I shook my head again. "It's late winter. We have shortages of our own."

"And that gives you the right to charge us more?" she snapped. "I should report you to the Germans!"

I didn't think she would. Even if she was angry with me, or wanted revenge, she still needed the food we provided.

"The city starves, while countryfolk count their money." She huffed but held out her bag anyway.

Without a word, I put the nine potatoes into her bag, and she closed it up tight and left, leaving me feeling awful. She truly was a kind woman, so if she had become angry with me so easily, things must have become very difficult at home.

And while I wished I could have given her all my potatoes, her visit was soon followed by another woman, whose family was just as hungry. "We are grateful for every single bite," she whispered.

That was followed by the entry of a boy I didn't know, an *inconnu*.

He looked a little older than me and was definitely taller, with blond hair and blue eyes, and what appeared as an easy smile. But I wouldn't be fooled by his friendly appearance. I wouldn't do business with him. All he would ever know was that I was here, reading my book.

I glanced down at the pages, trying to focus on the words. It wasn't working.

"Do you have anything to sell?" His words were in French, but the accent wasn't quite right. He wasn't from France, but he was trying to sound as if he were.

I tilted my head. "No, I'm sorry."

"My parents and I are hungry. We've just arrived into town—"

"By car?"

He hesitated. "No. Another way. Please, if you have anything to spare, I will make it up to you one day, I promise."

When I said nothing, he quickly added, "In fact, I'll help you now. Several German soldiers arrived in town a few minutes ago, so you ought to be careful going home. They are still in the area."

If that was true, then I couldn't remain here any longer. I had work to do, a very different kind of work. I picked up my bag and put the schoolbook on the top again. *"Merci,"* I said. "I must go now."

"Jakob." He quickly added, "That's my name. What is yours?"

I shook my head at him, refusing to answer, then walked past him to leave the little building. I opened the door, quietly huffed, then closed it again. He really did look hungry. I reached into my bag and pulled out three potatoes, which I offered to him. He probably needed them more than we did.

Jakob took them with a humble nod, then cradled them against his chest as if they were precious gems. They were no gems, but this was wartime, and a single bite of food was worth more than any shiny rock.

"If I can ever help you, all you must do is ask," Jakob said.

I smiled at him, just a little, then turned and left the little building. He seemed nice, but he was still an *inconnu*.

And as Maman had so frequently reminded me, never ask help from a stranger.

CHAPTER
THREE

Rule: *A good agent can think their way out of any situation.*

Just as Jakob had said, there were several German soldiers in the road, dressed in grayish-green coats with fur linings around the neck and pants of the same Nazi green that were tucked into tall black boots. They shouted orders at one another as they unloaded their bags and supplies from large trucks. That concerned me. It appeared they intended to remain here for a while.

I could guess why.

Because of its thick forests and rolling hills, the Perche was the perfect place for resistance groups to hide. We called them partisans. They conducted raids and ambushes and helped to gather information to be sent back to the Allies still fighting this war. The Germans had a different word for the partisans. They called them terrorists.

Which had to be the reason they were here today.

Six weeks after the invasion, France surrendered, and the Germans immediately carved up our country, taking what they considered the best areas, or the most strategic places.

The Perche was in the part of France known as the Occupied Zone, which meant we were directly governed by the Germans.

Grandmère often described the Perche as it had been before the war: quiet and peaceful, a large forested region made of up small villages where everyone knew everyone else and helped one another as needed on their farms. She believed the best of people lived here.

The Occupied Zone included great cities such as Paris, Nantes, and Bordeaux, and the wealth of our farmland and mines.

Free France was to the south, but Maman said life there wasn't any easier than ours. "What's the difference between a government here run by the Germans or a government there that bows to the Germans' every demand?" she asked.

The Alsace-Lorraine region in the northeast had been quickly annexed into Germany. Almost overnight, the people there were treated as if they were now, and always had been, Germans.

Between Alsace-Lorraine and the rest of France was a Reserved Zone, meant for future German settlement. We called it the Forbidden Zone.

Until the war, my family had lived only fifty kilometers from the Forbidden Zone, near Auxonne, a small township only a couple of hours by car from the Swiss border. Farther east from Auxonne, the hills rolled higher, gradually becoming steep mountains and narrow valleys. There, the trees grew tall and thick and even more beautiful than here.

We had to leave because of the Germans. And now they were here.

Their presence surely meant they expected trouble or were about to cause some. I wouldn't have come into town today if I had known there would be so many. I certainly would not have brought food for the black market.

But I had to remember my mission: Help the resistance, help my father. Do my part for France. There was a lot I could do.

Because the Germans didn't usually suspect children.

Which is why I could do the Female Long Throw. Unscrambled, it read: Follow the German.

I was looking for one particular officer, Lieutenant Becker, who had arrived several days ago. The partisans were worried about him. He was described as a man with a mask—on the outside appearing polite and friendly, but when crossed, turning cruel and dangerous. It was said that he volunteered for the cold-blooded jobs, those that even the worst of other soldiers wanted nothing to do with.

Finally, I found Lieutenant Becker, sipping coffee in a

café in the town square. From a distance, he seemed pleasant enough, but once I entered, he briefly glanced my way and my heart skipped a beat. I'd seen death in his eyes; he had caused it. He craved more of it. Every part of me wanted to run away; I even turned back to the street. Then I remembered why I was here, that I needed to be here. So I walked past the lieutenant and another man seated beside him and sat in the back of the room. I pulled out one of my schoolbooks and kept my eyes low while listening to everything they said.

"How many times must we kick these people before they learn to stay down?" he asked in German. When rumors started of a coming war, my parents insisted I learn German. They felt it would give me an advantage, though they could not have had any idea how I would use it.

His companion was thin enough that his face appeared to be little more than bones covered in flesh, giving him a cruel look. He said, "We had hoped this past winter would freeze the partisans out of the forests. But if we succeed today, we will control the Perche anyway."

"We will find her today. And him." Lieutenant Becker impatiently tapped the table. "Let's join the others and organize a search."

My head tilted toward the soldiers. Who, exactly, were they searching for?

The lieutenant threw some coins on the table, then stood with his companion, and they walked out the door.

I couldn't follow too closely—that would be obvious. And it was a cold day, so it wouldn't make sense to appear as though I were casually wandering the streets.

I passed the table where the officers had been and smiled at the excuse I'd been offered. They had overpaid for their drinks.

With a nod from the shopkeeper, I picked up the extra coin and began to follow the men farther into town. Not too close—I wanted to draw this out as long as possible and see where they were going.

They walked side by side down the center of the road, letting the occasional motorbike or wagon move aside for them. They appeared to be headed toward the church, but just before reaching the steps, Lieutenant Becker turned and stared directly at me. His eyes were sharp and cold enough to send a chill into my bones.

"Come here, girl!" he ordered, placing one hand on his pistol.

That movement, and his stern expression, held me frozen in fear. I had never spoken directly to a Nazi before and everything I thought I'd say in such a moment, every lie I'd ever planned out, melted inside my head until the only thing left was the truth.

A truth that would get me immediately arrested—or shot.

I stumbled forward, my legs obeying an order my brain could barely comprehend.

"Why are you following us?" he asked.

I heard the truth echo in my thoughts. *I'm following you so that I can send a secret signal to the partisans not to come into town today.*

"Well? Speak, girl!"

Then, suddenly, my mouth opened, and the words began to spill out in German. "I'm . . . following you . . . sir . . . so that I can . . ." I swallowed hard and clenched my fist, then remembered the coin inside it. I held it up to him. "So that I can return this. You paid too much at the shop."

He studied me a moment, then took the coin from my hand. "You speak the mother language very well. What's in that bag you carry?"

"Books." I slid the strap off my shoulder, debating whether to tell him about the potatoes. If I told him, he'd suspect my involvement in the black market. But if I didn't tell him, and he found them himself, it would be much worse. "And a few potatoes," I added.

"Why do you have potatoes here in town? If you got them from the black market—"

"No, no." I had four left, which I pulled from my bag to show him. "We grow them on our farm. They're a gift . . . for you."

He took the potatoes. "That is very generous, *danke*." I turned to leave, but he added, "Wait. Come back."

I closed my eyes, summoning enough courage to turn and face him again. When I did, the coin was still in his other hand. "Let this be my gift to you, for the potatoes."

My fingers folded around it and I thanked him, though even as I spoke, I couldn't remember if I was thanking him in my language or in his. I hoped it was his.

He patted my arm, then turned with his companion to continue up the steps. When the church doors opened, I saw the room crowded with Nazi soldiers, a sea of camouflage uniforms and red badges. They were here to search for *her* and for *him*.

Whoever they were, my heart crashed against my chest.

The war had just come to the Perche.

FOUR

Rule: *Codes will both protect you and reveal you.*

The system for sending a message to the partisans was simple, but also very precise. I'd been taught by a girl named Yvonne who worked for resistance movements all over the country.

"If you make any mistakes, the partisans will suspect the Germans have interfered and will ignore the message," she had warned me.

All signals were to be exchanged at a brick wall on the edge of the forest to the north. The wall could be readily seen from the safety of the thick trees and was easy for me to reach from town.

During wintertime, our arranged signal was based on snowballs when snow was available, or bundles of twigs when it was not.

A single snowball meant nothing to either of us. Anyone could form a snowball and happen to leave it on the brick wall. An even number of snowballs meant there was no new information. Any odd number of snowballs signaled that a message was waiting for them. The greater number of snowballs, the greater the threat.

Today I made seven and spaced them evenly apart so that they could easily be counted from a distance. I used a different kind of paper each day, and today's was a torn piece of newspaper from the café. With a small pencil, I wrote the message in an English code that Yvonne had taught me.

Have Evelyn in Place for Show.

For this code, only the first letter of each word mattered, and each letter stood for a completely different word.

The H of the first word meant HIDE.

The E in Evelyn meant ENEMY.

The P was for the PERCHE.

The S was for SEARCHES.

I was telling the partisans: Hide. Enemy in Perche for Searches.

I crumpled up the newspaper, then stuffed it in the cavity of the wall behind a loose brick. Papa had used that same trick to hide things back in our old home. Many of our valuables were still stored behind bricks in the walls of our house, until we could return for them.

Each day, someone was sent to view the brick wall. Today, they would leave the shelter of the forest to retrieve my note, but it would be worth the risk. They needed to get everyone into hiding before the searches began.

Then I bundled my coat around me and hurried home, breathing more easily once I rounded the corner to our property. In the winter, snow balanced on the limbs of our trees, creating a beautiful patchwork of brown and white against our blue skies. But spring was my favorite season, when the first green buds peeked out, ready to unfold new leaves and blossoms, when the world around me began to awaken once again. I hoped spring would come soon.

But I hadn't taken more than a few steps onto the property before I realized it was too soon to relax. The barn door was ajar. I was always careful to close the door, and I was sure I had done so this morning. Maybe Maman or Grandmère came in after I'd left for town.

I walked toward the door to close the latch, then saw something in the snow. Drops of blood. Those definitely hadn't been there before.

I lowered my sack to the ground, then stared at the barn for what felt like a very long time, debating what to do. Someone must have entered the barn other than Maman or

Grandmère. The blood looked fresh, which meant they were probably still inside.

My heart drummed against my chest, and I was certain whoever was inside the barn could hear it. No matter how softly my feet landed on the snowy path, surely they already knew I was coming.

As I walked, I dropped handfuls of loose snow over each speck of blood. Leaning against the barn door was an old shovel that I sometimes used to clear a path when the snow fell too deep. Careful not to make more noise than was necessary, I picked up the shovel and readied myself to take a swing at the intruder.

For the longest time, I stood at the door, my feet like lead, refusing to obey my command to walk inside. My muscles felt frozen until, finally, I began to feel the shovel's weight and knew I'd either have to lower it and run away, or go inside.

I had to face whoever was inside. Grandmère was alone inside the house. She was too frail to help me attack the intruder, and we wouldn't abandon our farm to whoever was in there.

That's what my decision finally came to: the realization that I had no choice other than to go inside, confront the intruder, and force him to leave.

Maybe it was only a partisan, someone who had become

too cold and needed a warmer place to stay. But somehow, I knew it wasn't.

And there was blood.

I took a deep breath, whispered a prayer that I hoped would be heard, and opened the barn door, yelling in French, "Whoever is in here, you'd better leave while you still can!"

CHAPTER

FIVE

Rule: *When in need of a weapon, begin with what is around you.*

Nobody answered. Not at first.

I was halfway through yelling the threat again when a voice called back in English, "I'm British. *Parlez-vous anglais?*"

With a British father, of course I spoke English, though he didn't have to know that. So I only replied, "*Un petit peu.*" A little bit.

He grunted, then continued in English, speaking slower than was necessary. "My name is Captain Henry Stewart, with the Royal Air Force."

What was an Air Force pilot doing in the Perche?

And although his accent sounded as real as my father's, that still didn't mean I could trust him. The partisans had taught me to suspect everyone. Maybe he was a German spy, one who'd practiced the British language and accent. If he was, better that I find out now.

"If you're from England, you must know the best place in London to buy bread pudding." I began stepping around the barn toward the sound of his voice, keeping my shovel ready.

"That's a matter of opinion," he replied. "I prefer the puddings of Birmingham to any of those in London."

I rolled my eyes, irritated with myself. Anyone could have answered that question. Taking a few more steps, I asked, "And how close is Birmingham to Scratchy Bottom?"

Silence. Then, "Are you sure that's the name of a place? Or did you only hear it in the schoolyard?"

I hesitated. "I think it's a real place. My father told me about it."

"If you're not sure, then maybe *you* are the German spy. I'm not one of them, if that's what you're thinking. Now will you please come around the corner and help me?"

I rounded the corner to see a man in a dark gray British uniform, half lying on a pile of straw. He was probably near my father's age, though his hair was darker and his eyes were brown. But I quickly noticed his injuries, which were worse than I had expected. His uniform along his middle was soaked in blood. Pain was etched into the lines of his face, and he seemed to be having trouble keeping his eyes open.

I lowered my shovel. "Maybe you are a spy. That blood doesn't look a bit real."

He said nothing to that, only laid his head back down on the straw. "What's your name?"

"Sophie."

He closed his eyes, accepting my lie as easily as I'd told it. "Corn syrup, cornstarch, food coloring. How many of those ingredients do you have?"

I shrugged. "Cornstarch, I think. You can't get the other items during the war."

"Nor can I. And I'd need a lot of it to create fake blood, so without that option, I just had to use my own."

My tone softened. "How did you get hurt?"

Captain Stewart let out a slow sigh, perhaps relieved that I finally believed him. "For now, I need to get this injury bandaged, and I'm terribly hungry. Will you help me, Sophie?"

I nodded. "Wait here." I brought the shovel out with me and returned it to leaning against the wall of the barn, then hurried to the house.

"You're later than usual today, Meggie." Grandmère had been stirring a stew over the fire but paused to look at me when I entered.

"I came back as soon as I could," I told her, adopting Maman's method of using a lot of words to say almost nothing at all. Which reminded me . . . "Has Maman returned?"

It was early afternoon. No errand should have taken her this long.

"Not yet." Grandmère saw my hopeful expression fall. "Your mother will be fine," she whispered. "The spirit of a French woman cannot be conquered."

That was true; our spirits would live forever.

But the body can die.

It was a horrible thought, one I knew I shouldn't have. One that twisted my gut and made my fists clench. I didn't want to think that way, but I'd seen for myself what could happen if a Nazi soldier became angry with someone. I just had to hope that wherever Maman was right now, no Nazis were there. Or that her errands would not anger them.

"I made a stew," Grandmère said. "It's thinner than I would have wanted, but the taste is good and it's a better meal than what many others will have today." She stirred the pot again, then asked, "Did you have any problems out there?"

"What?" I was thinking so much of Captain Stewart that I couldn't quite remember what problems she might have been asking about. I pulled out the money I had earned from the sale of potatoes and gave it to her. "There is one problem. I . . ." My mind raced. "Could you get your sewing kit? A button on my coat has come loose."

Grandmère frowned. Buttons were hard to come by during the war, so she would not risk losing a single one.

When she went upstairs for her kit, I opened the cupboard beneath the sink and pulled out an armful of rags, then quickly dished up a bowl of thin stew from a pot hanging over the fireplace. I was out the door only seconds later.

Captain Stewart was sitting up a little more when I returned to the barn. I gave him the bowl of stew, though he held it awkwardly at first. I couldn't understand why until he lifted the spoon to his mouth, and I realized his right arm was injured too. After a few bites, he switched hands and seemed to do better. He had a pistol against his side, but he appeared to be right-handed, so I knew he'd be slow even to draw his own weapon. A small shovel was strapped to one leg and the dirt on it appeared to be fresh. I wondered about that.

When he finished, I took the bowl but continued to stare at him, unsure of what to do next.

"Thank you for the stew." Captain Stewart grimaced as he shifted his weight on the straw. "It might be the best I've had since that time I was passing through Scratchy Bottom, England, in the far south of the country."

I smiled back at him. "I knew it was a real place."

He pointed to the rags still bundled under my arm. "Are those for me too?"

"Er . . . yes. But I don't know . . . I've never . . ."

"Just leave the rags here; I can wrap my own side. Who lives in your house?"

My eyes narrowed. "Why do you ask?"

"Don't be so suspicious. We're fighting the same enemy, remember? I'm looking for a woman named Sylvie Kenyon. Do you know her?"

A lump formed in my throat, and I only stared back at him.

Sylvie Kenyon was my mother. There was no reason why someone from the Royal Air Force should even know her name, much less come to inquire about her.

Rather than answer him, I asked, "Where's your plane, Captain Stewart?"

"It was shot down south of here. I managed to parachute out, but my landing wasn't the greatest, as you can see."

I began to think about what Lieutenant Becker had said when I was in town earlier today, about the search. Were all those Nazis here to search for Captain Stewart? Then my gut twisted. They were searching for a *him* and a *her*. Were they here to find my mother?

Captain Stewart pointed to the shovel strapped to his leg. "I saw you staring at this. If we have to parachute out of our plane, we use this to dig a hole to bury the parachute itself. We don't want the Germans to know where we landed and follow us."

But what if they had followed him? They'd come here!

My feet shuffled, but I dropped the rags near him and said, "I'd better return before my . . . before the people inside become anxious about where I've gone. I'll come out when it's time for evening chores and check on you."

"All right, but—" I stopped and turned back to him, waiting for the pain to fade from his face so he could continue. After several seconds, he spoke again. "Sophie, you won't turn me in, I hope."

No, of course I'd never do that. I knew we had to do everything possible to keep him safe, or even to keep him alive. But at what price to my family?

CHAPTER
SIX

Rule: *Never stop searching for answers.*

I f Grandmère was suspicious about why I had gone back
outside, she didn't say anything to me, and I certainly
wasn't ready to talk about such a big thing. I snuck Captain
Stewart's empty bowl into the sink when she wasn't looking.

She noticed the bowl a few minutes later. "Where did
that come from?" she asked.

The lie bunched up into my throat, so much that I knew
I'd choke on it if I didn't just spit it out. "I was so hungry, I
had to try some."

Her thin white brows furrowed. "When?"

"A while ago. You must not have seen me take some, but
it was delicious. The best stew I've had since . . ." I thought
about Captain Stewart out in the barn. It would be a cold
night. Somehow I'd need to get a blanket out to him. "It was

the best stew I've had since coming to live here with you, Grandmère."

Grandmère took great pride in her cooking, especially when she was forced to use fewer ingredients than she wanted. Her smile quickly faded as she said, "I had hoped we'd all eat together once your mother returned home. But if you've already eaten, I suppose it will just be her and me."

My shoulders slumped. I was incredibly hungry, and the stew really did smell as if it was one of my grandmother's best stews ever. But maybe hunger was what I deserved, after lying to her.

So instead of complaining, I asked, "Do you know when Maman might return from her errands?"

Grandmère glanced out the window, as if expecting my mother to be crossing the yard now. When she saw no one, her shoulders slumped too. I knew she was worried.

So was I.

"Your mother will return the first second that she is finished," Grandmère said. "In the meantime, I have an idea for you."

Obviously seeking a way to distract me, Grandmère pulled a tall glass jar off the shelf. I hadn't looked at it in months, and I didn't want to see it now.

"We must have hope." Every time she thought about Papa, those were Grandmère's words. She'd always made me want to believe it, but lately, her eyes said something different. She was losing hope for him.

So was I. Maybe there was no point in keeping this one last code unsolved.

For most of my life, Papa and I had shared a love of codes. Our game was to create something the other could not decipher. Neither of us yet had lost the game.

The day he left for the war, Papa had given me a tall jar of folded papers, each one with a different code. He believed he'd made enough papers for me to solve one code each week until he came home.

"You'll see," he'd said, as cheerful as he always was, "I'll be home just as you finish solving the last one."

Only one paper remained in the jar now.

I'd held on to this code for months, hoping to time the solution so that within seconds of putting the last letter into place, I'd hear a car approaching Grandmère's house with him inside. I'd run to him just as he raced toward me, both of us laughing and smiling. I'd fly into Papa's arms, then hug him so tight he would grunt for air. And I'd try very hard not to cry with happiness.

I couldn't begin to count the number of times I'd imagined it.

But that's all this ever was, a dream I'd too often imagined.

"I'm not in the mood to solve a code today, Grandmère," I mumbled.

"Your father will make new codes when he returns. Maybe after you solve this last one, you can begin creating codes for him. You still plan to be a cryptologist, no?"

Grandmère knew that as soon as I was old enough, I planned to get a job as a cryptologist in London, creating and deciphering codes to help with the war effort. For a long time that had seemed like such an exciting future. In the early months of the war, that was all I'd ever talked about. But now, after almost two long years, I just wanted everything to be over. I hated the idea that by the time I was old enough to work in London, this awful war still might not have ended.

Which was why I needed to help Captain Stewart. I couldn't sit here, distracting myself with a code. I had to help him.

But Grandmère had already pulled out the last folded paper and flattened it on the table in front of me. My mind was swirling in every direction—confused, worried, even frightened. If I did solve this code, it would feel like I was giving up on my father, like I knew he would not come home again.

I glanced down at the paper. Papa's final code was only two words: JAIMIE STAYED.

I didn't want to pick up the pencil, but now that I'd seen the code, my mind was already turning. Maybe I'd work on it, just a little.

I didn't waste time wondering who Jaimie was, because

that didn't matter. This was an anagram, I was sure of it. Which meant all I had to do was rearrange the letters to form new words, the message Papa wanted me to have. I found plenty of individual words:

MEAT. Since the war began, we'd had very little meat. On the rare occasions we did get some pork or chicken, we donated it to the partisans in the forest. They needed it more than we did.

DATE. Such as June 24, 1940, the date that France fell to the Germans. Or one day later, the twenty-fifth, when France was divided between the Free Zone to the south and the Occupied Zone, where I lived. Or some date in the future when all this would end. I prayed day and night that it would end with Allied victory, with freedom.

Other words were there too: YEAST, TIDY, STYMIED, as in, Papa's puzzle had me stymied—I put my pencil down, frustrated. Even if one of those words was correct, the remaining letters couldn't be formed into any other words.

Determined to find a solution, I tried again, this time finding a word that I crossed out as soon as I wrote it: DIE. If that word was in the solution to Papa's anagram, I wanted nothing to do with it.

Finally, I did work out one phrase that used every letter, but I had no idea what it meant: MY IDEA IS A JET.

If I'd done it correctly, then the solution to this code was another code of its own. What did it mean?

SEVEN

Rule: *When a secret is shared, it is no longer a secret.*

Frustrated, I set down the pencil. "I can't solve this one."

"Of course you can, but maybe not today." Grandmère pursed her lips. "I know that your heart wants to be in the fresh air right now. How many times have you glanced outside? Would you see to milking the cow?" Eagerly, I jumped up and started toward the door. She added, "Leave your coat here while I fix that button. You can wear a few layers of your other clothes for now."

My heart leapt. Grandmère had not only given me an excuse to be outside, but also a reason to go upstairs first.

I gave her my coat, being sure to tug hard on the threads of the lowest button as I did, then hurried up the stairs. Once inside my room, I opened the window and tossed out a blanket from my bed. I threw on a few layers of clothes, then went downstairs again.

Grandmère had turned on the radio, always tuned to the London broadcasts, and was in her favorite chair to sew the button. Two things worked to my advantage: her poor hearing, and the position of her chair, facing away from the kitchen. My mother had left some rolled crepes out on the counter. I grabbed two and snuck out the door. My next stop was to retrieve the blanket from beneath my window. It had become caught on the lower branches of a tree, but after a few hard tugs, and several broken twigs, the blanket came loose, and I dragged it to the barn.

I stopped at the barn door and knocked. There was no answer, so I quietly called, "Captain Stewart?" When he answered, I entered.

I noticed a bulge around his middle and assumed that was where he had wrapped the rags I'd brought out for bandages. He was still lying in the middle of our stack of straw, but the bits that had been stained with his blood were gone. I wondered what he had done with them.

His eyes immediately flew to the crepes in my hand. "Are those for me?"

They were filled with apple jelly, so I knew how good they would be, and how rare a treat this would be anywhere in France. One of them had been meant for me, in place of the supper I would no longer eat. But even from here, I could practically see his mouth watering, so I handed both of them over, along with the blanket. He ate both crepes in only six bites, then smiled. "*Merci*, Sophie. I don't think I've ever tasted anything so delicious."

"Where is the dirty straw that you were lying on?" I asked. If he had been foolish enough to toss it outside, I would have to retrieve it before it was seen.

He frowned back at me. "I looked for a place to hide it here in the barn. I found a few loose floorboards—"

My heart sank. I knew exactly where this conversation was going.

From inside his jacket, Captain Stewart pulled out my journal. My record of my father and my daily goals since they had left.

"Normally, I wouldn't invade your privacy," he said. "But the Nazis wouldn't hesitate, so neither will I."

I froze as Captain Stewart opened the journal to the entry I had made earlier that morning. He pointed to the anagram I had created for it: Female Long Throw.

"This one has hundreds of possible solutions," he began. "Assuming it's a simple code, I can narrow it down to words that make sense on their own. So 'Lemon Glow Father' is out." His eyes narrowed. "But what about, 'We forgot hall men'? Who are the hall men?"

I shook my head. "There's no such thing."

"No, there isn't. But perhaps this code is giving you instructions regarding a crashed plane nearby: 'Low Flange, Rot Hem.'"

I stepped back, becoming genuinely frightened by his tone. "I don't even know what that means!"

"A flange connects two separate pieces of a plane, holding them together. But if the seam—or its *hem*—were to go rotten, the plane would come apart midair and crash." Captain Stewart closed the journal and tossed it at my feet. "Enough of your questions about who *I* am. Maybe I should ask who you really are. Am I safer taking my chances out there with the Germans?"

EIGHT

Rule: *Question everything.*

I was slow to pick up the journal, mostly because I was stalling for time until I could think of a response. How stupid I had been, to think mixing up a few letters would fool anyone, or that a few loose floorboards provided a safe hiding place for a notebook that could get me arrested. I was furious with myself, but I still had to answer Captain Stewart's question.

One possibility was open defiance, to insist that he had no right to question me after all I'd done for him, after all the lies I'd told in the last several minutes, for his sake!

Or I could kick him out of the barn. If he thought he'd be better off with the Germans, then maybe he should go out there and find out how wrong he was!

Or I could leave the barn and go tell Grandmère the truth. Even if she was angry with me for hiding Captain Stewart here for so long, she'd know what to do.

That seemed like the best of my options. I even turned with my journal in hand when Captain Stewart said, "I found one more solution: 'Follow the German.'" He sat up taller in the hay, grunting with pain as he did. "Sophie, please tell me I have it wrong."

My eyes darted, but he was waiting for an answer, so I said, "I never do anything too dangerous. I just watch the Nazis' movements when they're in town."

"And report on them to who?" I didn't answer, and he finally let out a heavy sigh. "I have a daughter about your age. We sent her to the countryside outside London during the Blitz. I cannot imagine how I would feel if I heard she was trying to spy on the Germans."

We knew about the Blitz, the near-daily bombings in London and other areas of Great Britain. Maman said that was why she hadn't wanted us to go to Britain with Papa.

Captain Stewart pointed to the journal in my hands. "Burn that. You have some good codes in there, but every one of them can be solved, so all you are doing is building a mountain of evidence against yourself. If that is found by the wrong people, you will end up in a Nazi camp. Do you understand what that means?"

I understood plenty. All this time, I'd thought I was protecting my family, but instead, I had put them at terrible risk.

He sighed again. "Burn that journal, Sophie."

"My name isn't Sophie," I whispered. "It's Meg."

He paused a moment and stared at me, then his eyes softened. "It's good to meet you, Meg."

I put the journal in a pocket of my sweater, then grabbed a milk bucket. "I have afternoon chores to do."

"I'd offer to help but—"

"You're injured; I understand."

I put out a stool and led our milk cow out of her stall. But I'd no sooner gotten to work when Captain Stewart asked, "How did you become interested in codes?"

I hesitated, then finally decided to trust him with a little more information. "My father and I had a game of trying to create a code the other could not solve. I know he made them easier for me, but not *that much* easier. I'm trying to solve one now, in fact. It's also an anagram, but the only way the letters all fit—"

I stopped there, catching the words in my throat. I had pulled only one phrase from his anagram that made any sense: MY IDEA IS A JET.

Didn't Captain Stewart fly a jet?

Was it possible that my father knew Captain Stewart would come here one day? Maybe his code was a message about Captain Stewart?

That couldn't be. My father wrote that anagram nearly two years ago. He could not have known then that I would be meeting Captain Stewart now.

But still, could this really be only a coincidence?

"Are you all right, Meg?" Captain Stewart asked. "You seem distracted."

I began milking our cow again. "I'm fine. I just was thinking about that code. I need to get back to it soon and check the decoding."

"Can you solve anything other than anagrams?" he asked.

"Of course!" Papa used to say that there were as many secret codes as there are stars in the universe. I loved substitution ciphers the best. Those codes replaced every letter with a different letter, symbol, or number.

"Let me see that journal of yours again."

I hesitated, but it seemed to have caused Captain Stewart pain just to reach out his arm, so I didn't want to refuse him. He turned to a back page, wrote something on the paper, tore it out, then gave it back to me.

I studied what he had written while leading the cow back to its stall, then turned around. "Do you want me to solve this?"

"If you can."

"There are no spaces between the letters."

He grinned. "You said you were good at codes."

I was, but I'd also noticed something he might not have thought was important. Captain Stewart hadn't consulted a code sheet when he created this code for me, and he wrote it too quickly to have encoded it as he went. The only way he could have done this so fast was if he already had a substitution cipher memorized.

Fighter pilots had no time to memorize code sheets.

I was beginning to think that Captain Stewart wasn't a pilot. I'd wondered before if he might be a spy, but hadn't taken the thought too seriously.

Until now.

If he was a spy, who did he really work for?

CHAPTER NINE

Rule: *Simply be smarter than your opponent.*

I finished my chores, then told Captain Stewart I had to return to the house. "If I'm out here much longer, my grandmother will become suspicious," I explained.

He pointed to the journal back in my pocket again. "You will burn that?"

"Yes, I promise." But not yet. I had other things on my mind first.

Grandmère was just putting biscuits in the oven when I came inside. "You took longer than usual," she said. "Was that old cow giving you trouble?"

"No, no. Everything is fine." I gave Grandmère the bucket of milk, then looked around. "Maman still isn't back? It's getting dark."

"I'm sure your mother is on her way, or she will be soon. Shall we play a game while we wait?"

I patted my pocket with the journal inside, then said, "If it's all right, I'll just go to my room. Thank you for fixing my coat."

"You are a good girl, Meg. I am always happy to help."

Normally, we tried to remain together in one room after dark, to save candles now that electricity was rationed. If Grandmère had let me come upstairs so easily, that was significant. Maybe she felt she could better keep a watch for my mother if I weren't around. I wanted to watch for her too, though I knew from hours of waiting for Papa that it didn't make anyone come through the door any faster.

Or come through it at all.

With every passing minute, I became increasingly worried. My mother had never, *never* been gone this long. Even if she really had been on errands, it was the end of the workday and shops were closing. Where was she?

I tried to focus on Captain Stewart's code. Anything to keep from thinking about my mother.

The letters were written out in a long string.

QMFBTFCSJOHNFTPNFXBUFS

Right in the center, I picked out the word "JOHN," but since the rest of the code was meaningless, that was almost certainly a coincidence. Whether his code was in English or French, the most commonly used letter was "E." I thought it

49

would be safe to assume the most common letter of his code—"F"—was also an "E."

QMFBTFCSJOHNFTPNFXBUFS
  E E   E   E   E

I also assumed his code was written in English, since he and I had spoken in English. If that was true, then my next step was to think of what word likely began the phrase.

The second most common letter in English was "T," and the most common word was "the." So it would make sense to assume the first word of his phrase was "the."

I tested that for a while, but when that led me nowhere, I began studying the wide gap of letters between the second and third "E." At least one vowel had to fill that gap.

I became stuck there too. Captain Stewart certainly hadn't made this easy on me.

If the "F" in his code was an "E" in the alphabet, maybe that wasn't a coincidence. What if all the letters were simply shifted ahead by one?

If that was true, then the first letter of his code, "Q," would become "P." The second letter, "M," would become "L," and so on. Almost instantly, the first word became PLEASE, near proof that my theory was correct. Seconds later, I had his message.

I gasped, stuffed his code into the pocket of my sweater, and raced back down the stairs. As I had suspected, Grandmère was near the window, looking out. She jumped when she saw me, but in one exchanged look, we both understood. Maman still hadn't returned. The pit that had been lodged in my gut all day was growing heavier by the minute.

"I, er . . . forgot one of my chores outside." I reached for the lantern and lit it, then went back to the kitchen for a tall mug. "Also, I'm thirsty."

"I should say you are!"

I had to be careful this time, knowing that I was being watched. I filled the mug from the pump in our yard and took a long sip, or pretended to. I couldn't have Grandmère see me refill the mug and then carry it into the barn full.

Nor could I knock on the barn door, but I opened it slowly while singing a little tune so that Captain Stewart would know it was me.

His eyes were heavy, as if he'd been sleeping, but he sat up taller in the straw when I entered. A smile widened across his face when he saw the mug of water.

"You solved it, then?"

"The pattern was simple."

"But the trick was seeing the pattern. You must be very good with codes."

"Codes aren't nearly as interesting as being a pilot." I pulled up the milking stool and sat facing him. "What really fascinates me are the planes. I saw a Spitfire up close once, during an exhibition before the war. It had only one yellow knob. Can you tell me what it was for?"

His eyes narrowed. "I'm not as familiar with the Spitfire."

"Oh? What was your plane?"

"The Lysander." He was quick to answer that one.

"I've studied all about Lysanders." That was yet another lie from me, but since it was in pursuit of the truth, I figured it was acceptable. "Which model is the fastest?"

He hesitated again, this time for too long. I stood up, accidentally knocking over the stool when I did. "You're no fighter pilot, and maybe you're not a captain either. Tell me the truth now or I'll report you."

"To whom?" He shook his head, and even chuckled slightly, which threw off my concentration. Nothing about this was funny.

"Clever girl," he said. "Maybe too clever for your own good. I think you already know who I am."

"I think I do too." Again, I reached for the shovel that was leaning against the barn wall. Just in case I needed it.

CHAPTER
TEN

Rule: *Worrying does not make anything better.*

aptain Stewart eyed the shovel in my hands. "Put that down. I'm still a Brit, lass. I'm just not a pilot."

"How'd you get those injuries?"

"That part of my story was true. I did parachute out of a plane, and I did crash in my landing. But the plane did not."

"Then what are all the Nazis in town looking for?"

Captain Stewart's tone became serious. "Lower that shovel, please, Meg."

"I heard one of the Nazis say they had come to search for a him and a her. Were they talking about you?"

"Probably. But I also think they are interested in some people I was supposed to meet yesterday. There is someone else I need to locate—"

"Sylvie Kenyon."

He raised a brow. "Yes. She's a radio operator."

"Like the radios in our home?"

"This is different. It's the kind of radio used to transmit a message to someone far away, such as back in London. A message the Nazis wouldn't approve of."

My mother never would be involved with anything like that. Would she? "Sounds dangerous."

"It is. Here in France, most operators only last about six weeks, but Madame Kenyon has been with us for about eight months."

"Oh." My pulse began racing. "So you need her to send a message to London?"

"Not this time. I came to give Madame Kenyon a message." His eyes fixed on mine. "Do you know her, Meg? It is vital that I speak to her."

I was the first to look away, and when I did, I asked, "Are you sure that Sylvie Kenyon is a radio operator?"

"She's one of the best we have."

A knot formed in my chest. Where was my mother?

Captain Stewart seemed to notice my distress. "Have I said something wrong?"

"Meggie, come quickly!"

I recognized my grandmother's voice, and now I really was worried. I dropped the shovel and raced back to the house. Grandmère was at the door and motioned me inside, then quickly closed and locked the door behind me.

To my surprise, the first person I saw was Jakob, the boy

I had given the potatoes to earlier that morning. He stared back, clearly as surprised to see me as I was to see him.

"Why are you—" I began.

But my mother leaned forward from a chair where she had been sitting, facing the fire. "It's all right, Meggie. He helped me get home."

I still didn't understand, but I rushed to Maman's side. That was when I saw her right foot lifted up on a stool. The ankle was swollen, and her legs were badly scraped.

I stood back, suddenly stiff as a board. "What happened?"

"I will explain everything, I promise." Maman's eyes flicked up to Jakob. "But for now, we have a bigger problem."

He said, "The Nazis are out tonight, doing searches from house to house. You're farther from the center of town so you have a little time, but they will come."

"What are they looking for?"

"I heard they're searching for a British spy."

Grandmère folded her arms and looked at me. "Meggie, do you have anything to tell us?"

At that very moment, we heard a faint knock at our door. My pounding heart shot into my throat. If they had come already, we were doomed.

ELEVEN

Rule: *Take responsibility for your actions.*

The four of us in the room stared at one another, none of us knowing what to do. The knock came again, and from the other side of the door, I heard a voice say, "Meg, let me in."

All eyes flew to me. I turned to my mother and said, "Please don't be angry. I didn't know what else to do."

I stepped forward and unlocked the door. Captain Stewart must have been leaning against it so heavily, he practically fell into the room. Jakob rushed forward to help me catch him, and together we braced his weight.

"*C'est ma faute,*" he began, using perfect French to take responsibility for being here.

"Meg?" Grandmère looked at me.

"I'm sorry, it's really my fault," I said. "I found Captain

Stewart in the barn, injured. I've kept him a secret from you all afternoon."

"That explains a lot." She stepped closer to him and sniffed. "I can smell the tea on him. He's British all right."

Captain Stewart turned his head toward Jakob, still speaking in French. "You're one of the people I was supposed to meet."

"We reached the meeting place, but saw blood," Jakob said. "I came into town in hopes of finding you."

Captain Stewart's attention turned to my mother. "And I came to find you."

She looked directly at the captain. "There are bears in the woods."

"Not for much longer, I think," he replied. "Madame Kenyon?"

Jakob caught my eye, as confused as I was, until I realized what was happening. These were code words, a way they could identify each other.

Maman's shoulders fell. "I received your distress signal, but that alerted the Germans to where I was. I had to leave before I could send your message to London."

Captain Stewart pressed his hand against his injured side. "Then no one knows what happened to me. We need to send that message."

"Impossible." Maman shook her head. "My equipment

is damaged. I have no way of contacting London, and certainly not while there are so many soldiers in town."

Captain Stewart tried to take a step forward, then faltered. Jakob bent to help as Grandmère said, "Put him on the sofa."

"No," the captain said, slumping over in pain. But through gritted teeth, he said to my mother, "We need to talk, and then I'll leave."

"You're injured," Grandmère said. "You need help."

"Meg has been a great help to me today."

"I'm sorry," I began. "I just wanted—"

"You did the right thing," Maman said, reaching for my hand.

"The next phase of my mission involves Jakob," Captain Stewart said. "He and I will leave. We've put you in too much danger already."

"You won't get any farther than my gate," Maman said. "You're here now, so let's just decide what to do about it."

"Give me a horse," Captain Stewart offered. "We can be kilometers away from here by morning."

"You're not taking our horse!" Grandmère said, placing her hands on her hips. "Do you know how much it's worth?"

"We don't have much time," Maman said. "If the Nazis are coming to search our home, they must not find anything." Her eyes rested again on Captain Stewart. "Including you."

Captain Stewart finally allowed Jakob and me to bring

him to the sofa. He grunted as we lowered him to the cush-
ions, then he lay heavily against one side, looking as if he
were close to passing out.

"I'll tend to him," Maman said. "Jakob, I owe you too
much already, but I need to ask for another favor. Will you
go back outside? Take a lantern with you. Search everywhere for any sign of this man having been here and erase all
of it. No blood, no footprints, nothing."

"Of course I will." Jakob glanced over at me and grinned.
"Thanks again for the potatoes."

He grabbed the lantern and darted out the door. The
second it shut, I whispered to my mother, "He's a stranger to
us. Why do you think we can trust him?"

"Maybe for the same reason that you fed him," Maman
countered. "Now listen carefully. Go upstairs and clean out
everything that might cause us trouble with the Germans.
Burn all your father's codes, then gather any pictures of him,
or anything else that identifies him. If you are not sure what
to do with something, gather it up too. Grandmère will help
me down here."

Without another word, I flew into action. My mind was
spinning with possibilities—all of them so awful if I were to
make a single mistake. I couldn't overlook the tiniest object,
or any detail that my eyes had become accustomed to. There
was so much to look at, so much to see, I could barely keep
my thoughts straight.

Maman and I had left most of our possessions at home when we came here, and we'd always been careful in Grandmère's home. Still, I had a small picture of our family on the windowsill of my room that would have to go, along with the one last unsolved code of Papa's. I hurried downstairs to find Maman leaning over Captain Stewart, adjusting the bandage around his middle. I heard Grandmère back in her room. I couldn't imagine what she might have in there to be cleaned out.

"You say you landed in a tree?" Maman was asking him. "That wasn't good aim."

"It was a cloudy night, or I would have been fine." He smiled faintly. "The moon is both our enemy and friend. Our boats cannot reach shore with it, but as you can see, our parachutes cannot land without it."

Maman glanced back at me. "I know my room the best. Stay with the captain while I search it."

She left and I crossed over toward the sofa, sitting in the chair where my mother had been seconds ago.

"I only came to the door to tell you I was leaving," Captain Stewart said. "You shouldn't have brought me in here—it's too dangerous."

"You should have told me the truth about yourself from the beginning." Even as pale and pathetic as he looked, I still felt angry with him. "You should have told me everything, if you cared at all about keeping me safe."

Captain Stewart frowned. "Is that speech for me, or for your mother?" I hesitated and he added, "I'm willing to guess that you haven't told her about your own fight against the Germans."

I lowered my eyes. "Are you really a spy?"

"It's more accurate to say that we are professional troublemakers. The more trouble, the better. Some call us the League of Ungentlemanly Behavior, but in the end, we're a group of misfits who lack the good sense to conduct this war in a proper way. Our task is to do everything the regular military cannot do."

"Are you allowed to be telling me this?"

A sigh escaped the captain's lips. "Absolutely not, so I must count on you for secrecy. But I am telling you for a reason. If I don't get out of this one—if the Nazis should find me tonight—I will deny that you had anything to do with my being here. I'll claim the same for your mother and grandmother, but they won't believe it, not if all of you have helped to hide me. Do you understand?"

I shook my head. He was saying too much, too quickly, and all I really understood so far was that I had put my family into terrible danger by bringing the captain in here. I had made a grave mistake, though I still didn't know what other choice I'd had.

And as I would soon learn, it was a choice that would lead to other dangers I never could have imagined.

TWELVE

Rule: *Be careful—the smallest detail can betray you.*

Neither Maman nor Grandmère had finished searching their rooms when Jakob burst through the door. "They're in the area. I just saw the headlights!"

Anyone in a car these days was likely to be the Germans. Petrol was expensive and heavily rationed, so most of us had returned to bicycles, horses, or simply walking where we needed to go.

Grandmère peered out the window. "I think they're at Madame LeClair's farm now, but we'll be next."

With a heavy grunt, Captain Stewart made himself sit up. "Is there any place all of you can hide? They're only interested in me."

"You're the one who must hide." Grandmère turned to Jakob. "Are you finished outside?"

"Yes, except for the straw," he said. "I don't know what to do with that."

"Bundle it and bring it in for a fire." Grandmère walked to the fireplace and stirred the ashes with a poker to rekindle a flame. "Don't let any straw fall along the way here, not one piece. Meg, you'd better help him. Hurry."

I followed Jakob out the door, watching carefully for any evidence of Captain Stewart being here, but Jakob had done a good job hiding everything.

As we walked, he looked back at me. "Many of the French have learned to accept the German occupation, or even to help them. Not you?"

"No, never." I turned to him. "How can we accept what is clearly so evil?"

Jakob stopped to stare at me. "The Nazis are evil, not the Germans."

I shrugged. "Is there a difference?"

"Yes, Meg. There is." Without another word, he walked ahead of me into the barn. His lamp was still lit, but he began immediately to bundle the straw with twine from our barn. As he did, I used the lantern to search every place where Captain Stewart could have been. I found a few small pieces of straw that might have had blood droplets on them, but with so little light, they also could have been specks of mud. I wasn't taking any chances. They went into the tied bundles.

Jakob carried them back to the house while I followed behind with the lantern to be sure nothing dropped to the ground. Once inside, Grandmère already had the fire going again. One by one, we added the bundles while Grandmère swept the floor around us.

Maman was sitting near Captain Stewart and they were speaking quietly. I watched them, intensely curious about what they could be saying. At one point, Captain Stewart nodded over at me. Maman caught my gaze, offered me a comforting smile, then turned back to him.

"You've done us a great service tonight," Grandmère said to Jakob. "I've prepared a bag of food as part of our gratitude. I wish we had more to spare, but this should get you most of the way to Spain, if you're careful."

"Spain?" I asked him.

"It's a neutral country," he said. "They're not for or against either side in this war. My parents and I must get there."

"Why?" I asked, but he only lowered his eyes, quietly refusing to answer.

"I'll meet you tomorrow," Captain Stewart said to Jakob. "Just stay at our meeting point, as long as it is safe."

Jakob nodded back at him, then darted out the door and into the night. Grandmère locked the door and said to Captain Stewart, "I believe the time has come to get you hidden."

He grunted as he returned to a seated position. He pulled

a folded yellow paper from his uniform and gave it to Maman. "This is why I came. I don't know what it says, but your husband insisted that I put it directly in your hands." Captain Stewart gave me one final look. "I owe you my life, Meg. Now be smart, and save yourself tonight."

I might have to do more than that, I realized. If it became necessary, I'd do whatever I could to save my entire family.

CHAPTER
THIRTEEN

Rule: *Always be listening—especially when they don't know you're there.*

Together, Maman and I helped Captain Stewart limp into Grandmère's room behind the kitchen. She had moved her small metal-frame bed just enough to reveal a hole beneath the floorboards.

"Your grandfather built this during the Great War twenty years ago. That was supposed to be the war to end all wars, was it not? This hiding spot was created to hide things from the Germans." She drew in a slow breath. "Though we have never hidden a person before. I do not even know if you will fit in there."

"I'll make myself fit." Captain Stewart put his feet into the hole and sat on the floorboards. He looked at my mother first. "They know a radio operator is in the village, but they do not know it's you. Don't give them any reason to suspect otherwise."

"There's a reason I've never been caught," Maman said. "I know what to do."

"We all know what to do," Grandmère echoed.

Maybe I knew, I wasn't sure. Over the supper table, we had frequently discussed how to avoid any confrontations with the Germans, and what to do if they couldn't be avoided. From my own experiences, I had learned how to escape the attention of the soldiers, how to see without appearing to look, how to listen while it seemed that my attention was elsewhere.

Yes, I supposed I did know what to do. Tonight, I had to become as invisible as possible.

Captain Stewart lay inside the hole, though he had to roll half on his side so that his knees didn't poke up too far. In the small gap that remained, I placed the items we had gathered from around our home, which meant he had no room at all to move. Grandmère smiled down at him, then replaced the floorboards. She and I shifted her bed back into place, and we looked at each other.

"What is our plan?" Maman asked.

"We need to go to bed," Grandmère suggested. Maman began to protest, but Grandmère said, "These are unannounced searches. If we are still awake, it will look like we are expecting them."

"You're right," Maman said. "You both had better get ready for bed. I still have some work to do."

Maman kissed me good night, and I went up the stairs but stopped there. It would be impossible to sleep tonight, and I wouldn't sit in my room and wonder what was happening downstairs, what work Maman still had to do on such a dangerous night.

I heard a chair scoot back from the table, but otherwise, the home became almost unbearably silent, interrupted every few minutes by Maman's heavy sigh and the sound of paper crumpling, followed by a spark in the fire. Every dangerous thing that could not be hidden had to be burned.

I straightened, breathless and in a sudden panic, thinking about the journal of my codes, and of all the resistance work I'd done. Captain Stewart had been correct—it was foolish to keep it, yet it was just there in the pocket of my sweater. They would easily find it.

I tiptoed downstairs. Maman was at the table bent over yet another paper. Two crumpled sheets were already beside her. She began to crumple this one, and then her head perked up. Without turning around she said, "You should be asleep, Meggie."

"I was so worried about you all day," I said, suddenly fighting back tears. "Where did you go?"

Maman pressed her lips together and nodded. "Sit with me, my darling."

I did as she asked, letting my eyes wander to the yellow

note, folded again, and a paper she had been working on, with a few letters on the page in meaningless order.

My attention returned to my mother. "Do you work for the resistance?"

"Shh." Maman's eyes darted. Then she stared directly at me and nodded.

I lowered my voice further. "You're a radio operator? What does that mean?"

She leaned in to whisper, "I connect the partisans in the forest with the spy offices back in London. What I tell each of them helps in their planning of secret missions."

Maman didn't seem to realize how I was connected to her work. The information I gathered in town was passed to the partisans . . . who then passed it to my mother.

If the situation weren't so serious, it would have made me laugh out loud. How much simpler life might have been if Maman and I had worked together rather than snuck around each other.

I almost told her about my own secret work. I even opened my mouth to say the words, but before I could, she pushed the yellow paper across the table, toward me.

"This is what Captain Stewart gave me earlier," she said. "He wanted me to have it specifically, but it doesn't make any sense."

"Who sent it?"

"It must be from your father, but I can't understand it."
Maman's eyes misted. "I would never willingly put you in
danger, Meggie, you know that. But I'm sure this letter
means more than what it says. I know how good you are
with things like this, and I thought maybe you could try."

I unfolded the paper, and indeed, the letter was written in
my father's handwriting. It was in English, which was always
the language of his codes. But this didn't appear to be a code.

Dearest wife, Daisy, and Mom:
One day I'll return, you'll see.
Nothing can stop me from climbing
to you. Watch perfectly as
the sadness becomes numb.
Remember my smiles, brightened
under tender skies by the sea.
Straighten the spine, Daisy.
Take courage, even when hurting,
have faith until this battle
ends. Until then, be calm.
Regards,
Rosbif

We hadn't heard from him since the day he left. If he
finally had the chance to send us a message, why would it be
so strange?

I read through the note twice before looking up at Maman. "Rosbif?" It was the French word for roast beef, a nickname for the British due to the way they prepared their meat.

Maman smiled, lost in memory. "I used to call your father that when we first met. Just an innocent way of teasing him."

I thought that was brilliant. Papa had signed the letter in a way that we would know it was him, but without identifying himself, or any of us, if the enemy should find this.

"What about—" I began, but Maman shushed me.

Her eyes had wandered to the window behind me. She took a sharp breath as moving lights swept across the wall, briefly highlighting her face. I heard the sound of an engine and my heart stopped.

Maman's hands balled into fists. "They're here, Meggie. The Nazis have come."

FOURTEEN

Rule: *The best hiding places are sometimes barely hidden at all.*

Maman called to Grandmère a warning that the Nazis had arrived, then turned to me. "You must burn that note."

"We can't," I protested. "Not until we know what it is."

"If it's found, they'll kill us. They'll find your father!"

"I can hide it." My hands began shaking. "I promise to hide it, but we cannot destroy it."

The car engine outside stopped. Maman looked back to the front door. We were out of time. She motioned for me to hurry upstairs.

I started that way, then remembered the reason I had come down in the first place. "My journal!" Before Maman could ask, I raced to the door where my sweater was hung and dug into the pocket. Outside, I heard the crank of doors opening, then closing.

I pulled out the journal and tossed it on the fire, though it slid off one log to the edge of the flames.

"There's no time for that," Maman said. "Get into bed and keep that note hidden. Be safe, Meggie!"

A knock came to the front door as I raced up the stairs, undressing as I ran. In my room, I stuffed my clothes under my bed, then pulled on a nightdress.

Maman still hadn't answered the door. Outside, the Germans began shouting, *"Öffne die Tür!"* By their tone of voice, they were not making a request; it was a threat.

"It's late," Maman responded in polite French. "What do you want?"

"We are conducting searches." Then the German doing all the pounding added, "We will break down the door if we must."

By then, I had slid into bed, but I wasn't finished. I needed to braid my hair, though it had nothing to do with vanity. I had a plan.

Downstairs, Maman finally opened the door. "Search everywhere!" the German commanded.

I wasn't yet finished with my braid. My fingers twisted the strands as fast as I could, winding them around one another, trying to pull them tight enough that a strand wouldn't come loose and expose my secret.

"Is there something you're looking for?" Maman asked. "Something I can help you find?"

"*Nein.*"

I finished the last braid, folded Papa's note, and pushed it into my hair at the nape of my neck. I wound the braids into a bun, then felt around in the darkness for a pin to hold the hair in place. I found one, two, then . . . where was the third pin? I always kept several by my bed. I needed a third.

"Search upstairs!" the German ordered.

The extra pins must have fallen to the floor when I cleaned out my room earlier. But footsteps were already pounding up the steps.

I lay flat on my pillow, pulling up the blankets around me.

There, I froze. A shadow blocked the light coming in from my door. One of the Germans must be right in my doorway.

He whispered to someone with him, "Asleep."

"Then let's search the other rooms first," came the reply.

I waited for the shadow to leave, then waited again for sounds of searching in the room beside me. I let my right arm flop over the side of the bed, and there I felt around the floor until finally, I found a pin. I was just beginning to pull my arm back up when the shadows returned. I had to let my arm dangle again, and the pin dropped back to the floor.

This time, the shadows were accompanied by flashlights that beamed into every corner of my room, ending directly on my face. Then came the order, "Wake up! *Schnell, schnell!*"

I didn't need to pretend to be frightened. I popped up straight in bed, my eyes so wide the flashlights hurt them. I pulled the covers up around me and tried to lean closer to the wall. One of my braids was coming loose. If it fell, the note would fall with it.

Two soldiers began a search of my room, and surprisingly, they were polite about it. They didn't dump anything out or search as closely as I would have expected, which made me think they were looking for something bigger. Such as a British spy, for example.

One of them noticed my braid falling out of the bun. He crouched down on the floor beside me and looked at it. I had to force myself to look at him, so that he wouldn't see the note. The soldier merely smiled and picked up the pin I had dropped. He gave it to me without a word, then gestured that I could use it in my hair.

I nodded back and tried to put in the pin, but my hands were still shaking too much to fix it properly, so I knew it did me little good.

When they had finished, they gave me a polite nod, then one of them said in French, "You may go back to sleep. Sorry to have disturbed you."

They left the room, but downstairs, the search continued.

Through my window I saw flashlights in the barn, and I desperately worried that Jakob and I had made some mistake there. It would have been so easy to overlook something.

From downstairs, a voice carried up to my room, one that put a heavy weight on my chest, making it hard to breathe.

"Whose journal is this?" This was Lieutenant Becker, the man I had followed earlier in town.

"That is mine," Maman said.

No, it was mine. But I was sure it must have burned by now.

"I do not think so, madam. This appears to be a child's writing." Maman didn't answer, so he continued, "I have a few questions for you, and for your mother and daughter as well."

Maman answered, her voice as calm as Becker's was sharp. "My mother is an old woman with a failing memory. She won't remember enough to answer your questions. Ten minutes after you leave, she won't even remember you were ever here. And my daughter is young and needs her sleep. Perhaps you could speak to her tomorrow."

"Perhaps we will," Lieutenant Becker said. "This is the last stop on our searches tonight. Would you be so kind as to put me and my men up for the rest of the night? That will give you and me plenty of time for all the questions I still have, and we would consider it a great service."

I could almost hear my mother's heart pounding. Or

maybe that was mine, I didn't know. But I was terrified, for me and my grandmother, for Captain Stewart, and especially for my mother. Because she probably was hiding secrets far more dangerous than anything in my journal.

And I had secrets of my own.

Secrets that could get all of us killed.

FIFTEEN

Rule: *The more dangerous the enemy, the more kindness is needed.*

If I slept that night, it was only for minutes at a time, followed by long stretches of staring at the ceiling, listening to everything happening downstairs.

Maman had delayed the questioning as long as she could, taking her time to offer blankets to the soldiers or showing them places where they might get a little rest. There couldn't have been more than four soldiers here—they'd all come in one Kübelwagen, but with the time she took, it felt like a whole squadron was downstairs.

With that settled, she offered Lieutenant Becker a cup of tea, which he refused, then a cup of coffee, though he especially refused it once she explained it was not made of coffee beans, but roasted acorns we'd collected from the forest.

"Acorns?" His voice registered his disgust. "The French

are supposed to love great food. Now you offer me a drink that is not food at all."

"The French must have something to eat," she said. "We do what we can with what little remains."

"The shortages are temporary," he said. "The war is temporary. Once we are victorious, there will be no more need for rations. Please, have a seat so we can talk."

From up in my room, I leaned forward, hoping to hear every word they spoke. Dreading to hear the words—terrified of them. But I still had to know what they were saying.

Becker began, and now he sounded far too polite. "May I ask how you injured your leg?"

"A riding accident this afternoon, here on our property. I'm not the best with horses."

"Did you go into town this afternoon?"

"My ration card is full for the week. I had no reason to be in town."

"I see." I listened carefully for any change in the tone of his voice. Did he believe her? She spoke so well, I almost believed her, and I knew the truth.

He continued, "Now, where is your husband?"

"We do not know," Maman said, which was the exact truth. "We have had no contact from him since the war began."

None, until tonight.

I thought again of my father's note. My mind had fixed on one particular line, something that might have meaning only for me. He had asked us to remember his smiles.

"Nothing in a code is done by mistake," Papa once taught me. "Everything you see is there for a reason."

Papa had written "smiles." As in, more than one smile. I doubted he was writing about our happy times together.

Instead, when I was very young, Papa used to write poetry in a brown hardcover journal, and he read to me from it each night. Before I was old enough to know what poetry was, I simply called his writing "my smiles."

"Read me a smile," I used to say.

I hadn't thought about that poetry journal for years. Why would Papa want me to find it now?

A light switched off in the barn, drawing my attention to the window to watch one of the soldiers ending his search there. Papa had a trunk in the barn of everything of his that he had brought from home. Maman said nothing was in there but some old clothes and a few books.

Books.

I needed to look inside that trunk!

But not tonight. Downstairs, Lieutenant Becker had moved on to questions about our lives here in the Perche. "Without a father in the home, how do you earn money?"

"It isn't easy," she said. "We grow our own food, and my mother has some savings."

"How do you spend your time?" he asked Maman.

"Like all mothers, I pass too many hours in the queue, waiting for our daily rations."

"And do you ever sell your food on the black market?" he questioned.

Maman paused here, and I leaned farther forward, desperate to hear her answer. Whether she lied or told him the truth, he would have a reason to arrest her.

Finally, Maman said, "Would you be any different if you had to support a family?"

A long pause followed. I wished I could peek into the kitchen. Was Becker frowning at her, considering an arrest? Did Maman look as frightened as I felt? Did she know she had given him such a dangerous answer? Because she had all but admitted her guilt.

Our guilt.

My guilt. I was the one who sold our food on the black market.

Finally, Becker answered her question. "I believe I would do the same as you have done. Though I question the wisdom of allowing your daughter to sell the food for you. Marguerite, is that her name?"

"Yes." Maman's tone was stiffer now.

"We found her bag in the barn, a bag I saw earlier today in town. Does she often wander about the town?"

Another pause. My mother only knew I went to town to

sell food. She didn't know why I stayed when I should have come straight home.

"My daughter must be bored, or a little lonely," Maman said. "There is little here in the Perche to occupy the mind of a child."

"She seems quite intelligent, and curious. Perhaps too curious."

"Meggie is only a child."

"The terrorists who occupy the forest behind this home have no regard for life. Why would your daughter's life be any different? If they thought they could use her—"

"Meggie is not involved with them." I knew my mother well enough to understand the desperation in her tone. She could sound as confident as she wanted, but even she wondered if her words were true.

"Yes, but there is this journal. Many of the pages are burned, but I am curious about what I can still read, and why she would have burned it."

"Those were just games between her and her father. She must have outgrown them."

"Yes." Becker's tone darkened. "Perhaps what started as games have become more serious to her." Another long pause followed, and he added, "As you say, she is a child, so we will let her sleep tonight. But I will have questions for her tomorrow."

Maman yawned. "I'm very tired, Lieutenant. Could we continue this tomorrow?"

"Of course, madam," he said.

The chairs scooted back and Maman quietly dismissed herself. Only then did I finally fall asleep for good, though it was a restless sleep filled with nightmares. The only dream I remembered after waking up was the worst of them all, because I soon realized it was no dream.

Tomorrow, I would have to face questions from Lieutenant Becker. Questions to which he already knew every answer.

Saturday, February 28, 1942
658 days since I've seen Papa

My eyes opened to the sound of the Kübelwagen starting up. Even then, I remained in bed, perfectly still and silent. I wouldn't get out of this bed until I was certain that every one of those soldiers was gone.

As soon as I could no longer hear the sound of their engine, Maman called up, "Meggie! Come downstairs."

I threw off my covers and hurried down the stairs. "Is everything all right?"

Maman didn't answer, and the strain of last night was evident upon her face. Dark shadows rimmed red eyes. She must have been crying. Maybe my eyes looked the same, and maybe for the same reason.

"Help your grandmother," Maman said.

Grandmère was on her knees in her room, the bed pushed back as it had been last night and the planks of wood removed.

The bag that we had placed into the hole with Captain Stewart was at Grandmère's side, but she was leaning over to speak to the captain.

"I don't think I can get out of here." His voice was weak, but at least he was alive.

"You must get out," Grandmère said. "We must tend to that wound." She looked up at me. "Can you help him?"

I sat on the floorboards near his feet and put my legs on either side of his, then held out my hands. "I can pull you up," I said.

His smile was faint but genuine. "I'm a grown man."

"I'm a farm girl, and stronger than you think." Then I smiled too. "And if you don't take my hands, we'll drag you out by your feet. I guarantee that will be harder on you."

"The French may offer their *mercis*," he said. "But no mercy."

If Grandmère understood the joke, she didn't seem to think it was as funny as I did. Captain Stewart grunted as he twisted onto his back, and when he did, I saw fresh blood on his uniform. That worried me. But he took hold of my hands, and I gave a hard pull upward until Grandmère wedged in behind him to help lift him to his feet.

Grandmère noticed the blood too and threw a look at Maman, who was already tearing up an old sheet for fresh bandages. I supported Captain Stewart's weight as we walked him over to the same sofa where we had laid him out last night.

He was heavier, weaker on his feet than he had been last night.

"Can I have some water?" he asked. "It was quite warm down there. And maybe something to eat?"

I fetched him a glass of water while Grandmère went to the stove to make him some eggs. At least with our chickens, we usually had eggs.

After I delivered the water, Maman said, "You should change into civilian clothes, in case you're seen. Meg, go out to the barn and find some clothes for Captain Stewart from your father's things."

My jaw practically fell open. Since Papa left, Maman had carefully protected all his possessions like they were sacred. It surprised me to see her willing to give up any of those items now.

Perhaps that showed how desperate the situation was.

I nodded and ran to the barn. The soldiers had definitely searched this place. The piles of hay had been moved, our tools were all in a different order, and Papa's trunk, which we kept in the very center of the barn to protect it from rain and snow, was left slightly ajar due to a knitted scarf of Papa's.

I picked it up and buried my face in the fabric, amazed that it still smelled like him: of fresh-cut firewood and cinnamon tea, his favorite. Now that I knew he was alive, my aching to see him again was so much worse.

The other items inside the trunk were a mess too. Maman would be upset if she saw this. If I'd had more time, I would have organized it, but not today.

I pulled out a full change of clothes for Captain Stewart, then stared down at the books in the bottom of the trunk. I saw a Sherlock Holmes story, a hymnal, a guide to skiing the Alps—one of our family's favorite activities—and Papa's brown book filled with his poems. My smiles.

Papa wanted me to find this book, I knew he did, but why?

The full sentence of his letter had said, "Remember my smiles, brightened under tender skies by the sea."

I was holding the book he wanted. But nothing else in the sentence made sense. Perhaps one of the poems inside would explain it.

I flipped through the pages, glancing from one poem to another and shaking my head. Not a single poem made any reference to tender skies, or the sea. These were silly poems to entertain a young child, nothing more.

Besides, he had written these poems six or seven years ago, long before war broke out, long before he had any idea that he would be missing now.

I had the right book, but also a sinking feeling that I might never understand why he wanted us to find it.

I closed up Papa's trunk, then returned to the house. Maman was finishing with wrapping a new bandage around Captain Stewart's side, and Grandmère was burning the old bandages. I gave him the clothes. Maman winced to see Papa's clothes in someone else's hands, but she only said, "You may change in any room of the house, but *la toilette* is out back."

He nodded, thanked all of us, then grimaced as he stood and shuffled out the back door.

"It's good that we have a few minutes alone," Maman said, putting her arm around my shoulders. "Captain Stewart and I have a plan."

I cocked my head. Something about the way she said it worried me. I wished I could close my eyes and plug my ears and refuse to hear what she was saying, just as I used to do when I was little.

But the times were far too serious, and I'd seen too much to ever be able to go back to a simple childhood again. So instead, I straightened my spine, as Maman always taught me to do, as Papa had suggested to me in his letter, and said, "What is the plan?"

SEVENTEEN

Rule: *Define the purpose for every mission.*

Grandmère's thin white brows pressed close together. She sat beside Maman, shaking her head. "Surely there's another way."

But Maman held up a hand, stopping that conversation. "We are lucky that Lieutenant Becker was called away this morning, but he will return, and you know how serious that will be." She turned back to me. "Be honest with me now, Meggie. What work have you done for the resistance?"

"Nothing more than you were doing." I pointed to Maman's ankle, bandaged and still swollen. "Lieutenant Becker won't care about me. He was here for you."

"No, he is here looking for Jakob's parents, though I'm sure Captain Stewart's arrest would be a fine prize as well."

"And you, Maman! Why would he believe your story of

a riding accident when he knows a radio operator escaped from them yesterday?"

Maman's sigh was heavy. "We both made mistakes yesterday. But he has no evidence against me, and I'll find witnesses to support my story, if necessary. We must find a way to protect you, though. He intends to question you when he returns this evening. You cannot be here."

My heart fluttered. "You're sending me away?"

"We have no choice. There is too much at risk if he questions you. So this morning, I told the lieutenant about my aunt in Paris who is very sick. Little does he know that we will receive a letter from her today begging you to come and help take care of her. Of course, I will have to send you to Paris at once."

I was confused. "We have no family in Paris."

"I tried to tell her that too," Grandmère said.

"It is only a story. You are not going to Paris, but you must go." Maman's eyes welled with tears. "You're so much like me, Meggie. More than you might know, but I want you to understand that what I am about to ask is only because I know how brave you are, how smart, and how strong. Tell me why you were helping the resistance."

I bit my lip, barely able to look at her. What I had to say would sound foolish and naive, but it was the truth. "I hoped it would be a way to help Papa. He's with the resistance, isn't he?"

Maman sighed. "In a way. He was recruited into the same organization that Captain Stewart belongs to, right from their earliest days. Do you still have that letter from your father?"

I pointed to my braids, at the bun. "It's in there."

Maman smiled through her tears. "Of course it is. Right after the war began, do you remember that telegram your father received from London? I know you do; how could any of us forget that day? It came directly from the prime minister's office, regarding a new, very secret organization. Even I did not know what it was, not until I was contacted by them as well, to help the resistance here in France. They are called the Special Operations Executive—the S.O.E."

Grandmère said, "Captain Stewart is with the S.O.E. too. One of London's spies."

"Yes." Maman's eyes shifted to the door as it opened again and Captain Stewart shuffled in wearing Papa's clothes, even looking like him a little except he was leaning heavily on the door to close it. Maman told him, "I was just about to tell Meggie what you said to me."

His eyes shifted to me, and it took him a long time to speak. Not because of his strength, I thought, but because he didn't seem to want to say the words.

Finally, he began. "Harper Kenyon was recruited to help design some of our secret weapons, but eventually he asked to work in the field. Last year, he participated in a mission in western France that successfully destroyed an electric station, which of course made the Germans very unhappy. Your father was captured and sent to a German prison camp. He might not have survived that, but the Germans discovered he was an engineer, so they moved him to work in one of their factories."

"I told Harper he should have been a poet," Grandmère said. "I knew engineering would be nothing but trouble."

"Mother, please," Maman whispered. Turning to me, she said, "Of course your father would never willingly help the Germans, so he began sabotaging their work. Captain Stewart believes he was discovered. His life is in danger."

"That's my mission," Captain Stewart said. "You met Jakob Durand yesterday. His father, Albert, helped your father get to a safe house where he is waiting for rescue. Albert is also the one who passed along that message from your father, the one on the yellow paper. But Albert will not tell us where he is until we get his family into neutral territory."

"We've read the message," Maman said. "But we don't know what it means."

"Harper told Albert that his daughter would figure it out." Captain Stewart eyed me, but I only shrugged. A whole night of thinking and all I'd come up with was a book of his poems that still meant nothing to me.

"If she cannot decode the letter, then there is no reason to ask anything more of Meggie," Grandmère said.

My attention remained on Captain Stewart. "What exactly are you asking me to do?"

"In my condition, I won't be able to finish this operation," Captain Stewart said. "And time is of the essence. Your father's life depends on how quickly we act."

"My radio is broken," Maman said. "So we have no way to relay to London the situation. As far as they know, everything is going according to plan."

"But it's not. If the operation fails, then Papa might—" My words locked inside my throat, swelling until I almost couldn't breathe. "Oh," I croaked, then I began to cry too. "Maman, I can't do this."

"I've already created the plan for the Durand family to get to Spain," Captain Stewart said. "It should take a week to get there, maybe two if the weather is bad. If the Durands follow my instructions, they still have a chance to escape."

"And I want you to go with them," Maman added, simple words that made my brain spin. This wasn't happening. This couldn't be happening.

"We don't know these people," Grandmère said. "They are *les inconnus*."

"You've already met Jakob," Captain Stewart said. "And I don't know the other two, but I do know that London considers it the highest priority for them to escape . . . and I might add, this is now your father's only hope of rescue."

"This is too much for Meggie," Grandmère said. "Too dangerous."

"What other choice do we have?" Maman asked. "Is it any less dangerous for her to remain here and be questioned by Lieutenant Becker?"

"Listen carefully," Captain Stewart said to me. "The Durands know the plan, so all you must do is go with them. And if they need help, then you are the perfect person for it, even better than I am!"

"Why?"

"The Germans will not suspect a child, especially about something so important. If anyone asks, you can say that you have been living with the Durands in the countryside until the end of the war. That will explain why you don't know them well."

I didn't know them at all. Grandmère was right. They were strangers.

"Their plan is to go through the Pyrenees Mountains, directly into Spain," Maman said. "There are friends of the resistance along the way who will assist you and see you safely there."

"What about you, and Grandmère?" I asked.

"As soon as I'm able to get a message to London, they'll put a plan together to get all of us out," Captain Stewart said. "I know this is too much to ask. If any of us were in a position to do it ourselves, we gladly would."

"It's all right to say no," Maman said. "We will understand if you feel this is too great a burden to bear."

"But it's the only chance Papa has," I mumbled. And it might be the only chance I had as well.

Although I was terrified, though my palms were sweating and my heart was pounding louder than a drum, I knew what I was going to say.

The only thing I possibly *could* say, considering how important this mission was.

"I'll do it."

EIGHTEEN

Rule: *A good leader must take control of the mission.*

Maman and Grandmère began packing a canvas shoulder bag with food, a thick wool blanket, and winter clothes that I might need once we reached the mountains. While they worked, Captain Stewart sat next to me, holding his side as he said, "I need you to understand how important this operation is. The Nazis want the Durands and will do whatever it takes to find them. The family has been trained to maintain their cover story, but you must do so as well. You need to think of them as your guardians and treat them as such, even when you believe you are alone. Most importantly, don't do anything that might draw suspicion to you."

"Why are the Nazis so interested in them?"

"The less you know about that, the better." He quickly added, "Now, listen carefully. The Durands are not far from here. About three kilometers behind your home, there is a waist-high rock wall that extends east and west farther than you can see."

I knew exactly where he meant. Before the war, Maman and I used to hike to that very wall when we came here on visits.

Captain Stewart unfastened the spade around his leg and gave it to me. "Slightly to the north of that wall, you will see three tall pine trees that have grown around a boulder, their trunks bending for the rock. Near them is a shallow cave, set into a hill. That's where you will find our friends. When you are alone in the cave, find the large, round rock inside, and there you can dig down to a backpack I've hidden. It is for you, and only for you."

My eyes widened. "Don't you trust them?"

Captain Stewart sighed. "Your grandmother is correct about this one thing: They are strangers, even to me. Tell them, on my orders, the contents of that backpack are for your eyes only. If they look inside without your permission, you will cancel the mission."

"We can't cancel the mission. My father—"

"Those are your orders, Meg. You're one of us now; you're an unofficial S.O.E. agent. Keep that backpack with you at all times, and this won't be a problem. I remember the way you ordered me out of that hiding place this morning. You're perfectly strong enough to keep control of this family. Inside the backpack is a map. You can share that with everyone. They know the plan. All you have to do is help them follow it."

I wanted to say something brave, something that showed my confidence, but since I had absolutely no confidence at the moment, I merely held my tongue and nodded.

Grandmère handed me the canvas sack. It was heavier than I had expected, but when I slung it over my shoulder, I did everything I could not to let the weight show.

"Very good," Maman said. "You will be fine."

My eyes darted away. It was time to say goodbye, but I didn't want to cry now, nor to see her cry. So I quickly wrapped my arms around her waist, mumbled, *"Je t'aime,"* and heard her expressions of love in return, then did the same to Grandmère. But to Captain Stewart, I stood tall and gave him a firm military salute.

He smiled. "That's for regular military, lass, but you're S.O.E. now. You are part of the League of Ungentlemanly . . . of Ungentle*womanly* Behavior. No saluting for us."

Nor tears.

I smiled back, said a quick goodbye, then stepped outside and made myself take a breath. I forced myself to take the first step away from home, wondering if I would ever return again.

Probably I wouldn't, and that was my own fault. If I had not been so foolish as to keep that journal, things might've been different today. But there was no point in dwelling on past mistakes. Papa still needed my help.

I turned away from the road to begin walking into the wooded area behind our home. Careful to step in places where the snow was already worn down, I took the next step away from the house, then another after that, and another after that.

Maman once told me that surviving in an occupied country meant we had to learn how to live in the middle—somewhere between accepting our fate and outright resistance. With my next step, I left the middle.

I was now an unofficial spy, and part of the resistance myself. It was no longer my job to simply observe the enemy. Now I had to do everything in my power to sneak three innocent people into safe territory. And, somehow, to also rescue my father.

"This is not the smartest thing you've ever done, Meg," I said to myself.

And a voice quietly answered inside my head, "Nor is it the stupidest thing you'll do before this is over."

That voice echoed in my head for almost an hour, following my every footstep until I came to the wall Captain Stewart had told me about. From there, I walked northward, watching carefully for the three trees bent around the boulder. When I found them, the cave was a simple thing to spot after that.

With the first crunch of twigs beneath my feet, Jakob's head poked out from the cave. "Oh!" He looked bewildered. "We expected Captain—"

I straightened up again. "I'm here to help you finish his mission."

"You? Really?" Jakob tilted his head, then disappeared inside the cave again. I heard talking and a chill ran down my spine. There had to be a mistake. I didn't know who Captain Stewart thought the Durands were, but Jakob was speaking in German. That was the strangeness in his accent—he was trying to hide the truth about himself!

Captain Stewart could not have known this, or he never would have helped them. Even their family name was a lie. Durand was a French name.

I considered running, getting as far from these people as possible while I still had the chance to escape.

Jakob's head poked out again. "Our agreement was with Captain Stewart."

I gritted my teeth, then said, "He is the one who sent me here."

"We are grateful, but we cannot accept your help."

A man emerged from the cave beside Jakob. His white hair was combed to one side, covering one bald patch and revealing another. His round glasses gave him a serious look, and his white beard gave him a grandfatherly look, though he seemed younger than that.

He was studying me too. When he finally spoke, it was in French, though his German accent was thick. "My name is Albert Durand. Jakob tells us that Captain Stewart is seriously injured, which puts us in a dangerous position. You must understand that we cannot place our safety in the hands of someone as young as yourself."

I grunted and lowered the bag from Grandmère, then looked around me, ready for the speech I'd practiced a dozen times on the way here. I pointed northeast. "Paris is that way. It's loaded with Nazis, defeated Frenchmen, and women who match their outfits to the gas masks they carry. Do you think anyone there will help you? Or take any other direction through these woods, and you'll meet some partisans who'd be very interested in you. As soon as you're taken prisoner, they'll trade you back to Germany in exchange for some of our people. That's fine by me. Trading you is a much easier way to get my father back."

Monsieur Durand's face softened. "Harper Kenyon is your father?"

"I know how much you all want to get to Spain," I said. "I will help you get there; it's what my father would want me to do. But you can try it on your own if you think you'll do better."

He and Jakob looked at each other, but then a third person in the cave emerged, a pretty woman with dark hair pulled into a tight bun, a trim build, and cautious eyes when she looked at me. But she soon smiled and said to her companions in near-perfect French, "We'll see how she does to get us out of these woods, then make our decision. My name is Liesel Durand. We are grateful that you would be willing to come and help us."

I didn't smile back, but only nodded and said, "We should leave. Use our daylight while we can."

"Captain Stewart said we would only travel at night."

"Not in these woods, that's too dangerous. If we meet any partisans, I can explain things." At least, I hoped I could. It'd take some clever talking to make the partisans trust these people, when I certainly didn't. Glancing over at the cave, I added, "Before we go, Captain Stewart left something for me."

"There's nothing in the cave," Jakob said. "Only a gas stove and a—"

"Maybe you could give me some privacy."

The group looked at one another again, but I didn't even blink. They needed to take me seriously from the beginning. If I couldn't earn their respect now, for the rest of this trip I'd never be anything but a child tagging along on their adventure.

"Leave the cave, please, and wait out here," I said, trying to be clearer than before.

Monsieur Durand left first, followed by Liesel, who I

assumed was his wife, and then by Jakob. With only a polite nod as we passed each other, I walked inside.

The cave was deeper than I had expected. From Captain Stewart's description, I had thought it'd be little more than a rock overhang, but instead, the Durands could have fit comfortably in here. Someone had rolled a large rock inside the cave to lean against or sit on, but there were blood droplets on one side. This must have been the rock Captain Stewart wanted me to find.

It took all my strength to roll the rock from its place. I had to brace myself against the cave wall and push until it budged just a centimeter. Once it started to move, the rest became easier.

Sure enough, the soil beneath the rock had been disturbed. It was packed down, but only because a heavy rock had been sitting on it.

I used Captain Stewart's spade to dig. Since he had dug up the soil only within the last few days, this was easy work. Only a few centimeters down, the spade found its target. I began pushing out the dirt around it, until a canvas backpack started to poke through.

It was heavy, so I used the stick to pry up the backpack, then filled the hole back in, burying the spade with it, since I feared it would be too heavy to carry. I unrolled the top of the pack, eager to see what spy gear Captain Stewart might have. Had my father designed any of it? Whatever I found, it had to be the highest level of secret if the three Germans with me weren't even allowed to look at it.

And I was quickly disappointed. There was a map of the area printed on silk, a flashlight, and a small camera. The straps on it were so short, they'd barely fit around my hand. Nothing else in here was of much use to anyone, and certainly not to a spy.

The strangest thing inside was a raw turnip, which I supposed a person could eat if the only alternative was starvation.

There was also a compact umbrella, a pencil and paper, some coal, modeling clay, a water thermos, and a few other items. Nothing of interest.

I leaned against the rock I had moved, angry and fighting back tears. Papa couldn't have designed any of this because these things were useless. They wouldn't even help me get these people out of the woods!

If these items represented what it meant to be a spy, then the S.O.E. would mean nothing to the outcome of this war. And now I was a part of it.

My mission to rescue my father hadn't even begun, and I had already failed him.

NINETEEN

Rule: *Knowledge is a powerful weapon.*

I s everything all right in there?" Madame Durand asked.

I wiped my eyes with the back of my hand, then picked up the silk map—the one thing Captain Stewart had said I could share with the others—and set it aside.

"I'm fine." My voice sounded thick, so it was obvious that I was anything but fine. I had to do better, or they'd send me away, and I couldn't fail now. In a more cheerful tone, I added, "One more minute."

I took a few deep breaths, forcing myself to calm down, then stared at the rest of the items I'd pulled out of the back-pack, trying to make sense of them. Surely these things were here for a reason.

The umbrella, in case of rain.

The pencil and paper, if the spy had to leave a note or decipher a code.

Coal for heating. The clay . . . perhaps to stop up a water leak?

I poked around inside the backpack and saw a book at the bottom. It had no title, but the plain leather cover was well worn, so I knew Captain Stewart had used this book often.

I pulled it out and began thumbing through the pages. Different chapter headings caught my eye: Communications, Recruitment, Propaganda. Then a few pages later: Codes and Ciphers.

I stopped there, reading more carefully as the book discussed the purpose of codes, the various types of codes, and the security levels of each type—all things my father had taught me throughout my entire life.

Papa!

I'd nearly forgotten the note from Papa, still hidden in the bun made from the braids of my hair. Papa had told Captain Stewart that he knew I'd be able to decode the message. Maybe this book could help me.

I wished I had time to read it now, but the others were waiting for me and were no doubt curious about what I'd found in here. Indeed, when I closed up the bag and emerged from the cave with it, they stared at me with widened eyes.

"Where did you get that?" Monsieur Durand asked.

Jakob grinned. "Captain Stewart must've buried it before we reached the cave."

"What does he have in there?" Madame Durand asked.

This was the question I'd been dreading, because it required me to speak with an authority I knew I did not carry. "I'm under orders from Captain Stewart not to speak to you about what's in here. If you try to look, then this mission is over."

Madame Durand put her hands on her hips. "He assigned *you* to keep secrets from us?" She turned to her husband. "Albert, we will not accept—"

"We will not look," Monsieur Durand said. "Though you must understand this, young lady. We are not uneducated or unaware of the world around us. There is a reason the Allies want us out of German hands. If something in that backpack can help us, it is your duty to share it."

I hoisted the pack higher on my shoulders. "Those are my orders. Captain Stewart suggested I travel posing as your guest, as if I've been sent away from my family in Paris. You can call me Meg. What should I call you?"

They looked at each other. Madame Durand finally said, "You may call us by our names, Liesel and Albert."

I had never called an adult by only their first name, and certainly never adults who were strangers. I started to protest, but Monsieur Durand said, "How will it look to others if you are traveling with us like a close friend and yet you speak to us like strangers?"

Now I understood. "Very well, Albert and Liesel."

Jakob grinned again. "Why don't you call me 'Jakob, the greatest hero in all of Europe!'"

"If you're such a hero, carry that shoulder bag for Meg," Albert said. "She'll have enough weight with carrying Captain Stewart's backpack."

I passed the bag from Grandmère over to Jakob, who added a few items from his pocket. There wasn't much—a slingshot, some fishing line, and a fresh pair of socks.

Albert pulled out a shiny silver pocket watch. "It is seven-fourteen exactly, time to go."

Jakob smiled over at me. "You wouldn't know this to look at him, but back in Germany, he was a wealthy man. There is nothing he values more than that watch."

"Not even you?" I asked.

Jakob only glanced down while Albert said, "It keeps perfect time. There are no finer watches in the world than those that come from Switzerland."

We started walking, Jakob and me in front of his parents, who trailed a few steps behind, speaking in German, apparently not knowing I could understand them. I tried to listen in at first, then finally gave up. It was too much effort, and I didn't care to hear their opinions of me anyway.

But Jakob seemed happy to have me here, and I was surprised to find that I enjoyed his company too. He had an easy smile and was fun to talk to, though I quickly discovered he had the strangest sense of humor.

"What does a bear have in common with a banana?" he asked.

I thought about that for a moment, then shook my head.

He could hardly contain himself from laughing before bursting out with "One of them is yellow!"

He began laughing so hard he had to stop walking and lean over to catch his breath. I merely stood and stared at him, trying to figure out what exactly made it a joke at all.

Jakob finally glanced up at me. "Don't you understand it?"

"There was nothing to understand."

"Exactly! Here's another one . . ."

And on we went, with one awful joke after another, until they became so utterly ridiculous that I finally began to laugh too.

"I knew you'd like them!" he said. "How about this one? How does a jet cross the road?"

"A jet?" I stopped walking, my mind racing back to the last code my father had put into the jar, JAIMIE STAYED. I told Jakob about it, adding, "The only solution that seems to work is 'My idea is a jet.'"

Jakob shrugged. "That doesn't make sense."

"Captain Stewart parachuted here from a jet."

"Yes, but your father wouldn't have known that when he wrote the code."

I'd thought of that too but had tried to talk myself out of

it. No, I couldn't make that mistake. One of the primary rules for codebreakers was: Don't invent anything more than what is there.

But if it wasn't that, then I was out of ideas. And if I couldn't solve that simple code, why would I ever think I could solve the far more complex code that he had sent on that yellow note?

Jakob seemed to sense my disappointment. "There must be other letter combinations."

"It doesn't matter," I said. "That code was only a game between Papa and me. Even if I did solve it, the meaning won't have anything to do with this war, or why we're out here. I'm determined to put it out of my mind."

Which really meant I would think of nothing else as we continued on. Albert walked with a slight limp, so we were moving slower than I wanted, but Jakob helped him through the more difficult areas. And I heard Liesel gasp a few times as she lost her footing on the slippery snow or the ice that sometimes hid beneath it, but so far, she had remained on her feet.

I fell back to speak with Albert, asking, "Do you know where my father is?"

He blinked once. Then, "Yes."

When he didn't say anything more, I added, "Why won't you tell the S.O.E. how to find him?"

"Because I do not trust the S.O.E., no more than they

trust me." He sighed. "I know that sounds harsh, but I had to be sure they would keep their promise to me first."

My temper was warming, so I didn't answer. I wouldn't have anything nice to say to that.

Eventually, Albert continued. "Your father was working in a factory I supervised."

Curiosity got the better of my emotions. "What kind of a factory?"

"There is only one kind of factory in Germany, and that is one that supports the war effort. What does it matter if they produce food, or uniforms, or tanks, or . . . anything else? One day, your father was reported to me for suspected sabotage. There was no doubt of his guilt, so there'd be no doubt of his punishment. I helped him escape to a safe house, but who knows how long he will last there? The Gestapo is searching everywhere for him."

I stopped and waited until he had stopped too before saying, "Please, Albert, call London now and tell them where he is."

Albert sadly shook his head. "We are in danger too, Meg. Help us and I promise, your father will come home alive."

But he couldn't promise that, not if the Gestapo was looking for him.

Beside me, Jakob said, "We admire you for wanting to help your father, but I don't think you have any idea of how much danger you've put yourself in. Maybe France is not *at* war, but it is *in* a war, and life is different outside the Perche. Terrible things are happening all over Europe. We left Germany because we could no longer be a part of it."

I stared back at him without knowing exactly what to say. Finally, I whispered, "Part of what?"

Albert stopped walking. "What do the French know about the Nazi camps? The places they are sending their political prisoners, and the Jews they are arresting? What does anyone know of them?"

I tilted my head, considering his question. I knew the Perche was sheltered, but that didn't mean we were immune from the effects of the war. I had been in town the day the Germans came through and arrested all the Jewish families. Close friends of mine had vanished overnight. The Roma families who had lived in the forests were taken too.

I'd heard that the same thing was happening in many other countries, or worse. Whatever that meant, I hoped I wouldn't have to find out.

I suspected Albert did know. Something of horror flickered in his eyes, then vanished, leaving an expression of deep sadness.

He frowned. "The day will come when the world will know everything that has happened, or that may yet happen. It will change us as a people, all of us, forever."

Jakob stuffed his hands in his pockets. "I was taught

that everyone has three choices in life. To be part of the good, part of the evil, or to try standing in the middle. But I don't think that's true anymore. There is no middle. Those who refuse to choose one side or the other only get in the way of those who are doing good, and in that way, end up helping those who wish to do evil."

"So you left Germany because you could not be part of the evil?"

"No, Meg," Albert said. "We left because the middle became the evil."

I understood him better than he might have thought. In the Perche, our biggest threat wasn't the Nazis. It was our fellow citizens who might denounce us to the Nazis, turn us in for any suspected wrongdoing.

There was even a radio show about it, a program called *Répetez-le* that read letters from listeners who wished to get their neighbors or former friends or even family members in trouble with the authorities. Too often, the enemy was one of our own.

My thoughts were interrupted by the crack of a twig somewhere ahead of us. I raised a hand, motioning for the Durands to stop walking. They did, but more twigs ahead of us were cracking, then some to the sides, and some behind us.

I looked around, hoping to see a friendly face, or any face at all as long as no Nazi helmet came with it. When no one appeared, I decided to take my chances and loudly said, "My name is Meg Kenyon. I passed messages to Yvonne . . . Do you know her? We need safe passage now through these woods."

Seconds of silence filled the air, so many that I was becoming anxious about whether my words had made any difference.

Then a girl emerged from the shadows of the woods, dressed in a beret and trousers beneath a belted coat, and with a pistol in her hands. I recognized her at once. "Yvonne?"

"It's good to see you again, Meg." Her eyes shifted to the others. "But who are they?"

TWENTY

Rule: *Share information wisely.*

While Yvonne waited for my answer, other partisans began entering the clearing, all of them armed, all of them eyeing us with suspicion.

I gestured to the Durands. "I'll be staying with them . . . in the countryside." It was a stupid thing to say. We were already in the countryside.

Yvonne pursed her lips, suspicious. "Where do they live?"

"I . . . uh." My mind raced. "I don't know them well."

"I think you don't know them at all." She turned to the Durands. "Are you French? Jewish?"

"They're from Holland." I blurted out the first country I could think of that wasn't Germany or Italy. When Yvonne waited for more, I added, "But they don't speak French."

"No?" She walked over to them, looking at each one in turn. They stood still and silent, trying to remain calm, but Albert had bundled his hands and Jakob's mouth was twitching. Only Liesel kept up the appearance of calmness, though she was almost too calm. That in itself could draw the partisans' attention to her.

Yvonne spoke in a language I didn't know, though I assumed it was Dutch. *"Waarom ben je hier?"*

Liesel smiled and, to my surprise, responded in what must have been fluent Dutch. I didn't know any of the words, but she gestured to Jakob and his father and then laughed, and so did Yvonne. They chatted a bit more, and at one point I heard my name, then they laughed again. I didn't appreciate that, but I did know that whatever Liesel was saying was working.

Finally, Yvonne stepped back and said to the other partisans, "They'll camp with us tonight." Then she turned to me. "My apologies if I was rude to you before. I understand better now."

"Good," I mumbled, then turned to Liesel, curious about what she must have said to change the situation so quickly. But Liesel only winked and smiled back at me.

The partisans closed in and walked us farther ahead to their camp, if it could be called that. Shelters had been built with stacked rocks and dried mud, or sheets had been draped over ropes stretched between two trees to create a simple tent. If necessary, everything here could be taken down within minutes.

Liesel said something else to Yvonne, who then gestured to one of the larger huts. With Yvonne's permission, the Durands settled there, pulling out blankets from their bags to spread on the ground and rest. They gestured to me to join them, but I wasn't ready for that yet.

I said to Yvonne, "Could I sit by your fire?" My toes had gone numb from the cold.

"Of course. I'll have someone bring you a hot tea."

"Thank you. And what—" I gathered my courage, hesitant to ask a question with an answer I might not like. "What did Madame Durand say back there about me?"

"Only that she believed we were heroes, and she hoped we would be safe." Yvonne took my hands in hers. "We are safer, thanks to you. Your message yesterday probably saved a lot of lives. The Nazis didn't find a single one of us. We owe you a great debt."

Before I could answer, she released my hands and hurried away, asking for someone to make me some tea. I glanced over at Liesel, who nodded and smiled back. That alone began to warm me.

Someone placed a cup of tea in my hands, and I drank it until I felt warmer, then I pulled apart my braids and retrieved the yellow paper from my father, holding it against the light of the fire to read it.

Dearest wife, Daisy, and Mom;
One day I'll return, you'll see.
Nothing can stop me from climbing
to you. Watch perfectly as
the sadness becomes numb.
Remember my smiles, brightened
under tender skies by the sea.
Straighten the spine, Daisy.
Take courage, even when hurting,
have faith until this battle
ends. Until then, be calm.
Regards,
Rosbif

The strange bit of wording in the fourth line caught my eye: "Watch perfectly." What did that mean?

Watch might mean to look or to see. It might mean to guard or protect. But if those were Papa's intended meanings, he would have said, "Watch carefully."

If he wanted a *perfect* watch, perhaps he had a different meaning in mind.

Not far from me, the Durands sat beneath their tented

shelter. Albert pulled out his pocket watch, then snapped it shut and replaced it in his coat.

Albert had said that pocket watch was valuable because it kept perfect time. He claimed the most perfect watches in the world came from Switzerland.

Switzerland was just across our border to the east, and directly south of Germany. But it hadn't been invaded because, like Spain, it was a neutral country.

I sucked in a breath, then put one hand over my mouth.

I'd figured it out!

Watch perfectly.

Papa wanted us to go to Switzerland. That's where we would meet him.

I looked back over to the Durands, who were in quiet conversation with one another. They were expecting to go to Spain. That had been Captain Stewart's intention, and maybe it was a better plan. The Switzerland route would require us to remain in the Occupied Zone, which was far more dangerous than entering Free France in the south, and I'd heard the escape route to Spain through the Pyrenees Mountains was fairly established.

But Papa wanted me to go to Switzerland.

How would I ever convince the Durands to change their plans? To go through more dangerous territory, via an unmapped escape route?

I already knew the answer to my questions: They wouldn't.

They wouldn't . . . yet. One way or another, I had to convince them to change their minds. We were going to escape through Switzerland.

TWENTY-ONE

Rule: *True friends will always come to your aid.*

Eventually, Jakob came to sit by me near the fire. He waited until we were alone before lowering his head and saying, "You got us this far. My parents are impressed."

"Your mother got us into this camp, not me," I said. "It was a lucky thing that she speaks Dutch."

"She speaks many languages." Jakob glanced back at her as she sat in quiet conversation with Albert. "She was a translator."

"For the Nazis?"

He nodded and looked away. Which was a good thing, because I suddenly felt all bunched up inside. Liesel had seemed so nice, so kind.

But she was not only German. She was one of *them*.

Had she been there to translate almost two years ago, when the invaders marched across our borders, terrorizing our people, arresting anyone who didn't look like them or think like them? Did she translate for my father when they took him prisoner?

I nearly asked Jakob my questions, but Yvonne and some other partisans came to sit near the fire, and we both fell silent, even as knots continued to form in my chest.

Yvonne had some frybread with her, and when she passed it over to Jakob and me, we gratefully accepted. Then she said to me, "If you're here, then you must know all the things your mother did for us."

"I only know she was a radio operator." There hadn't been time for details.

"She's so much more," a dark-haired boy sitting beside Yvonne said. "Often, she's been our one connection to the outside world. How's her ankle?"

"She was having a hard time walking on it . . . when I last saw her." I already missed my mother terribly, and talking about her now reopened that wound in my heart. I added, "Do you know how she injured it?"

"Your friend knows; he was there." Yvonne's eyes widened. "Hasn't he told you?"

I glanced sideways at Jakob, who was keeping his head down, and I realized why. I had told everyone he was Dutch. He shouldn't be able to understand what we were saying.

Without waiting for my answer, Yvonne continued: "Your mother was midway through a transmission when the

Nazis discovered what she was doing. She grabbed her equipment and ran into the hills. Her only escape led her toward a steep ledge. It was either jump or wait to be arrested. So she jumped. We had a few partisans in the area who would have helped her, but she waved them off. She didn't want the Nazis to see them and know they were there. So she limped or crawled, or whatever she had to do, keeping hold of that suitcase the entire time. The next time we saw her, your friend was helping her walk, although she didn't have the suitcase anymore. She must have hidden it somewhere."

"I see. So, she injured her ankle in that fall," I said. "Thankfully, we think it will heal all right."

Yvonne nodded. "She's a strong woman. There are few jobs more dangerous than hers. When the operator gets into a safe position to transmit their codes, it takes time to establish a connection and send the message. They have to do it quickly and then get as far from that position as possible, because it's likely the Nazis heard the transmission and are on their way to find the operator." She paused again. "Your mother is incredibly brave. You should be proud of her."

I was proud, of course. But I was also angry with her for keeping this a secret from me, or maybe angry with myself for not having figured it out on my own. And embarrassed because it was my job to be observant and to find out everything that was going on beneath the surface of the Perche. I'd failed to even discover the truth about my own mother.

"Well, you had all better get a good sleep tonight," Yvonne said. "It sounds as if you've got a long road ahead, and things won't be easy."

The boy next to her leaned in. "Listen carefully. Once you leave the Perche, if you want to survive, then don't trust anyone. An offer to help might be bait to turn you over to the Nazis. The government in Vichy are French puppets on strings pulled by Hitler himself. France even pays the Germans to be here, if you can believe that. Our police are his police; our militia is his Gestapo. Even the best people here will not help. They are hungry, and no one will risk their rations for you. So keep your head down and your eye on the border. Where do you intend to cross?"

I was supposed to say we were headed toward the Pyrenees Mountains in Spain, but that was no longer my plan. So I waited until after Jakob had left before I answered.

"Switzerland," I said. "We'll go over the Jura Mountains."

"That's too risky," Yvonne said. "The Pyrenees would be better."

"No, it must be Switzerland."

Yvonne nodded. "Very well. Go by train to Dijon, and if you get as far as Dole, that will put you on the edge of the Forbidden Zone. It's nearly a hundred kilometers from there to the border, all of it filled with Nazi posts and patrols. Anyone wishing to enter must have a special set of papers. If you want to cross, you'd better get help from one of the locals. Ask for Pierre. He will help if you tell him my name."

I arched a brow. "Pierre? That's a common name."

"Just ask for him, and he'll find you."

I wanted to ask how that was possible, but Jakob had returned by then, so we fell silent.

"In the morning, we'll bring you to the edge of the woods," Yvonne said. "We owe you that much, for all you and your mother have done for us."

"Thank you." I stood to walk back to the shelter where Jakob's parents had been all evening, keeping to themselves. Jakob joined me, but as we walked there together, he leaned in and asked, "What were you talking about after I left?"

"Nothing much."

"Oh." A beat passed, and then he said, "Eventually, we'll need to trust each other."

This time, I didn't answer him.

I couldn't.

TWENTY-TWO

Sunday, March 1, 1942
659 days since I've seen Papa

Thanks to Yvonne's help, by early afternoon the following day, we reached the eastern boundary of the Perche. I hadn't realized until this very moment how safe I had felt in the Perche, as if the woods that surrounded the little towns kept our secrets and protected us from the worst of the war. Wasn't that exactly what Jakob had tried to tell me yesterday, how sheltered we were?

But now, I stood at the edge of the forest, facing a broad landscape. All I could see ahead were wide-open areas with gently rolling hills and distant horizons. In another month or two, this would all become farmland. A few months after that, the harvest would come, and the Germans would take what they wanted and send it back to their country. The rest would be rationed and sold here. Some of it might be snuck onto the black market.

As peaceful as the land around us now seemed, I also knew the closer we came to Paris, the more my familiar world would be overtaken by tall buildings, a faster pace, and more Nazi soldiers.

"Captain Stewart suggested our best route to the Pyrenees Mountains would begin by taking the train from Paris," Liesel said. "But based on what the partisans told us last night, I think we should reconsider."

"Meg, I believe you have a map," Albert said.

"We should keep walking," I said.

But all of them had stopped, so I huffed and walked back to a tall and almost-flat rock near the side of the road. I pulled out the silk map and they immediately spread it out and began scouring the details for options.

"It's a hundred kilometers to Paris," Jakob said, tracing his finger along the map. "Every step puts us closer to the thickest population of Nazis in the country."

Albert began stroking his beard, deep in thought. "That's true. Paris is the last place we should go."

"We have to go to Paris," I said.

They looked at me for an explanation, but I didn't have one, not yet. The truth was that I needed more time to figure out how to convince them to go to Switzerland, and a hundred kilometers of thinking time seemed about right.

"If the Pyrenees are to the southwest, then why are we walking in the very opposite direction?" Liesel asked.

"Because of the trains," I said. "If we get to Paris, we can get the right train to . . . wherever we are going."

Albert shook his head. "We can catch a train from the nearest station, either to reach Paris more quickly or, better still, to find a southbound train that will take us directly to the Spanish border."

"Agreed," Liesel said, echoed by Jakob.

With no other choice than to tell them my plan, I took a deep breath, then said, "I have another idea. We should escape through Switzerland."

"Switzerland?" Liesel vigorously shook her head. "Absolutely not. The plan is to go to Spain!"

"Just consider Switzerland."

"Why?" Jakob asked.

I hesitated, wishing I had taken that hundred kilometers for thinking, because there was no logical reason for us to go to Switzerland. I knew that better than anyone.

But that was where Papa wanted me to go.

Desperate for any argument in my favor, I pointed to the map, putting my finger over the town of Auxonne. "This is where I used to live. I know this area. My father took us skiing in the Alps every winter. I know those mountains. I know nothing about the Pyrenees."

"You do not need to know them," Jakob said. "There are locals who will help us get through."

"Do you know who they are?" I asked. "Do you know

their names? Which villages they live in? Do you know anything about them other than that they exist?"

"Who will help us get through the Alps?" Jakob asked.

"That's my point—I can do it! We do not have to depend
on finding a resistance fighter or bribing a smuggler who
may turn around and betray us. I know where the border is,
and more than one way through it." I lowered my voice.
"Routes the Nazis do not know."

"How can you be sure of what they do and do not
know?" Liesel looked to her husband. "What do you have to
say to this? Will you let the opinion of a child change Captain
Stewart's plan for us?"

Albert sighed deeply, then turned to look directly at me.
"There are things you are not telling us. What is your true
reason for wanting to cross the Alps?"

My eyes darted away, but when I looked back at him, he
was still staring at me, waiting for an answer. Finally, I said,
"I have a note from my father. After he's released, he asks
me to meet him in Switzerland."

Albert nodded thoughtfully. "Were those the words he
used? That he wanted you to go to Switzerland?"

I bit down on my lip and shook my head. Nothing
in the code specifically said Switzerland. But I had inter-
preted the clues correctly, I was sure of it.

What if I was wrong?

Albert's tone was kind but firm. "You're only guessing,

then, and I'm afraid that is not enough reason for us to change plans. When your father wrote that note, he had no idea that you would be traveling with us, so it cannot be true that he was giving you instructions."

"Maybe—"

"We will stay with our original plan," Albert said. "Which also means that we will walk until we find the next southbound train."

I looked from him over to Jakob, who only shrugged at me. Then to Liesel, who was still frowning as if I had won the argument rather than her.

Maman had told me the Germans could not be negotiated with, and these three had just proved her right.

I wished I had never come with them.

TWENTY-THREE

Rule: *Make judgments carefully.*

For the time being, I had no choice other than to travel along with the Durands, as Captain Stewart called them. I had other names in mind for this family, most of which would have shaken my grandmother to the core if she heard me speak them aloud.

How I missed her, and my mother.

Especially Maman.

I'd become used to my father being gone, and we hadn't always lived with Grandmère.

But I'd never been a day without my mother.

This time, Jakob was at the rear of our group. His parents were walking ahead of us, but I kept a constant eye on them.

She was whispering to her husband now. I heard the words "child," "mistake," and, most distinctly: "Send her home. We're better off on our own."

Jakob must have heard it too. He bumped one arm against mine and whispered, "Don't worry about that. It's not because of you."

"It is."

"No, Meg. You just have to remember that some people go about with all their emotions balanced on a very thin line. I don't know why. Maybe because something has gone wrong in their lives."

"Is that true for your mother?"

He watched her for a moment. "I think so. You didn't cause those things to go wrong; you only upset the balance in her emotions."

"What happened to her?" I asked.

"My father knows, but she won't tell me. I only know that the last time I asked, she got this look in her eyes like her whole world was falling apart, so I don't plan to ask again. I do feel sorry for her, though."

I knew I should feel the same way. A truly good person would, but I didn't. Maybe because my own emotions were on a similar thin line, and far out of balance. I said to Jakob, "My family's world *did* fall apart. Nearly everything was taken from us when your country invaded. Your mother was part of that. She worked for *them*. I'll help your mother, but I will never feel sorry for her."

He stared over at me. "I didn't think you'd be like this."

"Like what?"

"The kind of person to believe everyone is the same, just because they come from the same place."

"But you are all the same! Do you know why I was helping the resistance? Because after Germany defeated France, the Nazis told us they'd be different than we expected. And at first they were. They were polite and friendly and helpful. Then they took our food. They emptied our museums and robbed us of anything of value. They've arrested the Jews for no crime other than existing peacefully among us. They took my father, for attempting to defend the country *they* invaded! All this, from the enemy that tried to tell us they were different."

Jakob nodded curtly. "So you see my family as the enemy. Me as the enemy."

"You are German. So I suppose—"

"If that's the way you think, then my family is also one of *them*." Jakob stuffed his hands in his pockets. "And you are only one of millions of people we've conquered."

Jakob strode ahead, leaving me to walk alone. Which might have been a good thing. Because I didn't know what I would have said next. I only knew that an ache had formed in my chest. I didn't want to think of him as an enemy.

But how could I ever think of him as a friend?

We continued walking in silence. I was hungry and

thirsty and wanted to stop for a rest. Blisters had begun to form on the bottoms of my feet, and my shoulders protested with the weight of Captain Stewart's bag, which seemed to grow heavier with every kilometer we crossed.

But the Durands were not complaining, so neither would I. I just kept walking.

While making plans of my own.

I understood why they wanted to stick with Captain Stewart's plan, but I could no longer follow it. Nor could I go home, not if Lieutenant Becker still wanted to question me about my journal.

Once the Durands were safe, I'd have to continue on to Switzerland, even if I was going alone. Papa would be there. I knew he would be there.

And so we continued on in silence for another couple of hours. Finally, Liesel turned to Albert. "I'm exhausted. Could we take a few minutes to rest?"

He nodded and checked the time on his pocket watch. We had been traveling through farmland, with row after row of tall dried cornstalks left over from last fall's harvest. But we had come to a little clearing with dirt and a few large rocks beneath a tall oak tree.

Jakob pulled out a canteen from his bag. "I hear a river nearby. I'll find us some water to drink."

"I'll come with you to help," Albert offered.

Liesel had already sat down on a nearby rock in the

shade, facing away from me to adjust a pretty gray scarf around her neck. I preferred the sun. It was warmer here.

It was also as far from her as I could get. Rather than having to speak to her, I reached into Captain Stewart's bag and pulled out the leather-bound book, the one with no title or author printed on the cover. Since the moment I'd seen it, I had been eager to know more about this book. All I had done earlier was flip through the pages.

Turning my back to Liesel, this time I started from the beginning, and my eyes immediately widened. In only the first few words, I knew exactly what I was holding.

This was Captain Stewart's spy training manual!

I flipped through the book, pausing every few pages to read the chapter titles with rules for the spies listed below. Everything was in here—the art of disguises, how to withstand an interrogation, what to do in an emergency . . . and there it was again, the chapter on codes.

I stopped there, almost short of breath for the excitement building in me. Page after page described the various types of codes, some of them ones Papa had never told me about, nor that I had ever before imagined. How to create them, how to send them safely, how to break them. Not only that, but page after page of ways to create invisible ink, or how to make it reappear on the page. I'd never even thought of invisible ink before.

My mind raced. What if Papa's yellow note contained a

secret message hidden on the paper itself? Was that possible?

I scanned the list of ingredients for invisible ink. Some of them I'd heard of, such as milk—did Papa have milk, wherever he was? Milk was simple to detect; just heat the paper and the invisible writing would darken. Many of the others were chemical names I'd never heard of, but I doubted Papa could get any of them while he was in hiding.

"Am I bothering you?"

I slammed the book shut, hearing Liesel's voice behind me. I wondered how long she'd been standing there, how much she'd seen.

"What are you reading?" she asked.

"Nothing." That was a foolish answer. Obviously, I'd been reading *something*. "Just a book Captain Stewart had in his bag."

"Another secret, I see. Can we talk?"

I replaced the book and rolled his backpack closed, then stood to face Liesel. "Of course."

"I wish to apologize for my behavior earlier today. I believe that Captain Stewart's plan is best for us, but I had no wish to offend you. We are grateful for your help."

An apology was the last thing I had expected to hear, and her kind words took me off guard. I faltered a moment before saying, "Oh yes, of course. I'm sorry too . . ."

I didn't know why I was apologizing. I wasn't sorry for anything, so I let my sentence fade out with no further explanations.

"Captain Stewart must have a lot of faith in you, to send you here to help us," she said.

I shrugged. "I think mostly he believed I'd be safer here than at home."

She smiled. "That was our reason to leave as well. We had to bribe a man to seal us into shipping crates for transfer out of Germany by train. It took us as far as Orléans. From there, we had to get to the Perche to meet Captain Stewart."

I said, "He must have thought highly of you as well to agree to this mission."

She shook her head. "He came on assignment from London. And from what I understand, he wasn't particularly excited to be helping us."

"Why not?"

She widened her arms. "Who among the Allies wishes to help a German these days?"

We fell silent until I said, "Jakob told me you were a translator. Did you work for the Nazis?"

"In my profession, it is impossible *not* to work for the Nazis in some way."

"What did you translate?"

"Everything I was asked to translate." She shifted her weight. "Diplomatic communications, intercepted messages. Sometimes codes. I understand the note from your father is in code. If you wish, I'm happy to help you with it."

"No, thank you." I lowered my eyes. "He believed that I'd be the only one who could solve it."

She smiled. "You and your father must have a special bond, if he knew you alone would be capable of deciphering his code. No wonder you want to see him again in Switzerland. I'm sorry that it is not possible for us to change our plans for him."

Before I could answer, Jakob came running toward us. "Get away from the road!" he called. "Hurry, hide everything!"

Albert was not far behind, though in his hurry to leave the patch of cornstalks, he tripped, and the canteens of water dropped to the ground.

"I'll get them," Liesel said. "You take the heavier things and get them off the road."

She began gathering everything he had dropped while I grabbed my bag and raced behind Albert and Jakob into the rows of cornstalks. With her arms full, Liesel joined us on the ground, and we all ducked low. I worried we weren't low enough. I could still see the road, which meant anyone on the road could see us.

Seconds later, we heard the sound of a truck slowly

approaching. I glanced up long enough to see a German Opel Blitz park directly in front of where we had just been. The canvas fabric over the truck bed parted and at least ten Nazis jumped out.

"Ach, no." Albert groaned.

We all looked over at Albert, who was quietly patting his pockets. As the Nazis filled the clearing directly in front of us, he whispered, "I believe that I dropped my glasses."

TWENTY-FOUR

Rule: *Little mistakes can lead to disasters.*

For the next several seconds, I didn't breathe. I hardly dared to, when the slightest draw of air seemed to echo louder than the soldiers not ten meters away from us.

Those who had already exited the vehicle were laughing, tossing orders at one another, exchanging opinions of how lucky they were to have been assigned to France rather than "the filthy countries."

Beside me, I heard Jakob breathing, the rustle of the cornstalks when Albert shifted positions. I definitely heard Liesel whisper to Albert, "What if we are caught?" and even heard the slight tick in his neck when he shook his head to warn her not to speak. With all that, how could I breathe, and add to the noise?

The heavy German boots came closer to us, responding to someone's order to eat quickly so they could move on.

One of them would sit in the exact place where I had just been.

The soldiers were laughing and talking with one another, though I was too afraid to make sense of their conversations. I did understand that they were opening cans of food to make a lunch, and I immediately detected a horrid smell. I wrinkled my nose in disgust.

Beside me, Jakob quietly sniffed. I turned to see him grinning, which I could not understand. Not in this moment.

From beneath the tree, one of the soldiers shouted in what I was certain had to be a string of curse words, and then hurled the can into the cornstalks. It landed on Jakob's shoulder and rolled directly in front of his face, and his smile instantly disappeared.

The odor from the can was foul, but I also worried that the soldier would be ordered to come into the cornstalks and retrieve the can.

Indeed, it did sound as if some order was given, but that was almost immediately followed by someone else saying, "*Was ist das?*" A question that put a lump in my throat.

I glanced over at Albert, who was shaking his head. He turned to Jakob and pointed at his eyes. They had found his glasses.

One of the soldiers began walking toward us. I saw the cornstalks bend and crush in his path, felt the vibrations of his heavy boots on the soft earth beneath us, and saw birds fly from where they had perched on the ground, frightened by his approach. He was so close, and my heart was pounding so loud, I didn't understand why he couldn't hear it too.

He called in German, and when we didn't respond, he spoke the same words in French: "If someone is out there, it will go better if you show yourself now."

When we still gave no answer, I heard a click, and then he began firing his weapon into the cornstalks. One of the bullets pierced the can of half-opened food, a stew that oozed from the container, some of it back-spraying onto Jakob's face.

The soldier tilted his rifle down, using it to push the cornstalks aside so he could see better. Behind me, a rustling sound caught the soldier's attention. He took another step toward us and a knot formed in my throat. His boots were only centimeters away. If he stepped again, he'd find us.

The rustling sound was repeated, only this time a bird flew from behind us, high into the air.

"*Genug!*" the officer in charge ordered, then demanded the soldier return from the field and gather around him along with the other men.

He showed them the glasses. "These are German made," he said. "Most likely they were dropped by a soldier like you who came this way earlier today. We cannot be this sloppy. Nor can we allow our enemies in this country to get possession of them and turn the lenses into weapons."

Something soft fell to the earth, and I heard a sound almost as awful as when the soldier had fired his weapon. A crunch of glass and metal.

They had just crushed Albert's glasses. And from the look on his face, this was a disaster.

We waited exactly where we were for several minutes after the Opel Blitz left, none of us moving or even whispering a word. Finally, Albert nodded. Jakob lifted his head first, then sat up and motioned to the rest of us that everything appeared safe.

He immediately stood and gathered a few fallen leaves from the ground, using them to wipe the splattered stew off his face. Then he crouched down and picked up what remained of the glasses. The frame was badly bent, and only a broken edge of one lens was still attached.

"How is your vision without glasses?" I asked Albert.

"Up close, I can see fairly well. But even that tree in front of us has lost its detail. At the road, the entire world is a blur. Beyond that, I could not identify a friend from an enemy."

Albert was half-blind without his glasses.

And I was supposed to help him cross through Nazi-occupied territory, and then lead him over an entire mountain, filled with enough hazards to challenge even someone with perfect vision.

Our situation had just gone from dangerous to absolutely impossible.

TWENTY-FIVE

Rule: *People are individuals, not categories.*

We continued our journey in a far more somber mood than when we had left earlier that morning. Jakob walked ahead with me to watch for any trouble. Liesel and Albert walked directly behind us. She was doing her best to act as his eyes whenever necessary.

"Something has been bothering me," I said to Jakob. "When the German opened that can of food and it smelled so awful, I saw you smiling."

That same smile reappeared on his face now. "I wondered if maybe it was one of the cans I helped to pack." When he saw my confusion, he added, "It was part of a volunteer effort back in Germany, for the Hitler Youth. We were sometimes brought to the factories to load the cans of food into crates to be shipped out to the soldiers. Shortly before my family left Germany, we spent a day loading crates of beef stew. We worked fast, so no one had time to watch what anyone else was doing." Now his smile widened. "No one saw the nail in my hand as I punched a tiny hole into every can I touched. Air in a sealed can of food will ruin it. Maybe I was hit with one of the very cans I spoiled!"

I smiled along with him, but he was also making me think in a way I never had before. I asked, "You did that to your own people?"

His smile immediately fell. "*They* are not my people. My people are the ones who fight them. My family wants nothing to do with *them*."

"At least your family is free."

Something flashed in Jakob's eyes—not anger, but a hint of pain. He blinked that away, then gestured to Albert and Liesel. "You're speaking of them? You don't understand, Meg. To get this far, we've had to leave everything behind—everything! Our friends and families, our home country. We will be branded as traitors in Germany, and everyone who ever knew us will have to bear that shame. Does that sound like we're free?"

Albert must have been listening, because he said, "We know who we are . . . who we were before. All we ask is that you look at us for who we are now trying to be."

Jakob added, "As I said before, we are not all the same."

Nor were we here in France, I supposed. I'd seen for myself the French women who flirted with Nazi soldiers, heard the stories of one family denouncing another to the authorities for hiding Jews, buying or selling on the black market, or for secretly listening to the radio broadcasts from London. I'd listened to those same radio broadcasts myself, so I knew there were also a lot of French citizens who continued to fight for our freedom, who resisted German control in any way possible, even if all they could do was wear blue, white, and red, the colors of our flag.

I apologized to Jakob, who only grinned and said, "Also, I tell much better jokes than other Germans."

I frowned back at him. "Your jokes are the *better* ones?"

"Of course! Let me tell you about the one with the frog and the cat . . ."

We continued walking, passing small farmhouses and barns and fields with the occasional patch of snow. They were almost ready to plant again.

I thought of Grandmère and all the work I did to keep that farm running. She'd never be able to manage it all without me, not even with Maman's help. They needed me to help plant her fields and to care for the young crops. If those fields weren't planted, they'd go hungry next winter.

Without me.

Liesel called ahead, "Tell us about your family, Meg. I know a little about your father, but what about your mother?"

"I, uh . . ." I wasn't sure where to begin. Had Jakob told them that my mother was a radio operator for the resistance?

I only said, "My family used to be happy. We used to be together."

"That's why you want to go to Switzerland," Albert said. "Allow me to propose another solution. After your father is rescued, couldn't he come to Spain?"

My spine stiffened. "My father's note said that I should go to Switzerland."

"It couldn't say that, Meg." Jakob frowned over at me. "Captain Stewart was supposed to be on this mission with us, not you. Your father was never giving you instructions on where to go."

Deepening my frustration, Liesel added, "If you don't mind me asking, I find it strange that your mother would send you out to help us, rather than coming along herself. Is she ill?"

"No, but she injured her foot . . ." I hesitated there, checking my words. ". . . in a riding accident."

Then I glanced back at Jakob, realizing he would know I was lying. He knew exactly why my mother was injured. But Jakob only stared back at me, expressionless. He was letting me lie to his own family.

Jakob was a difficult person to figure out.

"I believe we should find a place to sleep for the night," Albert said. "We have gone a long way today, but we are nowhere near Paris. We should not be looking for shelter too close to curfew."

"I'll run ahead and see what's available," Jakob offered.

He hurried past me, and I fell back to walk beside Liesel as she continued to lead Jakob's father along the path.

"I hope it did not bother you to talk about your mother," she said. "It's only that every time I look at you, I think about my daughter, and wonder if she ever talks about me too."

"You have a daughter?" My heart thudded against my chest. "Where is she?"

"Germany." Liesel smiled faintly, and it quickly faded away. "I had no choice. They put her in the care of another family so that I could concentrate on my work. She was forced to join the League of German Girls, as all our daughters are. For her sake, I had to continue to work for the Nazis."

"They forced you to become a translator?"

"I used to teach languages at the university. Then, several years ago, I received a visit from some representatives of the Führer, asking me to do some translation work. At the time, none of us knew what he believed, the future he wanted for Germany. There was no reason for me not to do it. The Nazis liked my work and paid me well at a time when no one, especially no woman, was paid well for anything, and so I continued to work for them. Eventually, I began translating documents marked as 'Secret' or as 'Classified,' documents with plans and messages that frightened me, so I told my supervisor I wished to leave. He informed me that at the level I now was, I could not be allowed to leave, that I was required to work for them."

"And you had to agree, because of your daughter."

Liesel quickly brushed away a tear that had fallen to her cheek. "Once this mission is complete, I will get her back . . . somehow. This war has done terrible things to many people."

It certainly had been terrible for my family. This war seemed to me like a chain of dominoes stacked on their ends. With the first invasion, one tile had toppled another, and then another and another. And not only in the destruction of governments and traditions and border lines but destroying dreams for the future and traditions of the past. Destroying families.

Including, I supposed, the connection between a German mother and her daughter. Surely, Albert ached for her too, though he hadn't spoken a word throughout this conversation. I wondered if their daughter was near my age, or, if there had not been a war, if we ever could have been friends.

Because, certainly, I could not consider Liesel's daughter an enemy. She had nothing more to do with this war than I did.

"What's your daughter's name?" I asked.

Liesel closed her eyes a moment, as if trying to picture her. Then she whispered, "Her name is Margarete. I called her Meg."

TWENTY-SIX

Rule: *Watch everything, while making it appear you've seen nothing.*

Jakob returned after a short time with news of an abandoned home where he thought we might take shelter. I wanted to talk to him about Margarete, about his sister. I'd always wished to have a sister, or even a brother, but Maman said I'd been a miracle baby and that I nearly had not survived my birth.

Now I would have to survive the Durand family. We were only on our second day of a mission I had codenamed simply as: Rescue. I was beginning to wonder if I would need an even greater miracle to complete this mission.

Maybe the Durands were seeking a miracle too. When Liesel and Albert spoke to each other, it was often of loved ones they had left behind. They were both worried for what might happen to their friends and family members as punishment for their leaving. Surely Margarete was included in those fears.

Jakob must have felt the same way, but so far, he hadn't said a word about any of that. I knew he must be terribly worried for his sister.

"Your mother told me about Margarete," I said as he was leading us to the abandoned home. He looked confused at first, and I added, "Your sister, with my same name. I remember that you told me your mother's world had fallen apart. Is that why, because she had to leave your sister behind?"

Jakob tilted his head and thought for a moment. "I'm sure that was very difficult for her."

It was an odd response and not at all what I'd expected. Didn't it bother Jakob too?

"I think I found a good shelter for the night," he said, changing the subject far too quickly. "But I was surprised to find that it wasn't the only abandoned home. I saw at least two others in the area."

"How unusual," Liesel said.

"Not really," I said. "A lot of people left when the Germans invaded, going south, or to England if they could. My family left our home in Auxonne too. We've never returned home, and I'm sure many people here never did either. They believe it's safer in Free France."

"Maybe it is for now," Albert said. "But sooner or later,

the Nazi appetite for power and control will turn its eyes to the unoccupied zone. Southern France will not remain free for much longer."

If it even was free now. According to Grandmère, everything the Vichy government did had to be approved by Germany, and in its hurry to get Germany's approval, Vichy too often betrayed us, its own citizens.

We were pleased when Jakob showed us the house he had found. It was far from any neighbors and enough off the road that our presence shouldn't raise any suspicions. Nothing of value remained, but a few logs were stacked near an old fireplace, and a water pump in the yard still worked. I noticed a telephone on a desk in the front room and excitedly picked up the receiver, hoping to hear a connection. But the phone was dead, and I set the receiver back down, disappointed.

The telephone sat on a little table. I opened a drawer and drew in a hushed breath. Inside was a small gold menorah. A Jewish family had lived here.

I sat on the floor, holding the menorah in my hands. When we first went to live with Grandmère, the Jewish family next door had a daughter about my age, Véra. She was friendly and loved to laugh, and we quickly became friends. Almost as quickly, Germany began placing restrictions on her family—on all Jewish families. Our government in Vichy protested . . . but only because the Germans had not gone far enough. After blaming the Jews for France's loss in the war, Vichy forbade

Jews from going to the movies, banking, working in the more prominent jobs, and even from owning a radio. Véra's family used to come to Grandmère's house and listen to the radio with us. Then one day they stopped coming. A month later, they disappeared entirely. But it was not Germany who had taken them. Vichy had given the orders.

Others had disappeared too. A Roma family who'd lived in the forests. Even two men in our town, because it was rumored they were romantically involved. I didn't understand how that could have mattered to their Führer, but Maman said the same things had happened elsewhere, and not only in France but throughout Europe.

I wondered if the people who had once lived here had simply disappeared too, and where they were now.

Albert built us a fire while Jakob looked around outside to be sure that we were in a safe place. Liesel offered to put a meal together from the supplies Grandmère had put in my canvas bag. I knew I should offer to help, but instead, I went to the back of the house and began digging into Captain Stewart's bag again.

I opened his spy manual to a new section, one titled "Surveillance," which seemed to be instructions on how to observe someone from a distance without them realizing they were being watched. Of course any spy would need those skills, so I ran my thumb down the lines to read carefully.

The rules were simple and logical. The person who is watching shouldn't stand out in any way—there should be no reason for anyone to notice them. When possible, more than one person should be at the scene, so that if the target becomes suspicious, that second person can take over. They should stay close enough to obtain the information they need but remain at a distance otherwise. And if their cover is blown—

I glanced up, feeling the weight of someone's eyes on me. Sure enough, Jakob was peering through a nearby window. When he saw that I'd noticed, he backed away.

I closed the book, wondering what I should do next. Had he simply been curious about what I was doing, or was I the target of *his* surveillance?

Captain Stewart told me that although London had cleared these three for the mission, he didn't know the Durands, and I guessed that was not even their true name. And while for the most part they seemed kind and sincere, the truth was that after two days on the road with them, I didn't know them either. And what I did know gave me every reason to be careful.

I did know that Liesel had been a translator for the Nazis.

I did know that they left behind a daughter that no one other than Liesel wanted to talk about.

And I did know that Jakob had been watching me. I just couldn't explain why.

TWENTY-SEVEN

Monday, March 2, 1942
660 days since I've seen Papa

J akob never did explain why he had been spying on me, but when I saw him the following morning, I wanted an entirely different explanation.

"We need to talk about your sister," I began.

He only shook his head. "Liesel shouldn't have told you about her. We agreed that none of us would discuss other family members."

"Not even your own sister?"

"Especially not her." He stood, shoved his hands into his pockets, and left the room, adding only that "My father says it's time for us to go."

Nearly an hour into our walk, Jakob finally began speaking to me again. "How did you figure out that your father would be going to Switzerland? Was it in that letter from Captain Stewart?"

"Yes."

"Can I see the letter?"

I thought about that a moment, then shook my head. "He intended it for me."

"Yes, but sometimes it helps to have someone else look at it. Though if you really want it solved, ask my mother. She did a lot of code making before."

"I'll think about it."

"Are you sure you decoded it correctly? What if you're wrong?"

That was something I hadn't fully considered, and the thought sent a chill through me. What if I persuaded the Durands to go to Switzerland, and it was the wrong place?

Without waiting for my answer, Jakob said, "This is why it's best for us to stay with the plan. We're going to Spain. That's what we agreed."

"That's what you all agreed." I stopped walking too and shoved my hands in my coat pockets. "I think I'm correct about the code. So I can help you get to Spain, but I won't stay there. My father will be in Switzerland."

"You're going by yourself? Do you have any idea how difficult it would be to get there on your own?"

I wanted to argue back, but I couldn't. He was right. I needed to stay with the Durands, at least for now.

The Durands' plan for today was to continue on the road until we came to a train station. They preferred to catch a southbound train, but I figured they'd be happy to catch any train at all as long as no Nazis were on board.

"A station can't be much farther ahead," Jakob said. "Sooner or later, the right train will come."

"It isn't wise to wait out in the open," his father said, snapping his pocket watch closed. "If a train is too long in coming, we'll keep walking."

I was the first to spot the train station, on the outskirts of Dreux. I knew of this place since many people came from here to buy our food off the black market. We began walking faster. None of us wanted to arrive a minute too late, then be forced to wait hours for the next opportunity.

"I hope we haven't missed the right train already," Liesel said.

"One might be expected soon." Jakob pointed to a nicely dressed woman who was waiting at the stop. "Any reason to worry about her, Meg?"

My instincts were likely no better than his. But I squinted to see her better, thinking of the mother who had been so angry when she heard the price of our potatoes. If it was her, or anyone I had sold to in the past, we would have to move on. But she turned slightly in our direction and I didn't think I recognized her, nor did she seem interested in us. I shrugged. "I don't see any reason to worry, but I really don't know."

Except within only a few more steps, Albert raised a hand. "Stop!" We did as he asked, each of us looking around for any sign of what had drawn his attention. I heard nothing, but he cocked his head, then in a low voice, said, "Get off the road. Now!"

Jakob scrambled back to help his father, who was squinting so hard to look around that he tripped over a rock at his feet.

Liesel pointed out a thicket of trees in the distance. "Can we make it?" she cried.

We had to. We were almost there when I heard what had caught Albert's attention.

Engines.

Which almost always meant Nazis.

Liesel and I ran ahead and were making good time, and then I heard an "oof" behind us and saw that Albert had slipped on a patch of snow and fallen.

I raced back to help Jakob pull him to his feet. Together, we hurried into the trees.

Liesel had arrived ahead of us and sat with her back against the trunk of a tree. I removed my bag and clutched it tight against my chest as I crowded in beside her. When the engines grew louder, I turned to look out through the underbrush, seeing a line of camouflage green trucks on the road.

"No," she cried. "No, turn around. Faces are easy to spot."

So I turned and sat beside her, then Jakob and his father did the same at the tree next to ours.

"That woman at the train platform." Liesel took a few panting breaths before continuing. "Did she see us run?"

"She must have seen us." Jakob glanced over at me. "If we were in Germany, she'd definitely report us. Is it the same here?"

I wasn't sure how to answer. I'd heard stories of people being turned in for crimes as simple as the possession of an extra ration card, or for being out minutes past the ten o'clock curfew. So yes, it was possible that she would say something. Maybe even likely.

The trucks pulled into the small parking area beside the train station and cut their engines. It was quiet only for a second or two before orders were shouted. I couldn't stand not looking anymore, so I turned, watching the trucks empty of German soldiers, who lined up on both sides of the steps to the boarding platform. They stood at attention, raising their arms in a salute as one more man exited the truck.

He shouted an acknowledgment of service to Hitler, and my blood ran cold. I knew this voice. I'd heard it before.

This was Lieutenant Becker, the man to whom I had given the spare potatoes after I'd been caught following him. The man who had come to my home and questioned my mother, and who wanted to question me.

Had he come looking for me?

Jakob and I exchanged a glance. His brows were pressed low and his mouth set in a tight grimace. I wondered if he was thinking the same thing. This could not be a coincidence.

TWENTY-EIGHT

Rule: *Most people are good and will want to help you.*

Lieutenant Becker began making a speech to the other soldiers, loudly proclaiming Germany's superiority, and adding that if they were to give honor to the Führer, they must complete their mission here in France.

I didn't catch the rest of what he said, but Liesel did. As he continued speaking, she whispered, "They have orders to find any resistance members and arrest them." She listened a bit more, then said, "Or to shoot on sight if they try to run. But they are here today because . . ." Her eyes widened and her voice trailed off.

"Because why?" I asked. But Liesel only shook her head, refusing to answer.

I turned from her to Jakob and his father, both of whom were staring back at me as if a spotlight was aimed directly at my face.

I whispered, "Are they looking for me?"

Albert nodded. "They are looking for someone who fits your description. They said this girl is believed to be part of the resistance, because of a partially burned journal they found."

My shoulders sank. Yes, that was me.

Jakob gave me a grim smile. "Well, Meg, you're one of us now. We are all fugitives here."

We heard the rise of another engine, this one from an incoming train. I turned to look toward the platform again and saw Lieutenant Becker speaking to the woman on the platform. She gave a loud laugh and tossed her hair. Flirting.

We called them Grey Mice, the French women who paraded around with Nazi soldiers as if they were welcomed guests in our country. These women weren't traitors to France, but most people felt they were the next closest thing.

"We need to go," I said. "Now."

The woman had begun looking around the area. Lieutenant Becker waved two more soldiers forward, and they all listened intently to whatever she was saying.

"She is telling the Germans where we are," Jakob said, scowling.

"There's nowhere for us to go!" Liesel said.

The train pulled into the station. Several soldiers got off the train and several more began boarding. But Lieutenant Becker remained with the woman, and now both of them were looking around. Surely he was asking about us, about *me*. And she knew exactly where we were. I almost couldn't breathe for fear of what would happen as soon as she pointed out our location.

Finally, the woman pointed across the road, in the opposite direction of where we were, and the two soldiers who had been listening lifted their rifles and went in the way she had directed them, away from us.

"She just saved us," Jakob breathed.

I began breathing easier too. She was not a Grey Mouse at all. I had judged her unfairly. Jakob's words from yesterday came to my mind, that all people were not the same, just because they came from the same place.

Lieutenant Becker gestured at the woman to board the train ahead of him, then gave a sharp salute to his soldiers before following her. After a few more tense minutes, the train whistled and began rolling away. The soldiers who had exited took the waiting trucks away.

"Too many Nazis use this station," Liesel said. "It's not safe for us. The trains may not even be safe once we reach Paris."

"*If* we reach Paris. We will have to wait here until all those soldiers are far away," Albert said. "That may take some time."

"What shall we do while we wait?" Jakob asked.

I smiled. "I have an idea. It may at least ensure that no other soldiers come to this area for a while."

The Durands leaned forward, interested in what I was hinting at. I reached into Captain Stewart's backpack and pulled out a bag full of small metal bits, each bit with four sharp points. Any way they landed on the road, one sharp point would always face upward.

Jakob's eyes widened with interest. He must have already known what they were. So did his father, though he wasn't smiling at all. Liesel shook her head.

I said, "Captain Stewart's book talked about these. If we go back and scatter them along the road, we can create a lot of flat tires."

"And create a lot of trouble as the Nazis look for whoever put them on the road," Albert pointed out.

My smile widened. "But how will they look for us with popped tires?"

"No." Albert spoke more sharply than I'd heard him before. "We agreed. No more violence."

"A popped tire isn't violence," Jakob protested.

"It's an attack. You know how I feel about this, Jakob, *why* I feel this way."

"But it isn't the same!"

"To me, it is."

Jakob grunted with frustration. He glanced over at me,

muttering loud enough for all of us to hear, "*Your* father would let you do it, Meg. *Your* father trusts you."

"Enough!"

Jakob stood, ignoring our warnings for him to stay low, then marched away toward a small hill nearby.

"He should not be out there alone," Liesel said. "None of us should."

Her eyes shifted to me, and I stood. "Let me talk to him."

I ducked low to follow him, keeping myself hidden should a Nazi happen to reappear at the station.

Jakob hadn't gone far. He was seated on a small rock behind the hill. At the bottom of the hill, a winding stream rolled past us. He had found a fistful of rocks and was tossing them into the river one at a time.

"He has no right to treat me that way," Jakob said.

"He's your father," I said. "He's only looking out for you."

Jakob snorted, then mumbled, "No, he isn't."

I put one hand on his arm. "Maybe my suggestion was too risky. If he feels—"

"I know he's looking out for me, Meg. What I mean is, no, he isn't my father. Liesel is not my mother, nor are they even married."

"What? But—"

"My name is Jakob Dentz. There is no Durand family."

I shook my head. "I don't understand. You said—"

"I'm supposed to tell everyone he's my father, because that's what our papers say, our false papers that Captain Stewart arranged for us. We've all kept our first names, but obviously our last name isn't real."

"Oh." Then, more quietly, "Where are your real parents, Jakob?"

Jakob opened his mouth, then closed it. "Gone."

Gone? Like my father was gone? I almost asked, but something in his expression warned me that I didn't want to know the answer. So all I said was "I'm sorry." Then, after a long silence, I added, "At least you have some kind of parents now."

Jakob only frowned. "I didn't know Liesel until we were preparing to leave Germany, but I definitely knew Albert. He's the reason my parents are gone. I'm traveling with these two because they're my only chance for freedom, but as soon as we cross the border, I'll get as far from Albert as possible."

"Why?"

Jakob shook his head. "If you knew who he is, you'd do the very same."

Again, I wanted to ask for more information. But not now. It would be safer for us to return to Jakob's family . . . who weren't his family at all.

He reluctantly followed me back there, though once we entered the glade, Liesel said, "Albert and I have been talking. Since we know they're looking for us, perhaps the best thing we can do is to keep their attention elsewhere while we continue on the road."

Albert sighed. "After that scare, I need a little more time to rest. But if you and Meg wish to leave some trouble behind, do it quickly and carefully, and then we will be on our way."

I grinned and reached for the tire spikes, rolling up Captain Stewart's bag again before I left. Jakob kicked a foot in the snow a moment before he forgot his anger and let himself smile. "Let's go."

TWENTY-NINE

Rule: *Sabotage the target of highest value for the least amount of risk.*

In less than ten minutes, Jakob and I had scattered enough road spikes to flatten the tires of the next twenty vehicles to cross this road. If I were a better person, I might've felt guilty, but as it would almost certainly be Nazi tires with holes in them, Jakob and I just laughed. My only regret was that we wouldn't be here to see it.

When we returned, Liesel and Albert were waiting for us at the side of the road. She handed me Captain Stewart's pack, stating, "We kept it safe for you."

Had she?

The moment I took it, I knew something wasn't right. It had been rolled up differently than when I left it.

They had looked through it, or at least one of them had.

I closed my eyes, cursing my mistake. Captain Stewart had told me not to let anyone else see what was in this backpack. He'd told me to keep it with me at all times, and then I'd gone and left it unattended, practically inviting them to look.

We'd only been away for ten minutes. How much could they have seen in that time?

All of it.

I forced out a thank-you for the pack, then slung it over my shoulders. Jakob eyed me, sensing something was wrong. I said nothing as we set out along a footpath near the road. If we had to hide again, it was better if we were nearer to the trees.

That turned out to be a good decision, since we did end up hiding only an hour later from a Nazi service vehicle carrying a load of tires in its truck bed. It was followed by another vehicle with the same number, then a Kübelwagen with an entire squadron of soldiers.

"They're looking for us," Jakob said, and then a laugh sputtered from him. "Do you really think we damaged that many tires?"

"This is no time for laughter," Albert said. "We must go faster."

Jakob groaned. "Can't you be happy that our plan worked so well?"

"How do you know it worked? Only because they haven't caught us . . . yet."

That silenced Jakob for some time, which made the next

several hours of walking miserable for me too. I had nothing to say to Albert or Liesel, and Jakob had nothing to say to me. So the afternoon dragged on, each of us wrapped up in our own frustration. The only distraction was the occasional need to dodge off the road at the sign of other people, or especially, at the sound of an approaching engine.

The sun was low in the sky when we entered another forested area not far from Paris, and near to the Palace of Versailles, the home of the royals before the French Revolution. The palace had long served as a reminder that wars had come to France before, and we'd always survived them. So we would again.

We camped that night inside the walls of a crumbling abandoned home just past the village of Saint-Lambert. We had little shelter from the cold wind that whistled through the gaps in the walls, but we built a small fire in a protected corner and huddled closely around it to keep warm.

Ever since my conversation with Jakob, it had been hard for me to think of anything other than what had happened to his parents, and who Albert and Liesel really were. Captain Stewart had said the Nazis wanted Albert back. He had treated me kindly thus far, but if Jakob blamed him for the fate of his parents, then he probably wasn't as good a man as he pretended to be.

I stared at Albert and Jakob seated together around the fire and Liesel, a little farther away, adjusting the gray scarf around her neck. From all outward appearances, they got along just fine, though now that I knew the truth, I saw the formality between them. Their relationship was more like a business partnership where they helped one another out of necessity, rather than affection. If they were trying to pass as a French family, this would have to change.

There was no easy way to start this conversation, other than to just start it. I blurted out, "You need to work on your cover story as the Durand family."

"Cover story?" Albert turned to Jakob, tension mounting in his expression. "You told her?"

"Meg deserves to know who she is trying to help," he retorted.

Before another fight started, I said, "If I'm questioned, I should know the same story that you would tell them."

"Why should any of us be questioned?" Liesel said. "We've done well so far."

"No, Meg is right," Albert said. "Her story needs to agree with our story."

I leaned in toward them. "Captain Stewart's book talks about cover stories, how to make them sound real. I'll never learn all the details of your life, not in the next few days, but I have an idea for what we can say to anyone who asks. A lot of children from the cities have been sent to the countryside where it's safer. I could say that my mother contacted you as distant cousins. You came to pick me up and bring me home with you."

Liesel sat up straighter. "Yes, yes, that's good. We can easily adjust our story to fit with yours."

I nodded. "But the three of you also need to act more like a family, like a real family."

"What do you mean?" Confused, Albert looked at Liesel. "I have been perfectly polite at all times."

"This isn't about politeness; it's about affection. I know how my parents were, how they *are* when they're together. They're comfortable. They look at each other, they smile at each other. Papa doesn't ask Maman if she needs his hand. He just takes her hand."

"We are as close as we intend to be," Liesel said sharply. Too sharply.

So I let the matter drop. I didn't know what I'd said to make her angry, but clearly I had.

"We will never be the same as a real family," Albert mumbled.

After the worst of the tension had passed, Jakob leaned back and smiled. "As part of my cover story, I'm going to decide that you two are annoying parents and that I don't have to listen to a word either of you say."

Albert's face reddened. "You will not—"

"You're not really my father, so I can do what I want."

"For our purposes here, I am your father, and you will do exactly as I say."

"If you continue like this, I will withhold your meals," Liesel said. "We will not tolerate your disrespect."

"Why should I care?"

"Do not speak to your mother that way!" Albert caught himself before the last of his sentence. "I mean, do not speak to Frau Durand that way."

After a tense moment, Jakob and I began laughing. When they looked over at us, I said, "*Now* you are beginning to sound like a real family."

Sometime soon after, I must have drifted off to sleep, only to be awoken by Albert, who whispered for us all to hear, "I have a surprise for my family. Look up, quickly. All of you."

I kept my wool blanket tight around me as I sat up. The fire had gone out, but smoke was still rising, and I wondered if maybe Albert had stamped it out so that we could see the sky a little better.

"What?" Jakob began. Then he looked up. "Oh!"

I said nothing, and only watched as our full moon slowly went dark. "What is it?" I mumbled.

"A total lunar eclipse." Albert chuckled. "The moon has just passed entirely within Earth's shadow. How I wish I could see it clearly for myself."

As he finished speaking, the eclipse became complete. It

was as if the entire Earth went dark. I felt it in my heart, as if I was losing hope for myself, for my family.

Just as quickly, the first glint of moonlight sparked again, the tiniest shimmer at first, but slowly it widened, and light began to return.

"Remember this always," Albert said. "There is nothing so dark that light cannot find its way back." His eyes turned to me. "There is nothing so lost that time cannot return it to us again."

I glanced up at the eclipse and smiled. Here, so far from my family, and in such desperate circumstances as we were, I thought that eclipse might be the most beautiful thing I'd ever seen.

Tuesday, March 3, 1942
661 days since I've seen Papa

Because we needed to avoid Versailles, which was surely filled with Nazis, our walk the next day was longer than it should have been. Maybe that was for the best. It gave the Durands time to practice being a family.

Which, oddly, made me a little sad. Liesel took Albert's arm as they walked, reminding me of my parents. Jakob began calling them Papa and Maman, and every time he did, I cringed inside. It only made me miss my own parents more. I thought I noticed him cringe too, and maybe for the same reason.

We were in the suburbs of Paris now, and with every step closer to the city, we saw increasing numbers of Nazi soldiers. Signs of their presence were everywhere. German flags hung from our buildings, notices in shopwindows were posted in the German language, even our street names had been changed to German words.

But worst of all was seeing French citizens going about their lives as if they didn't notice any of it. Too many of them spoke to the Germans like friends or ignored them as if they were fixtures on the sidewalk, never to go away.

That was a possibility, of course. If Germany won this war, and as far as I could tell, it looked like they would, then this was a permanent occupation.

I looked over at the Durands, wondering what they thought of this. Did they want Germany to leave France as much as I wanted it? Did they see themselves as part of the occupation?

When we finally came to a street where we were alone, the Durands seemed to relax. My mind was still turning with questions.

"Are you all right?" Liesel asked me. This time, she brushed a hand across my hair as she spoke, and I bristled against it. I wasn't any part of their false family.

"I'm fine," I muttered.

"Albert and I think it might be a good idea to stop at a market and pick up some food to replenish our supplies. After all, with some luck, we have a long train ride ahead."

"You need a ration card," I said.

Her brow wrinkled. "Food is rationed here?"

"You didn't know that?" I asked.

"We've passed many farms here. Where does all that food go?"

Did she really not know? Every long night that I'd gone to bed hungry flashed through my mind. Hunger was a dull ache, always a part of life here. But Maman said that starvation was worse; it was pain, and we should be grateful for what little food we had. I tried to be grateful, but right now, I was angry.

"Our food goes to Germany, along with anything else they want, and we are forced to make do with what remains." I squinted over at her. "If you ate well in Germany, then it's only because someone here went hungry."

"I know hunger, better than you think," she replied. "When the Great War ended, life in Germany became nearly impossible. The penalties we suffered were severe, many of them imposed by France. Some people, good friends of mine, died of hunger. Was that any fairer than what France is facing now?"

"So this is a punishment?"

Albert coughed, and beneath his breath said, "Others are on this street now." In a low voice, he added, "Nobody should be hungry, Meg. You are right about that. Perhaps you and Liesel will try to buy some food so that we are not among the hungry tonight."

I lowered Captain Stewart's bag, then unrolled it and dug into a pocket near the top, withdrawing a blank ration card. He had about a dozen in there, so I figured he wouldn't mind if we used just one.

From there, we found a quiet alley where Jakob and Albert could wait. Jakob gestured to Captain Stewart's backpack. "No one will look in it," he said. "Trust me."

I had to. It wasn't the kind of bag a girl my age would wear to shop in a general market. I passed it over to Jakob and hoped he was worthy of my trust.

"Crackers, cheese, dried meat if it's sold here." Liesel was beginning to make her shopping list. "We need food that can travel easily and that won't spoil."

But when we entered and began to go down the mostly empty aisles, she looked at me. "Where is the food? We have our ration card."

I had my eye on a blond woman ahead of us. She held a baby on one hip and tears were rolling down her cheeks. She called to the clerk at the front of the store. "No flour again today?"

No one answered.

Remembering Liesel, I said, "The ration card limits what we can buy. It doesn't guarantee anything."

"Enough of these rations!" the blond woman yelled. "My children need bread!"

A single jar of baking powder was on the shelves in front of her. But there was no flour. No sugar, or oats.

"Please, madam . . ." the clerk said, rushing over to her.

"No! There must be flour somewhere in France. Where is it?"

The clerk reached over to calm her, but she flung out her arm, knocking over a bottle of oil behind her. Glass shattered and a puddle of oil began to seep into the wood floor.

Now the clerk folded his arms. "That bottle must be stamped on your ration card."

"That was your fault, not mine." The woman turned on the clerk. "Perhaps it is also your fault we have no flour. Is there bread in your home, monsieur?"

He stepped back, a sudden look of guilt on his face.

A second woman shouted, "I shop here every day, and every day there is less on the shelves. Does the food go home with you as soon as it comes in?"

"Please, please calm down," the clerk said, though other people in the market, now both men and women, were beginning to murmur too. This wasn't good.

"We should leave," I said to Liesel, who had managed to find one box of crackers and a few thin carrots.

"Let's check the other aisle," she said. "We must have food for our journey."

"There won't be a journey if we are caught here." I grabbed her hand and began pulling her toward the door.

"Thief!" the clerk shouted. Whether he believed we were stealing the crackers and carrots, or he was hoping to turn the growing mob against us, didn't matter. Suddenly, the angry faces shifted our way.

I swiped one hand through the items still in Liesel's

arms, forcing everything to the floor. Shoppers around us, who only moments ago had passed these same items on the shelves, now dove for them, scrambling for anything they could get.

I pulled Liesel out of the market just in time to hear sharp whistles around the corner. That could only mean one thing.

"Act natural," I said. "Keep your head down, walk slowly."

Two French policemen were running toward the store, pistols in their hands. I briefly looked up, and we stepped aside to let them pass. One of them brushed roughly against Liesel's shoulder, but she only lowered her head farther as we continued on.

Other shoppers had been attempting to leave the market, but the policemen grabbed hold of them and shoved everyone to the ground.

"Who started this?" one of the officers demanded. "Answer now, or you will all be taken in for questioning."

No one responded. Had we not left when we did, we would have been lined up for questioning too.

Beside me, Liesel let out a breath of relief. "We might go hungry tonight. But I will be grateful for it."

And with those words, I finally understood what my mother had tried to teach me for all these months. Some things were far worse than hunger.

THIRTY-ONE

Rule: *Make decisions with as much information as possible.*

Once again, we had no choice but to continue onward, though we were already closer to Paris than any of us wanted to be. Even here on the outskirts, the city began rising around us, a constant swirl of people on foot or bicycle. The buildings were as tall and grand as I remembered from before the war, and the shops had far more variety than those in the Perche or my old home near Auxonne. The women who passed us were as fashionable as ever, and the men conversed with one another as if all was normal.

But it wasn't.

Looking closely, I saw men in berets, leaning in close to speak to each other until a Nazi soldier passed them by. I'd heard rumors of resistance fighters in berets. Perhaps these were some of them.

Nazi flags hung from our grand buildings where French flags had once flown proud. Signs in shopwindows read, *"Les Juifs ne sont pas admis."* Window after window forbidding Jews to enter.

A large sign pasted to a brick wall depicted a monstrous drawing of the Jewish people. A young couple passed it, their heads bowed down. Pinned to each of their coats was a yellow star marked with the word *"Juif."* My eyes crossed between them and the horrible drawing. That couple was no different than any of us, and I wondered how the other people here on the street couldn't see that. Maybe if we just looked at one another, if we stopped hating and pointing fingers of blame, maybe then we could stand together against the true enemies of France.

"Pardon."

A woman bumped my arm as she passed me by, her blond hair neatly combed beneath what must have been an expensive hat, and her coat was tied around her waist without a single crease. Yet as she walked away, I noticed that her silk stockings weren't stockings at all. She was barelegged but had painted a stocking line up her calves, and her shoes had wooden soles. The Germans had stolen the leather out of France.

She began to cross the street but had to wait for a line of Kübelwagens, those the regular officers traveled in. They were followed by a sleek and shiny car with a fin over the trunk passing directly in front of us. I'd never seen anything like that one before.

Beside me, Albert chuckled.

"What's so funny?" I asked.

"We Germans love our speed," he said. "That car is a Tatra, used by the highest-ranking officers. They might be the fastest cars on earth—able to go a hundred kilometers an hour. The problem is, you'd have an easier time driving a broken baby stroller than one of those. Take one too fast around a bend, and it'll flip over every time. I wager the Tatra has killed more German officers than all the Allied attacks combined."

Finally, we turned onto a road with no soldiers and quiet enough that we could relax a little. Only then did Liesel say, "It was a mistake to come this far. We never should have come to Paris."

"This was Captain Stewart's plan," Albert said.

"He made that plan because he knows what to do in case of riots, or police actions. We don't."

"I know what to do," Jakob said. "We get away from it if we can, but if we can't, then we have to fight."

"No, Jakob!" Albert stopped walking and faced him directly. "I was clear when I made this agreement that I would not lift a single weapon, nor allow anyone in our group to do so."

"But if it saves our lives—"

"Violence only takes lives. There is no other end to it."

"But—"

"Do not argue this with me again! You think because I allowed you to use those tire spikes that you will be allowed to escalate a fight against the Nazis. No, I will not permit it."

Jakob folded his arms. "I don't need you to permit me to do anything. You are not my father."

"I am standing in place of your father."

"No, you are pretending, and I am pretending, but you are not in my father's place and never could be. My father would never do the things you have done. That's why my parents are in prison and you are here, a free man!"

Jakob marched on ahead. Liesel hurried to catch up to him, leaving me alone with Albert, who only hung his head.

I couldn't leave without him. Someone needed to remain at his side to see what he could not, but I wished I could go and talk to Jakob, rather than listen to Albert offer explanations and excuses.

But I had no choice. He was going to make those explanations anyway.

"Jakob does not know the whole story," Albert began. "For the past two years, Jakob has worked for me, running errands as I needed them. I've become fond of him. I never married, and I believe I would have liked a family of my own."

"But what about Jakob's family?" I asked.

"Ah. Well, do you remember that your father worked for me in a factory, and that he was reported to me for sabotage?"

"Yes."

"At the time, he was with a small team of engineers, a team that included Jakob's father. Gradually, they became good friends, especially because they were the only two men who spoke English . . . or so they believed. The day your father was turned in for sabotage, Jakob's father was also turned in for hiding Jews. Someone had overheard them."

"Who?"

"I have no idea. I only found out when I received a telephone call from the Gestapo, telling me they were coming to arrest both men and to make sure to keep them at the factory. I had both men brought to me, and both men confessed." Albert's sigh sounded as sad as he looked. "I knew of a safe house, but they would not take everyone. I could not save both your father and Jakob's family."

Guilt pricked at my conscience. "So you chose my father."

"No, your father begged me to save the family, but Jakob's father made the decision. He said that if he were to run, that would be an admission of wrongdoing, and he insisted that hiding this family was the right thing to do. So I helped your father escape, and Jakob's father went home.

He and his wife got the Jewish family into hiding elsewhere, but they were arrested."

"Why wasn't Jakob arrested too?"

Albert rubbed his hand over his jaw. "Because I sent him on an errand, a very long errand that put him far from the factory that entire day."

I lowered my eyes. "Does Jakob know that you saved my father instead?"

"No. He has no idea that your father was ever involved. He only believes I did nothing to save his parents, which I suppose is the truth."

"Jakob's father made that decision, not you."

"Yes, but you see, I wanted to choose your father, for my own selfish reasons. I knew he was part of the S.O.E., so if I helped him escape, he could help me. That's when we came up with our plan."

I still had one other question, one I almost dreaded to ask. "What happened when the Gestapo came and both men were missing from the factory?"

His frown deepened. "They threatened to arrest me, to send me to the concentration camps. So I made them an offer. I had just completed an equation for a weapon they wanted to build. I said I would give it to them if they forgave my crime, and they agreed. I left Germany that same night— abandoned my home and the wealth from a lifetime of work—but that was better than giving them the equation.

Jakob had no choice but to come with me. I know he doesn't like this. I know he resents me and even believes I ruined his life. Maybe I did, but I also saved his life."

My shoulders fell as I thought of my mother. Like Albert, she had sent me away to avoid questioning by the Nazis. The only difference was that he had something to offer to save himself. Maman didn't.

I looked up at Albert. "What was the weapon?"

"Pray that you never hear of it." Albert was silent for a long time. "It would have killed millions, without costing Germany a single soldier. Maybe I took the coward's way out, but at least I got out."

"Yes, but how could you have designed that equation in the first place? How could you have worked for them?"

"I am a scientist," he said. "We were never given the option of choosing whether or not to work for the Nazis."

"Neither was my father, or Jakob's father. But they chose to resist."

"So have I . . . now." Albert ran a hand across his short white beard. "That's why I left. From now on, I will do everything in my power to stop the Germans from finishing the weapon that I started."

But he *had* started it. That was the problem.

He continued, "Part of making up for my past behaviors is to gain the forgiveness of those who have been hurt by my country. That includes you, Meg. We've begun to think of you as a friend, you know."

I had begun to think of them as friends too. But I needed to remember that I was on a rescue mission. All that mattered was getting my father back. I couldn't let my focus be swayed by friendship. During a war, friendships were far too dangerous.

Possibly Albert's was the most dangerous friendship of all.

THIRTY-TWO

Rule: *Trust your instincts.*

Jakob and Liesel were waiting for us when we caught up to them several minutes later. I pulled out the silk map and studied it with the Durands at my side. Liesel pointed to a mark of a train station in Boulogne-Billancourt, an area just outside the heart of Paris. "That's the closest station," she said. "And it connects to the main lines of the city. Perhaps that will take us to the border of Spain."

Albert was less enthusiastic. He pointed to a set of buildings near the train station. "I know the work that happens there. It was a car factory once, but it's a war factory now. The Nazis will build thousands of trucks this year, repair hundreds of tanks. I don't like the idea of using that train station."

"Look at the map," Jakob said. "We can't get to Spain from there anyway. We need to go to Paris for that." He turned to me. "What do you think, Meg? You probably know this area better than any of us."

I did know it. My parents used to come to Paris often, but rarely to Boulogne-Billancourt, except to pass through. And I did have a suggestion, though none of them would like it.

I said, "If we stay in Paris tonight, we can get a train first thing in the morning that will go almost all the way to Switzerland. I know the route because that's how my family used to get to and from our home. I understand that you all want to follow Captain Stewart's plan, but I really think our best chance is if we go to Switzerland."

Jakob stepped closer to me. "My vote is for Switzerland."

Liesel shook her head. "No, Jakob. We've made this decision already."

"Then Meg and I will go. We don't have to stay together!"

Albert said, "I propose that we let our emotions settle tonight. We can go to Paris in the morning, and then decide what will be in the best interests of all four of us."

We'd never come to the same decision. Albert and Liesel wanted to stick with Captain Stewart's plan and go south. I was determined to go east.

So was Jakob, apparently, and I was glad to hear it. If I did go to Switzerland, I'd rather have someone else with me.

By then we had reached the end of the street. I glanced back and realized the gray scarf that Liesel had worn knotted around her neck was missing. When I pointed it out, she clutched at her bare neck and began looking around the area. "I loved that scarf! Could we go back for it?"

"No," Albert and Jakob answered in unison. They looked at each other and laughed. I was glad for that. The tension between them had been too heavy for most of the day.

"Is there anything on the scarf to identify your name?" I asked.

Liesel shook her head. "No, but it was a gift from a friend. There is no other scarf like it anywhere."

"You brought another one, I think," Albert said. "A red one."

Liesel nodded, but looked at me with sadness. That friend must have been someone special for her to be so upset now. But none of us wanted to go back to search for it, apparently not even Liesel. She merely sniffed and walked on ahead of us.

Eventually, I pulled out Papa's yellow note, wanting to review his words as we walked. But still, I saw nothing new. Jakob heard me sigh and looked over my shoulder. "That's not the anagram about the jet."

"No, this is the one Papa gave Captain Stewart for me to solve. And the worst part is, he would have written things into the code that we might need to know. I have to solve this!"

"May I see the note?"

This was the second time he had asked. After a brief hesitation, I passed it over to him. He quickly looked it over, then gave the paper back to me. "I speak almost no English. I can read none of it."

I smiled and began to translate, keeping my voice lower than Jakob's parents could hear.

Dearest wife, Daisy, and Mom;

"Who is Daisy?" Jakob whispered.

I pointed to myself, and he nodded his understanding. Then I pointed to the next few lines.

Nothing can stop me from climbing
to you. Watch perfectly as
the sadness becomes numb.

"Watch perfectly." That took a little more translation, to help him understand that "watch" had two meanings in English. When he nodded, I pointed to the next line:

Remember my smiles, brightened
under tender skies by the sea.

Then I opened Captain Stewart's bag and pulled out the book of my father's poetry. On the first page, he had written the words "My smiles." I translated that by smiling at him and pointing to myself.

Jakob smiled too, then held out his hand for the book. If he wondered what this book could have to do with our journey, so did I. He flipped through the pages, though these poems were also in English. Finally, he handed the book back to me, apparently with no more clue than I had about why my father wanted it.

Slowly, I translated the rest for him, letting him absorb each line before I moved on to the next.

> Straighten the spine, Daisy.
> Take courage, even when hurting,
> have faith until this battle
> ends. Until then, be calm.
> Regards,
> Rosbif

Jakob arched a brow. "Rosbif?"

"Maman's way of teasing my father. He used a nickname that could only have come from him. Probably for the same reason he calls his wife and mother-in-law by their titles rather than their names, and why I am Daisy rather than Meg or Marguerite. He doesn't want any of us identified by this note."

"Maybe his only purpose was to tell you to go to Switzerland," Jakob said. "Maybe you've already figured everything out."

"Papa always said that every word of a code mattered. If he wrote twelve lines, then there are twelve lines' worth of information." My shoulders slumped. Suddenly, I was exhausted. "This is impossible."

"Your father clearly had faith in you," Jakob said. "See that you don't lose it in yourself."

I thought a lot about those words for the rest of the walk, wondering if Papa had been wrong to trust me with his code. He could have created something for Captain Stewart, or even for Maman. Why me? If I were really good with codes, I would have unlocked the simple anagram of JAIMIE STAYED. This was far more complex.

I became distracted only later that evening when we arrived in Boulogne-Billancourt and needed a place to sleep. A sign in one window advertised a room for rent. It was expensive, but based on what I'd read in Captain Stewart's spy book, this was a good spot. It was private, had more than one exit, and the rooms had clear visibility to the street. So twenty minutes later, the four of us crowded inside the room, where we were finally able to properly clean ourselves at a washstand, and to be truly warm. There was only a small bed, which it was decided Liesel and I could share.

I wanted to keep thinking about Papa's code, but I was so tired, I fell asleep almost immediately. There was no time that night for dreams. We could not have been sleeping for very long before the first bomb fell on Boulogne-Billancourt.

THIRTY-THREE

Rule: *When threatened, find a safe position.*

There were supposed to be sirens.

That's what Maman always told me—if an air raid ever came, we'd hear the sirens. That would be our first warning.

The sirens would be followed by flares to wake people up and produce enough light to run to a shelter.

Shelter! We had to get to a shelter!

I leapt from the bed at the sound of the first explosion. "Everyone, get up!"

Jakob was already standing at the window, staring out as if mesmerized by the colors lighting up the sky. "It's not directly overhead. Maybe we should remain here."

But Albert shook his head. "No, if more are coming, then we must get to safety. Surely there is a cellar for this building. Everyone, get your shoes on now!"

We all flew into action, all of us except Jakob, who was still staring out the window. "It's beautiful, in a strange way," he said.

I turned and immediately understood what he meant. Bright, glowing lights fell in long lines from the dark sky, like trails of fireworks. Except the explosion didn't burst into beautiful shapes or into other lovely colors designed to entertain. Instead, it became an orange glow that covered the entire sky, like opening the door to a blast furnace, one that was terrible and deadly.

"Get away from the window!" Albert said.

Jakob stepped back, and not a moment too soon. A bomb fell closer than the others, rattling the furniture and walls. The window where Jakob had just been standing shattered, letting in an acrid smoke that instantly burned my throat.

I grabbed Captain Stewart's bag and led the way out of our room, following other families who were also pushing through the hallways to the lower steps. By the time we arrived, the cellar was nearly full, but Liesel and I sat on Captain Stewart's bag to save space, and Jakob and Albert each sat on their bags.

It was dark in here, other than a few candles people had brought in, and with the low ceiling, this place felt to me like a tomb. I hated having that thought in my head.

When the last person entered the cellar, I was sure there'd

be no room for him, but everyone adjusted as necessary and finally he took a seat, desperately asking, "Marie, are you down here?" No one answered, so he called her name again, his voice wavering more this time.

The silence to his question created a weight in the room that was so thick, it pressed in around me. Marie wasn't here. After a few minutes, he let out a small cry and left the cellar, calling her name again.

"Do you think he'll return?" Jakob whispered.

I hoped he would. A part of me needed to know Marie was still alive. Was she his wife, his child?

For a few minutes, everything was quiet outside, and I wondered if it was safe now. I even whispered to Liesel, "Perhaps we should leave. Too many people are here."

But before she could answer, another wave of bombings began. They whistled a high-pitched sound as they fell, and I cringed with each one, certain it was almost on top of us, hardly breathing until it exploded somewhere farther away.

"Don't be afraid," an elderly woman next to me said. "If you can hear them, then they're not too close."

That would have comforted me, if I had not then begun to ask myself about the bombs I *couldn't* hear. There was plenty reason to be afraid of them.

This second wave of bombs was worse than before. The ground shook almost constantly with each impact, or from the damage that followed each explosion. Families huddled more tightly together, and I wished we would do that too. Instead, I wrapped my arms around myself and tried to believe we would survive this.

"Tell us something from Captain Stewart's book," Jakob prodded me, but I only shook my head. "Or remind me again of your father's code. I'll bet by the time this is over, we'll have solved it."

I appreciated him trying, but I could only shake my head at him while other voices in our cellar became louder.

"The planes were flying low," someone across the room was saying. "They must be the British."

"Bombing French civilians?" Liesel whispered. "Is that the free civilization we are joining?"

Perhaps she had forgotten the number of bombs Germany had dropped on France to force our surrender. I didn't like what was happening right now either—I was terrified and felt desperately alone. But there had to be some purpose to what the British were doing. Perhaps the trucks and tanks made in that nearby factory were worth the risk to our lives.

Then came the moment I'd feared most—the bomb I didn't hear. The first sign we had of trouble was the thundering sound of its impact, then the explosion, almost directly overhead. Bricks and mortar crumbled onto the floorboards over our heads, furniture above us, everything made of glass shattered.

Then all was silent.

"It's all right, it's all right," Albert whispered. "We're still alive. The worst is over."

But he was wrong. From across the room, someone cried, "It's burst the water pipes. The cellar is going to fill with water!"

THIRTY-FOUR

Rule: *The agent's safety is always top priority.*

N o one had to say the words. We all understood that we had to escape the cellar *now*. Even the bombs outside were less of a threat than the water already pouring into this room.

Those who had been seated nearest the cellar steps were the first to climb them again, only to call back down, "The door is jammed!"

"Something must have landed on it," Jakob said.

I nodded, trying to keep calm, even as panic filled my throat, my chest, my every thought. That *something* was probably the inn where we had been staying, which was likely now just a heap of rubble. We were buried alive.

"Send the strongest men up the stairs," Albert said. "I noticed some sticks of wood behind me. Take those to pry the door open."

Jakob and I passed the sticks forward to the men, and Jakob went with them to offer his help. I hoped they would hurry. I stood, but the water was already past my ankles. I lifted Captain Stewart's bag to keep its contents from getting wet.

"*Une, deux, trois!*" The men counted in unison, then together they rammed shoulders upward against the cellar door. It bumped open a little, then closed again.

"Stronger this time! *Une, deux, trois!*" Once again they lifted, the men groaning from their effort, then cursing when it failed.

"Again!" This time, they produced enough leverage that someone cried, "My stick is wedged in!"

That was Jakob! I looked at Liesel and Albert with hope. And fear. I was standing now but crouched low in this small space. The water was halfway to my knees.

The men tried again, and this time were able to push Jakob's stick in deeper, allowing them to get a second one in as well. Their work now turned to pushing their sticks downward, hoping to widen the cellar door.

Gradually, they worked a third stick into place and the door was easing open, though something heavy must have been weighing it down.

"I'm small enough that if you get a few centimeters more, I might be able to slide through and help from outside," Jakob said.

But would he be safe? I listened carefully for the sound of further explosions, but everything seemed to be quiet outside. Perhaps the raid really was over.

With the next effort of the men, the cellar door widened enough that Jakob stuck his head out, wedged his shoulders and arms through the gap, then the rest of his body slid out.

"Well, at least the *entire* house didn't fall," he called back.

We heard shuffling sounds, a large thump, and something rolling across the floor, and then the men pushed again. This time the door opened.

I had expected cool evening air to greet our freedom, but instead, a thick soup of fog and smoke and dust wafted down into the cellar. That terrified me for what we might find on the surface, but we couldn't remain here either.

"Women and children first," one of the men said.

Liesel brought Albert along with her while I managed our bags, holding them over the waist-high water. Everything was wet, except for Captain Stewart's backpack, which was now over my shoulders.

When I left the cellar, the water was nearly to my hips. Jakob was waiting for us on the main floor, or what was left of it. The wall to my left was perfectly intact. Oddly, there were even pictures still hanging in their frames. One picture, I realized, was of the man who had been looking for Marie. A woman with a pleasant smile was seated next to him in the picture. Was that Marie? I hoped he'd found her. Two other walls were half-destroyed, and the wall behind me was gone, nothing more than a pile of collapsed wood and plaster and rock.

While looking around, I realized I was shivering. On top of everything else, we were soaked through and it was a cold night. Nor was our ordeal over.

Albert cupped his ear with his hand. "More planes are coming. We must find another shelter."

"Where?" Liesel asked.

"I heard people talking about a concrete shelter nearby." Jakob grabbed Albert's arm. "Let's go!"

Once on the street, I was struck by the thick fog surrounding us. "Where did this come from?" I asked as we ran.

"The Germans would have set off smoke bombs," Albert explained. "The Allies can't hit a target they cannot see."

Which made it more likely they'd accidentally hit civilians. Indeed, I already heard the cry of a woman sobbing for her husband in a nearby building that stood half-destroyed.

"Let's keep moving," Jakob said. "The shelter can't be far."

Maybe it wasn't, but Albert had been correct before. A third wave was coming.

Low-flying aircraft cut through enough of the fog that when I looked up, I saw dozens of planes, some higher than others, some flying faster than others, but one by one as they reached their targets, their bellies opened and dark shapes dropped from them, falling through the air and ending in a bright flash of light, a thundering explosion, and the aftermath of crumbling wood and concrete.

"There's the shelter!" Jakob cried.

It was only a concrete room buried in the ground, but just as we reached the door, a man shook his head at us and said, "So sorry, my friends, but it's full." And he closed the door in our faces.

"Now what?" Liesel asked. "We are doomed."

"Entrez!"

We turned to see a young Nazi soldier in a Kübelwagen, motioning for us to get in his vehicle. We looked at each other, hesitating while the soldier seemed to struggle for the French words he wanted to say. Finally, he called, *"Gare!"*

"I think he's offering to take us to the train station," Liesel said.

Jakob darted forward. "I don't care where he's headed. It's better than here!"

Liesel and I crammed into the front seat while Jakob and Albert rolled into the back, and the soldier sped away, picking up a woman and two children along the way, all of whom crowded in beside Jakob and Albert. The soldier raced through the streets, dodging debris and emergency vehicles and even a family who had crouched in the center of the road, children in the middle, with both parents surrounding them, using their bodies as shields.

I peeked over at the German soldier beside me, his face tightly focused ahead, his left arm waving people away when they tried to dart in his path, hoping to get on the vehicle too.

After a terrifying few minutes, we had escaped the worst danger and were headed into Paris, though it was so dark, there was nothing I could see, not until the tall clock tower of the Gare de Lyon came into view.

"There it is!" Liesel pointed ahead. "We'll be safe there."

The soldier's head turned sharply toward her. *"Sind Sie aus Deutschland?"*

Liesel's eyes widened. She had spoken in French, but her accent was clearly German, and the soldier knew it. This was a critical mistake.

I pointed to the curb and asked him in French to let us off. Ignoring our request, his hands tightened around the steering wheel, until one of the children in the crowded back of the Kübelwagen fell off and his mother jumped out after him. The instant the soldier slammed on his brakes, I pushed Liesel out of the vehicle ahead of me, and Albert and Jakob ran with us. The soldier called for us to stop, but we continued running, hoping he would stay and help the child who had fallen instead.

We ran toward the station, pushing through the crowds to enter an enormous building with a tall, arched ceiling, lined with windows, darkened now in the nighttime. This station should have been mostly empty at this early hour.

"We must hide, in case that soldier comes looking for us." Liesel took one of Albert's hands, and Jakob had wound a strap from Captain Stewart's pack around his wrist, keeping us together. We found a quiet corner where we could sit and try to listen for the sounds of any bombers directly overhead. Listen for the bombs we could not hear.

But it was impossible. Too many people were crying or talking about what they had seen outside, what they had just escaped only a few kilometers away.

Still, we listened, and waited.

And prayed that the worst was over.

THIRTY-FIVE

Wednesday, March 4, 1942
662 days since I've seen Papa

Eventually, there was silence.

Not a true silence, though. Sirens echoed in the streets, each with a different pulse, ringing different notes, a symphony of confusion. Military sirens, police sirens, hospital sirens, all headed in a single direction, toward Boulogne-Billancourt. I couldn't imagine what it must be like there.

Here, there was only silence.

Liesel pushed some money into Jakob's hand. "Get us tickets on the first train out of here. Hurry!" He nodded and left, sending a shiver through me. It couldn't be safe to send him out alone. What if that soldier who had brought us here was still searching for us?

Gradually, the sun began to rise, and the room brightened. I looked at the Durands, and several others who had also clearly escaped the bombing. We were covered in a powdery plaster, like we'd been dusted in flour. Everything was coated in it—our coats and bags, our hair, our hands—making ghosts of us all, I supposed.

We looked like ghosts.

Even if I didn't want to think that way, sometimes I just did. I wanted someone to speak, or to make conversation—any conversation—just to remind us that we were still among the living.

Liesel pulled a second scarf from her bag—the red one—and wet it with some water she had been carrying. "Each of you, clean your faces the best you can."

I went first, and when I'd finished, I looked around for Jakob, but he still hadn't returned. Why not?

I spotted a propaganda poster on a nearby wall, of a kind German soldier standing protectively over a French woman and her children as the French army marched away. It read, "You have been abandoned—put your trust in the German soldier."

I thought again of the soldier who had rescued us. For a few minutes last night, we had been forced to trust him. It might be the only reason we were still alive, and yet the instant he'd suspected Liesel was German, his attitude changed. I wasn't sure what might have happened if we had not run when we did, but it wouldn't have been good.

"I saw the planes," one man standing near us said. "The

Allies dropped the bombs. It was the Germans who tried to protect us."

"The Germans are a weed within France," a woman responded. "The bombs are necessary to root them out."

Behind them, I caught a glimpse of Jakob, urgently waving at us. Relieved to see him again, I grabbed our bags, and Liesel helped Albert follow as Jakob led us down the steps to the train platforms.

"All the other tickets were sold out," Jakob said. "But we must hurry or we'll miss the train!"

Albert tried to ask where the train was going, but Jakob didn't seem to hear and only hurried forward. I supposed it didn't matter. Now that the bombing was over, within the hour, Nazis would flood into the area. We needed to be as far from here as possible when they came.

Once we were near the train platform, Jakob passed two tickets to Albert and Liesel, but before I could get to him, nearly everyone else on the platform also began pushing toward the train, whether they had tickets or not.

I understood why. If the planes returned for a fourth wave over Paris, or if the Germans retaliated with an air strike of their own, none of us wanted to be here to see it.

The crowd that pushed at my back to board the train was worse than even last night when we had pushed to enter the station. I heard the voices of some people begging the crowd to slow down for everyone's safety, but they were drowned out in the shouts to hurry and to reach the edge of the platform.

The Durands and I were swept forward to where the train was coming to a stop. When one woman pushed us aside to get ahead of the group, she knocked me into a stranger, and I tripped and fell.

Some people in the crowd tried to move around me, but others were stepping on my legs and hands, quickly apologizing, then moving on. I tried to get up, only to be knocked down again by the next wave of people.

"Meg!" Suddenly, Jakob was at my side, crouching low and propping me up by my arms. *"Zurücktreten!"* he shouted, ordering everyone to step back.

"So we have a Nazi among us!" a man said, kicking Jakob in the chest as he passed by.

Jakob fell back, letting go of me, but I rotated toward him, and we helped each other stand, then kept running for the train.

"Where are Albert and Liesel?" I asked. "Did they make it?"

"I don't know," he said. "Let's hope so."

He grabbed my arm and pulled me along with him so that we wouldn't be separated too. Ahead of us, a horn blew, signaling that the train was about to leave, and there were still many more people trying to get on. I wondered where all of them had come from.

The doors in front of us began to close. Jakob put one hand between them, letting it partially close on his arm. When they opened again, he pushed me inside, then I turned and yanked him inside the train with me. We both fell to the floor as the train began to leave the station.

"Are you all right?" I asked him.

He nodded, but said, "I have never felt hatred like that before, just for who I am." He took a slow breath to calm himself. "The family we hid in our home tried to describe hatred to me, but I didn't understand it before. The worst part is that I don't think I understand it even now, not the way they would."

"Meg! Jakob!"

We looked across the train car and saw Liesel frantically waving at us, so we stood and pushed our way toward her and Albert. All the seats had been taken, and the aisles were full, but we crowded together into the corner of the train car.

"Where is this train going?" a woman nearby asked her husband.

He checked his ticket, then said, "This train will travel nearly all the way to Switzerland."

Jakob shrugged. "These were the only tickets left." I wasn't sure that was true, but either way it didn't matter.

Albert and Liesel looked at me. "I hope you were right about your father," Liesel said, and with their stern expressions, I felt a weight settle on my chest. This was no longer a mission in which I was following along with their plans. It had just become *my* mission. I would be the one making the plans.

I hoped we were doing the right thing too.

Because we couldn't go back now.

THIRTY-SIX

Rule: *Never give up. The solution will come.*

N early half of those who had been on our train got off at the next stop. Maybe they had only meant to put a little more distance between themselves and the bombs.

After the crowds thinned, we moved from car to car until at last we found four available seats near the front of one train car. The sun was steadily rising, bringing more light into the train cars than I wanted. The other passengers in here would have a long time to stare at us. Surely they could see the guilt on our faces, our desperation to fulfill this mission. Did they wonder what was inside the large backpack I carried?

In hopes of calming myself down, I said to the others, "Can we just talk, like normal people?"

"About what?" Jakob asked.

I looked at them. "How did all of you meet?"

Albert smiled. "I met Jakob when his father came to work for me in the factory. But Liesel and I met only a few weeks ago at a dinner party. After some conversation, she quietly mentioned her desire to leave the country. At first, I was hesitant to reply—you can understand how dangerous it would be to admit that to the wrong person—but finally I admitted that I felt the same way."

"So you planned the escape during that first conversation?" I asked.

"Oh no," Liesel said. "A few days later I went to the factory to speak to Albert, to tell him it would be impossible for us to attempt any escape. Albert told me to trust him, that he would find a way."

Albert picked up the story. "Shortly after I made that promise, your father was reported to me. It was obvious that I could help him, and he could help me. He and I made the plans. Now all we needed was to get in contact with the S.O.E."

"That was the errand you sent me on, right?" Jakob turned to me. "The Gestapo knew how valuable Albert was to their work, so they watched him very carefully, more than they watched me. Albert only gave me an address and said the message I was carrying had to be delivered immediately." Now he looked down and his voice became more solemn. "When I returned, my parents were gone, and Albert told me I had to leave the country with him that same night."

"We have made it this far together," Liesel whispered. "Soon our troubles will be over."

Mine weren't.

"Tickets and papers, please." A conductor entered the back of our car and immediately people began reaching in their pockets or purses. Even in a bombing, they had understood how dangerous it was to leave home without papers.

Jakob pulled his papers from his pocket—forged papers, of course. The conductor probably wouldn't give them a second glance.

A sinking feeling opened up inside me. I had left my papers at Grandmère's. In all the panic and hurry of that night and ever since, it hadn't occurred to me once that I might need them.

"Where are your papers?" Jakob asked. I only stared back at him and his jaw fell open. "Meg, what will you do?"

"No papers?" Liesel's eyes nearly popped from her head. "That will mean an automatic interrogation, at best."

The conductor was still several rows behind us but moving our way faster than I would have liked.

"I must have forgot my papers," a woman in that row said to him. "I'm so sorry."

"You are required to have them with you at all times," the conductor said.

"Yes, I know, but it was the middle of the night, and the bombings—"

"There are no excuses," he said. "I'm afraid you'll have to come with me."

"No, please!" she cried. "I am a citizen!"

The train conductor raised his voice. "Attention, everyone, please keep your papers in hand until we reach the next stop. We have received word that this train will be boarded and searched. There is nothing to fear; it's only a routine search."

I locked eyes with Jakob. Then we both turned to look at Albert and Liesel, who looked equally nervous. We had every reason to fear.

Meanwhile, the conductor took the arm of the woman who would be questioned and escorted her from the train car, ignoring her cries for mercy.

When he returned, I would be next. I had to find someplace to hide, if such a place existed.

"Promise that you won't get off the train without me," I told them. "Promise me, no matter what."

"Why? Where are you going?" Jakob whispered.

I glanced at the Durands, who all looked as confused as I felt. I only shrugged, letting them know that I could not answer Jakob's question, or any other.

I wished I didn't have to bring Captain Stewart's bag with me—that would make hiding incredibly difficult, but I had no other choice.

So as not to draw attention to myself, I casually walked through the front door of the train car into the transom. Before going to sleep last night, I'd read in Captain Stewart's book that there were a few places a person could hide on a train when necessary. It might not be safe—the Nazis knew about these hiding places as well as the S.O.E.—but when desperate, it was worth the risk.

I waited to be sure that no one saw me slip into the bathroom. I locked the door and began feeling around for any loose boards on the walls or floor. Finding none, I stepped onto the toilet, feeling an icy breeze shoot upward from the hole that opened directly over the tracks. I tried to keep my balance as the train swayed back and forth, and I pressed against the paneling on the roof.

But nothing had any give, not even when I pounded on it with my fist. The only way I might get behind the paneling was to break the wood, and that was hardly a solution.

Cursing under my breath, I exited the bathroom and crossed to the train car ahead of the one where the Durands still sat. I guessed that ten minutes had passed by now. In another five minutes, we would reach the stop.

I had hoped to try hiding in the bathroom of this new train car, but it was occupied. So I hurried on, to the first car of the train.

This one was a first-class car, with a row of private

compartments alongside a narrow aisle. The compartments were likely full of government officials or Nazi officers. I couldn't think of a worse place to hide.

But what was I to do? I couldn't go back, and the brakes of the train were screeching to slow us down. The lights of the city were ahead. We would stop soon, and the train would be boarded for searching.

At the farthest forward compartment of the train car, a rope across the door held a note stating this car had been sabotaged by terrorists last week, so this compartment was closed for repairs. My heart beat faster. Maybe this was my answer! Or at least, it was my only choice.

I tried the door, but it was locked. Then I remembered a pocketknife inside Captain Stewart's bag, and the instructions I'd read for how to use the knife to pick a lock. I dug into his bag, feeling around for the knife. Finally, I found it near the bottom. The train had slowed nearly to a stop.

I pulled out the knife and flipped it open, then with shaking hands pressed the tip of the blade into the lock. The trick was to feel around for a latch that the blade could move. I wiggled it, wondering if I'd really know when the latch moved.

Then, out of sheer luck, I felt something shift, and the door opened. I grabbed the bag and dumped the blade inside it while I slid into the compartment, then closed and relocked the door behind me.

I took one step back and stifled a scream. I had nearly

stepped through a large, jagged gap in the floor, with nothing but open air and train track below. Losing my balance, I scrambled for anything to grab, and finally caught a piece of broken wood siding that had separated from the wall.

Beneath me, the tracks passed slower and slower until we screeched to a final stop. It wasn't enough to be in here. I still needed to hide.

From the aisle outside the door, I heard the conductor announce for everyone to keep their seats, adding, "You will be notified when you are allowed to disembark."

"Please don't let them leave me," I whispered, a prayer that I hoped would somehow carry to Jakob.

I couldn't fit Captain Stewart's bag through the gap in the wood siding all at once, but I removed the larger items and deposited them inside the wall one by one until the bag itself fit. Then I angled my body through the gap, dropping down on a metal plank, and squeezed so tight between the walls that I truly didn't know if I'd be able to get out again.

But I was here now, and I hoped my plan would work.

Because the heavy footsteps I had come to recognize so well now pounded through the train car where I was hiding, with orders being shouted in German. I didn't recognize the words, but that wasn't necessary.

The search had begun.

THIRTY-SEVEN

Rule: *Courage comes from within.*

The first-class compartment might've been the first one searched. My breath caught in my throat as a key was pressed into the door of my compartment. In French, I heard the conductor apologize for keeping the door locked and causing a delay in the search. The answer came in German: He had better not make the same mistake again.

Light from the soldier's flashlight filtered through the wood boards where I was hiding. I remembered Liesel's advice, that faces were the most identifiable, so I turned as far away from his light as possible and stayed as low as the small gap allowed.

"Could someone fit behind those boards?" the Nazi asked the conductor. The very boards where I now hid.

"Perhaps if they stood there while the wall was built

around them," the conductor said. "But the gap would be too small for anyone to climb through."

Too small for an adult, I thought, then hoped the Nazi would not think of the same thing.

One of them pounded on the wall almost in front of my face. Dust flew into my eyes and nose, and with my next breath of air, I felt a sneeze coming on. I held my breath but the itch in my nose worsened. I was going to sneeze!

"And what is this?" the Nazi asked. "Someone's ration card?"

"Strange," the conductor said.

My heart stopped. It must have fallen from Captain Stewart's bag when I was unloading it.

"Perhaps it blew in from the tracks below," the conductor said.

"Perhaps this train is carrying black market supplies," the Nazi said. "You had better hope I don't find any. Show me the next compartment."

The door was shut behind me again, but only a second later, the sneeze came. I did my best to stifle it, but even so, I waited, terrified that I'd hear my compartment door open again. How could they not have heard me?

Other doors opened and closed, which was all I heard from within these walls. Although the danger wasn't over, I began to relax a little. If there were any trouble, I'd hear—

Shouting.

"Jüdin!" The German word for a Jewish woman. It was followed immediately by orders shouted so loudly that I caught distinct words. Someone was under arrest.

"Please, I was only trying to return to my family!" The woman was speaking in French, but so quickly and in a voice so thick with terror that I wondered if the soldiers could understand her.

"You must come with us," one of them ordered.

"I've done nothing wrong. I . . ." The woman's protests gradually faded away, as did the heavy boots on the train floor, and when a door slammed shut, I knew they had left this train car.

But I had no idea what to do next.

I needed to get out of this tiny space and go back to where the Durands had been seated and hope they were still there. If the Nazis found this woman, they could have just as easily realized the Durands' papers were fraudulent. Or maybe the family simply became too nervous and left while they could.

The train began to pull away from the station, and with those first rumbles of the wheels beneath my feet, my heart sank.

Careful to avoid the gap in the floor, I pushed Captain Stewart's bag out of my little space, along with the other larger items I had removed earlier. Wood blocks had been built inside the wall to brace the paneling, and I used them as a ladder to slowly climb out. I was dirty, my arms and legs were scratched, and I was afraid of what I would find when I returned to where the Durands had been sitting.

I had to believe they were still there.

I began repacking Captain Stewart's bag, but hadn't counted on the wind that would be stirred up in here from the hole in the floor. The yellow note from my father was tucked inside his book of poems, his smiles, which was propped against the umbrella. But a bump in the train knocked the book to its side and the cover bounced with it enough for the note to fly free into the air. I leapt for it, clutching the paper in one hand, then fell straight forward, directly over the gap in the floor.

I would've fallen through, except for my other hand, stretched to the floor across from the gap. I looked down to the tracks below, rumbling faster and faster below me.

Straighten your spine, Meggie. That's what Maman would say—make yourself as tall as possible, then roll away.

Straighten your spine. My father had said it too, in his note.

So I stretched myself as long as I could, then slowly rolled until the gap narrowed and I was on a solid wood floor.

I waited there to catch my breath, grateful for the simple advice from my parents that had saved my life.

Now Papa hoped I'd use the same advice to save him.

Straighten your spine.

I sat up, my head cocked sideways. No, that wasn't what he had written. His words were *Straighten* the *spine*.

In a code, every word mattered.

What if he wasn't talking about *my* spine at all?

My eyes shifted across this little compartment, to where Papa's book of smiles still lay. The brown cover was thick with a binding that Papa had made himself.

The binding of a book was called a spine.

Careful to avoid the gap in the floor, I hurried to that side of the compartment and picked up his book. I pressed against the spine, and when I did, I was sure I felt something there. But what was it?

"Forgive me, Papa," I whispered.

I pulled out the pocketknife from Captain Stewart's bag and cut along the spine of Papa's book. Inside, between the bound pages, was a small note in Papa's handwriting. It read:

I hope you never need to use these.

Nothing more was in the spine itself, but now that I had the book open, I saw that the cover was really two thin pieces of pressed board, and something was between them.

I pried the boards apart wide enough to withdraw not

one but three items inside, and immediately caught my breath.

Three sets of false papers.

One for Grandmère.

One for Maman.

One for me.

THIRTY-EIGHT

Rule: *The enemy will push hard to win. The agent must push harder.*

Angling to see better by the light filtering through these half-boarded-up windows, I opened each set of papers, each including entry visas for travel to Switzerland. Maman's picture was there, but another woman's name was beside it. The same was true for Grandmère, so I already knew when I opened mine that the name would be different.

Sure enough, there was my picture, with my same birth-date, but my name was listed as Marguerite Fortier.

I wasn't sure how Papa had anticipated that we might one day need false papers, but he clearly had. The visas also confirmed that he wanted me to go to Switzerland.

The Durands had the same kind of false papers. They knew they'd be able to get past the border guards using them. I needed these papers too, especially before getting off the train.

Papa had given me the exact thing I needed!

I was equally excited that I had solved another part of Papa's letter.

So although I wasn't sure if it was safe to leave this compartment, I couldn't make myself wait a minute longer to go back to the train car and show my papers—my *false* papers—to the others.

I hoisted Captain Stewart's pack onto my shoulders, then slowly opened the compartment door. I absolutely could not run into any Nazi soldiers here, nor did I want to see the conductor, or, for that matter, any traveler whatsoever. I didn't want a single question about why I had been hiding in that compartment, or even why I was in a first-class train car.

No one was in the corridor when I peeked out. I tiptoed toward the transom and crossed to the next train car, but this time, a notice had been posted on the door, written in both French and German. It read:

All citizens are ordered to report to the Gestapo
any sightings of Albert Tabbert or Liesel Welk,
believed to be traveling together and in the
company of a French girl.

Nothing was written about Jakob, which was good news for him. Drawings of Albert and Liesel were at the bottom of the pages. The artwork wasn't an exact replica of their faces, but if someone studied the sign closely, they might recognize them.

My heart sank.

Had the Durands seen this? Surely they had. For all I knew, that poster was on the door of every train in France.

This was a disaster.

The first thing I did when entering the next train car was to look out the window. Now that I had papers, I hoped we'd stay on the train for as far as it would carry us. It was better than walking, and probably safer too.

I passed through that train car and entered the next one after that, the one where the Durands were.

Or ought to have been.

My breath caught in my throat. Their seats were empty, and not a trace of them remained.

The forward door of the train car opened, and a new conductor walked through. "*Pardon*, mademoiselle," he said to me. "Were you looking for the people who were seated there?"

"Yes. Do you know where they are?"

He frowned. "They left their seats when the train was searched. I believe they moved on."

I nodded, and tried to keep my expression even, no matter how my stomach was twisting. If they had already gotten off the train, then they were long gone by now.

"Take courage," he said. "Everything will be all right."

Take courage? Those were the exact words from Papa's note. That couldn't possibly be a coincidence. He walked on but I immediately stood and followed him. "Monsieur . . . monsieur . . ."

He turned back to me. "Yes?"

I suddenly felt shy, but I did have to ask. "Monsieur, my name is Marguerite—Meg. Do you have any information for me? Is there any reason I am supposed to talk to you?"

His smile was kind, but clearly neither my name nor my question meant anything to him. "I don't believe so. Now please return to your seat."

I thanked him and slumped onto the seat where Jakob had sat before. Papa had once taught me that while it was a problem to miss a message in a code, it was even worse to put a message into a code that was never meant to be there. I had forgotten that rule.

I stared out the train window for some time, with no idea of what I should do now. It was likely that I would never know what had happened to the Durands.

Even if I got off at the next stop, there would be no point in trying to go back for them. They wouldn't still be at the station.

And there was no point in me carrying on toward Switzerland, because unless Albert made it over the border, he wouldn't fulfill his promise to get my father released.

And I doubted he *could* make it over the border without my help. None of them knew the Alps the way I did.

Then a voice inside me whispered that maybe that was the point. Their plan had been to go to the Pyrenees Mountains. They had taken their first opportunity to go their own way and leave me behind.

I leaned against the side of the mostly empty train car, clutching Captain Stewart's bag in my arms and staring outside at nothing at all. There really wasn't much else to do but get off at Dijon, then return to Maman and Grandmère.

At least I knew Lieutenant Becker wouldn't be there. No, he was here in the area, searching for me. And searching for my friends.

They were my friends now, and still in terrible danger. But there was nothing I could do to help them.

CHAPTER
THIRTY-NINE

Rule: *Be cautious with good news, and hopeful with bad news.*

After nearly an hour, the rear door of the train car opened. I glanced back out of habit, rather than actually caring about who might be passing through. But my eyes widened when Jakob entered. He waved at me, and I nearly shouted his name with excitement.

He hurried up the row toward me. "We'll be in Dijon soon. Why didn't you join us?"

"Join you? Didn't you get off the train?"

His nose wrinkled. "Why would we leave the train? We just went to another car."

I burst out laughing. "Oh! The conductor said that you had moved on. I thought that meant you had left without me, not that you had switched train cars!"

Jakob leaned in, lowering his voice. "Albert wanted us to

leave this car because he was certain he recognized one of the Nazis who was searching here. But we wouldn't have left without you. Where did you go?"

"I found a place to hide. But the best news is that while I was there, I figured out a part of my father's code. It led me to these!"

I pulled out the visas. Jakob opened mine and grinned. "Marguerite Fortier? That sounds like a wealthy person's name. I wonder if that was his plan." Then his brow furrowed. "But your mother's papers are here as well, and your grandmother's."

My smile fell as I realized why he was concerned. Why hadn't I thought of this before? Without these papers, Maman and Grandmère would have no way of joining me and Papa in Switzerland.

"This is all wrong," I said, feeling the tension rise in me with every word I spoke. "Papa wanted me to solve the code when I was still in the Perche! He wanted all of us to come on this escape!"

"It will be all right," Jakob offered.

"No, it won't! I've got to fix this!" I pressed my hand to my mouth as thoughts swam in every direction through my mind. How could I possibly fix this?

I couldn't. As long as I had all the visas, Maman and Grandmère would be trapped here in France.

Jakob began leading me to the next car. Sensing my

frustration, he said, "Tell me more about Captain Stewart's book. Maybe something in there can help you."

"No, it can't." I'd read enough of the book to understand that. Nothing could solve a problem as big as this.

We passed through the transom, pausing to see another notice like the one I had seen earlier. Those notices would be another big problem. I felt utterly hopeless.

This new train car was mostly empty, which I thought made Albert and Liesel stand out even more. I wondered if they ought to have chosen somewhere less private.

"Meg, we were so worried," Liesel said when we returned. "We finally told Jakob to look for you, but we had little hope of him succeeding."

The door opened again, and the conductor came through and began looking over the papers of each passenger as he announced, "Next stop is Dijon." He stopped directly in front of us, his eyes resting heavily on Albert and Liesel before they shifted to me. "That will be the last stop on this line. Today, there will be Nazis waiting to speak to each person as they exit the train. If you hope to enter the Free Zone from here, be sure that you are ready for their questions."

After a quick glance at each of our papers, the conductor continued on to the next train car, but not one of us moved or made a sound.

He knew who they were, who *we* were.

If we made any mistakes, the Nazis would figure it out too.

Yet it was worse than even the conductor had guessed.

We weren't headed into the Free Zone, to the south. No, we had to continue moving east, into an area I knew only as the Forbidden Zone. The Germans claimed this was land they were reserving for the future occupation of German citizens, but we suspected there was a larger purpose at work: to keep people like us from escaping into Switzerland.

The instant the conductor left, I spread out the silk map. Liesel and Albert pored over it, occasionally glancing out the train windows in hopes of determining where we were.

"We have fifteen or twenty minutes, maybe," Albert said.

"We can go to the back of the train and jump off," Jakob said.

"You'll break a leg," Albert said.

"Better than being arrested!"

"Don't you have a plan for this?" I asked.

"That plan was made before notices were plastered all over this train!" Liesel turned to Albert. "If we surrender, it might go better for us."

"If we surrender, we will go straight to the camps," he said. "I'd rather jump from a moving train."

"No, we must remember our cover stories!" It was the only chance we had. I started with Liesel. "Where do you live?"

"In Orléans," Liesel said. "We moved there after France's surrender, so we do not know many people, or the area very well."

"How did you and Albert meet?"

Liesel only looked toward Albert, who firmly said, "We met at work two years ago after my first wife died. We'll tell them that Jakob is my son from an earlier marriage."

"And I was never married." Liesel blinked hard. "According to Captain Stewart."

Jakob sighed. "We've all studied our stories over and over. But what is *your* story? Why did your mother send you to live with us?"

I thought for a moment. "The Perche has become too dangerous, because of the partisans. You all were traveling for a funeral in Dijon, so you picked me up on your way there."

"And what is your name?" Jakob asked.

"Meg Kenyon."

Jakob groaned. "No, not if they are questioning you. What is the name on the papers from your father?"

I closed my eyes, trying to remember it. "Marguerite Fortier."

"Say that a thousand times until it rolls off your tongue. Say every lie on your papers until it is natural to you."

"Even so, we might be searched," Albert said, eyeing me specifically. "No one should have anything to make them stand out as suspicious."

Every single item in the backpack was worse than suspicious—they would identify me as a spy and lead the Nazis straight back to Captain Stewart and Maman and Grandmère. All I could hope was that they wouldn't think to search a young French girl.

But if they did, the most dangerous item in the backpack was the spy book. I tucked that inside my coat, keeping my right arm down so the book wouldn't fall out.

"I must go to the bathroom," Albert said. Jakob stood to help him, but he raised a hand. "The aisle of a train car is straight. I won't have any problems seeing my way there."

Seconds after he left, Liesel raised a finger. "I have makeup! Perhaps you could help me look more . . . French?"

I grinned and sat next to her while she pulled out a small bag of makeup. I had never worn makeup myself, but I'd often sat and watched my mother apply hers, comparing her look to those of the fancier women in Paris.

"Red lips," I said. "The brightest color you have."

"Captain Stewart suggested I pack this one." She applied a red lipstick and frowned. "Too much?"

"Not for a Frenchwoman. Now you need to soften your

hairstyle." She reached for it, but with no mirror, she'd definitely have trouble.

I stood in front of her. "Here, let me."

I pulled at some of the pins in her hair, replacing them where my mother would to create a wavy look.

And surprisingly, when I leaned back to check our work, Liesel really did look more French. It was still her, but less like the drawings I'd seen.

"What about you?" Liesel asked.

"There's no picture of Meg on their notices," Jakob said. "Maybe they won't pay any attention to her."

"We can't take that risk." Liesel pressed her bright red lips together. "If I can look French, then you can look older than twelve."

She began applying her makeup on me, lining my eyes, rouging my cheeks, and using the same bright lipstick for my lips.

She leaned back and smiled. "Now, what about your hair?"

"Down." Jakob shrugged at me. "I think keeping it down would be pretty . . . I mean, it'd make you look older."

I pulled my hair from its braids, finger-combing to loosen the strands. Liesel leaned back and smiled. "Perfect!"

"What about me?" We looked up to see Albert, only a much younger-looking Albert. He had shaved off his beard entirely and parted his hair on the side rather than in the middle. On a casual glance, he looked nothing like the man who'd stood here fewer than ten minutes ago and bore little resemblance to the drawing of him.

But Lieutenant Becker had seen me face-to-face, and the Nazis somehow knew we were headed in this direction.

I sighed. "Let's hope we've done enough."

I doubted the Nazis would be fooled by any of us.

FORTY

Rule: *At all times, remain loyal to your team.*

Pulling into the station, Dijon looked much like anywhere else. A beautiful building housed a ticket office
and waiting areas. The station platform was beneath an
arched roof, with room for several trains to come and go.

But in Occupied France, it also meant we were welcomed
by a line of Nazi soldiers, standing along what would be the
entire length of our train. We'd have no chance to sneak past
them all.

My pulse seemed to rush to the ends of my fingers and
tips of my toes. They almost ached with worry.

"I should leave the train on my own," I told the Durands.
"If I am searched, that will put the rest of you in even greater
danger."

"Thank you, Meg." Liesel squeezed my hands in hers.
"That book has taught you a lot. Remember all of it."

I had to remember that I was Marguerite Fortier. That was my name, it had always been my name, and I was the kind of girl who could have a name like that.

But truthfully, I was so nervous, I barely could remember my real name, much less the lies I'd soon have to tell.

"Let us go first," Albert said.

They looked at each other and drew in deep breaths. Then Albert took his false wife's hand and led her forward along the aisle with Jakob close behind them.

Orders to halt cut through the silence of the train. I watched through the windows as each exiting passenger was greeted individually by a Nazi soldier demanding papers, then beginning a series of questions.

Most people got through with a few brief questions, but off to the right, a soldier called for assistance, then two others appeared, handcuffed one man, and escorted him away.

Just before getting off the train, Jakob glanced back at me, his eyes now wide with fear. He must have also seen what just happened and wondered what mistake that man had made, and whether we were making the same mistake too.

The Durands left the train, their papers already in their hands. Then it was my turn to leave. I walked into the aisle on shaking legs. With Captain Stewart's book pinched beneath my arm, I took another step forward, feeling like I was walking to my own end. My papers were clutched in one hand, though I was sure the sweat on my palms must be wearing away the ink. Smearing the lies.

It was all up to me now. No mistakes.

I left the train, instantly aware of how cold the day was. The elevation was higher here, and the temperatures would be colder from now on. The hardest part of our journey was still ahead.

But before I could think too much of it, I was directed to a broad-shouldered German whose frown seemed to be his natural expression. I gave him my papers before he asked for them, and his glare only sharpened when I put them in his hand.

"Name?"

"Marguerite Fortier."

"Where do you live?"

The answer to this question, thankfully, was true. Papa had used our original address from before the war. I gave him the correct answer, but before I finished speaking, his next question came.

"Does your family still live there?"

A shout behind me caught my attention. I looked back toward the Durands, and to my horror, saw two Nazi officers handcuffing Albert and leading him alone off the platform. Before they saw me looking, I turned away, utterly terrified.

What had he done?

"Answer my question."

I looked back at the Nazi, but genuinely couldn't remember what we'd been talking about. I certainly couldn't remember the lie I'd planned to answer him with.

But if I didn't, I'd be joining Albert under arrest.

I turned around again, this time to watch Liesel and Jakob cross to the far end of the platform to wait for me, or for Albert. I hoped they were waiting for him, because that would mean they believed he had some chance of coming back.

That's what I decided to believe, because I couldn't bear to think of the alternative.

"You will pay attention and answer my question." The soldier's tone sharpened. He was losing patience with me. "Does your family still live at this address?"

"They . . . They . . ." My father was an escaped prisoner who was hiding somewhere in Germany until I could help him get free. My mother and grandmother were almost on the other side of the country. "They are home." I took a deep breath, then straightened up tall and looked him in the eye. "I was at my grandmother's funeral in Paris."

No, that wasn't the cover story we had planned! The funeral was supposed to be here, in Dijon. Wasn't it?

He glanced again at my papers. "I am sorry to hear about your grandmother. Everything is in order here. There will be no civilian trains from Dijon toward your home today. I hope you have other transportation plans."

"Thank you." Though I had no other plans. I had thought the trains would carry us farther than this.

Hoping not to draw attention to myself, I casually walked inside the train station to the far wall, where Liesel and Jakob were waiting. I stood a meter from them and lowered my head.

"Why did they take Albert?" I mumbled, as quietly as possible.

Jakob didn't look at me to answer. "We don't know."

Liesel lowered her head as well. "We can't stay here. Albert would understand that."

"But we can't leave him," I said. "We should wait until we know if he'll return."

Liesel subtly shook her head. "If we wait, they'll bring all of us in for questioning. I don't like this either, Meg, but we have no choice now."

"Albert is part of this mission," I hissed.

"Better that three of us succeed than none."

"Without Albert, I can't succeed. He is the one who will make the telephone call for my father's rescue."

But Liesel wasn't changing her mind, and Jakob only shook his head at me.

The last of the passengers left the train, which meant the

Nazi soldiers began filing off the platform and into the station. If Albert were with us, we could have left already.

But he wasn't. And might never be.

"Let's find a market," Liesel suggested. "Jakob, we need transportation to get us out of Dijon. Anything that's safe."

She and Jakob walked outside first, and three minutes later, I followed, joining them in front of the station with Nazi flags hanging from the upper story. Every Nazi flag I saw infuriated me, but these inflamed me more than the rest, because I knew Albert was still somewhere inside, behind those flags.

A small market was visible across the square. Liesel turned to me. "Do you have any money in that backpack? I have no more."

I unrolled the pack and pulled out a little money, which I gave to her. She returned a few francs to me for the market and gave the rest to Jakob. "Perhaps you should go in alone, Meg. I'll try to help Jakob make our next travel arrangements." She drew in a deep breath and looked at each of us. "Be safe."

Jakob and Liesel went one way and I went the other, but I had no sooner stepped inside the market before I knew this plan was a mistake. This shop was as thick with Nazis as the train station had been. They paid little attention to me as I darted between them, pulling two boxes of crackers here, a loaf of bread there, and a small package of cheese I managed to grab ahead of another woman who was reaching for it.

I took my place in line behind two soldiers who were laughing with each other about an entire family they had arrested that day.

Laughing over their fate.

Then one turned to me and grinned. "*Bonjour*, mademoiselle. You look as if you did not enjoy our story."

I lowered my eyes but did not say a word.

"It was only a Jewish family," he said. "They were breaking the law by not wearing their star. Come on now, smile!"

"Enough!" a voice behind me said.

The laughter immediately stopped, but my stomach hollowed out. I knew that voice, and it sent a cold shiver down my spine.

Lieutenant Becker was standing directly behind me.

FORTY-ONE

Rule: *In great danger, the agent must remain calm.*

He'd know my voice.

He'd know my face, even through these layers of makeup. How absurd it had been to think a little lipstick and rouge would do anything other than call even more attention my way.

The grocer was speaking in German. If I replied in German, Lieutenant Becker would recognize my accent. If I replied in French, the grocer might take offense, to flatter the soldiers in his store.

The lieutenant wasn't finished scolding the soldiers ahead of me.

"You embarrass yourselves in front of the locals," he said. "And you offended this girl between us. Apologize to her."

I shook my head and lowered my eyes. I didn't need an apology. I only needed to become invisible.

The two soldiers now turned around and faced me directly.

"*Verzeihung*," the one said, echoed by the other.

I nodded back at them, saying nothing. Heat seemed to scorch my face as the second soldier continued to stare.

"Lieutenant," he began. "Were you not looking for—"

"Stop staring; you'll make her uncomfortable," Becker scolded. "Get out of line and out of this store."

The one who had been staring looked down at me a final time before they both saluted Becker, deposited their groceries on the counter, then left.

"They do not represent all Germans," Becker said from behind me. "Please, *Fräulein*, it is your turn."

I stepped forward and placed my groceries on the counter, then kept my eyes fixed on the grocer while he totaled my bill.

"Ration card?" he asked.

I put forward one of Captain Stewart's cards, and the grocer stamped it. I looked at the total and unfolded the money clutched in my hand.

"Can you pay in marks?" the cashier asked, eyeing Lieutenant Becker. "German money is superior."

Captain Stewart had German marks in his bag, but there was no chance of me opening that bag here.

"I . . . I, uh . . ."

"I will buy her groceries," Becker said. "Here, *Fräulein*, give me your money instead."

He passed a handful of German marks forward. I turned no more than I had to and set my French money in his hands.

I didn't miss the familiarity of the moment, of only five days ago when I'd placed four rubbery potatoes in those same hands.

Only this time, mine were shaking so hard I had to pull them into fists, and then hope my legs were stable enough to carry me out of the market.

I whispered my thanks, then raced outside to find Liesel, faster than I should have gone, but I couldn't make myself slow down. Without taking time to explain, I grabbed her arm. "Where's Jakob? We have to get out of here!"

"Meg, what—"

"Don't say my name!"

"All right. But what about Albert?"

"I don't know, I don't know!" We couldn't leave without him, but if Lieutenant Becker was here, the situation had changed. Either we left as soon as possible, or we might not leave at all.

I glanced behind me just before we reentered the train station. Lieutenant Becker was emerging from the market, but he was in conversation with an older Frenchman. Before he looked up, I grabbed Liesel's arm and pulled her inside the station with me. We'd be less visible here.

Several people were milling about in the area, most of them appearing to be waiting for the train back to Paris.

"There you are," Jakob said, running up to us. "I found a man who will take us in his wagon as near to the Forbidden Zone as he can go. Of course, I had to pay him a lot for it, but no one else would even speak to me."

"That's fine," Liesel said. "Where is he?"

"Hitching the wagon. He'll be here soon."

I glanced back outside. "How soon?" In hushed tones, I told them about Becker and the Nazi soldier who seemed suspicious of me.

Jakob looked at the clock overhead. "The farmer promised to be here in fifteen minutes. We'll be out of Becker's reach soon."

"What about their reach?" Liesel asked.

My heart stopped. Two Nazis were entering the station, the same two who had been ordered out of the market before. So far, they hadn't noticed us, but a single glance in our direction could change all that.

"Let's wait somewhere else." My voice shook as I spoke. I had to calm down. I had to think.

"The farmer will meet us right outside the station," Jakob said.

"But if Albert is released, he'll be inside the station," Liesel added.

"Get the groceries into our bags, quickly!" I began looking for a bathroom where I could wash off this makeup.

But that wouldn't be enough. Even with a clean face and rebraided hair, I'd still be in the same clothes as before. Captain Stewart's bag had a men's shirt in it. I would have to make it work.

In the bathroom, I pulled my hair into a quick braid and tucked it all into a beret someone had dropped near the door, tilting it sideways for a more feminine look. Then I put Captain Stewart's shirt over mine, belting it on the outside of my skirt.

Nine minutes still remained when I walked out. Liesel and Jakob were sitting on a bench in a corner, heads down.

I stuffed Captain Stewart's bag under the bench so it wouldn't easily be seen, but the time was still dragging by without mercy.

Eight minutes.

Where was Albert?

Seven minutes.

"He won't make it," Jakob said. "Will we leave him?"

Six minutes, then five, and we hadn't decided what to do.

"They're looking at you," Jakob said, gesturing slightly with his head. "Those two Nazis."

I pulled out Papa's book of smiles and held it up in front

of me. Inside I had written his anagram, JAIMIE STAYED, the one I still had not solved. But I couldn't pay attention to that now.

Four minutes were left, then three remained. The crowd walked forward to get into line for an approaching train. We looked even more suspicious now, just sitting here.

"Let's go outside," I said.

"Wait." Liesel grabbed my arm. "One of the Nazis just left the station. Where is he going?"

I chanced a quick peek at the remaining Nazi. He was holding a notice in his hands and glancing down at it, then looking up at us.

Two minutes.

He began to walk toward us.

"Let's get outside and watch for the farmer," Jakob said. "Everyone act normal."

At a time like this, how could I possibly know what normal looked like? I held Captain Stewart's pack by one hand and kept my nose buried in the book.

One minute left.

And no sign of the farmer.

"Walk down the road," Jakob said. "He'll come, he'll come." But he didn't look as confident as I wished he did.

"That Nazi who left just walked back into the train station," Liesel whispered. "An officer went inside with him. Is that Becker?"

It had to be Becker.

"Walk faster," I said. No one was watching, for now. This might be our only chance to put some distance between us and the train station.

"There he is!" Jakob pointed to the corner ahead where an older farmer was riding toward us on a wagon loaded with hay.

"You first." Liesel grabbed me by the waist and practically threw me onto the wagon. Jakob tossed in his bags next, saying to the farmer, "Don't stop, don't stop!"

Liesel jumped into the wagon. Jakob followed and began covering me with the hay.

"Stay down," Liesel said. "We cannot let Becker see you if he passes by."

She didn't need to ask. I remained perfectly still beneath the hay, barely breathing, listening to the steady rhythm of the wagon wheels as they clacked along the cobblestone path, rolling softly back and forth with the tilt of the wagon.

Nobody spoke. Except for once, after only two minutes, when Liesel mumbled, "Oh."

And instantly the wagon stopped. Why did it stop?

Why did it stop?

I knew that I couldn't move. But every muscle in my body wanted to leap from where I was and run. I couldn't think of any reason that we had stopped here . . . wherever *here* was.

I fought the urge to move, even when the weight changed in the wagon, which I could not explain. Had someone gotten on, or gotten off?

Then we began to drive again.

And I still didn't know what had happened!

FORTY-TWO

Rule: *A good agent will always act with integrity.*

At least twenty horrible minutes passed before someone spoke. Jakob said, "It's all right, Meg. You can
come out."

I'd lain quietly for so long, I almost didn't dare to move.
Not until I heard another voice.

"Meg is here?"

I popped out from beneath the hay. "Albert?"

He was up front with the farmer and turned back to face
me. "I was so afraid for you, Meg. Every time I tried to ask
where you were, they put a finger to their lips to shush me."

"What happened back at the station?" I asked. "Why
were you arrested?"

"I forgot the answer to a question." A grin tugged at his
mouth. "I realized the only way to get out of trouble was to
forget the answers to all their questions." Now the half grin

turned to a full smile. "What is my name? I don't know. Where do I live? I don't know. Have I ever lived in Germany?" Albert began chuckling. "'Oh yes,' I told them. 'With the Führer himself. We are great friends.' That's when they sent me away. Kicked me onto the road saying that I wasn't worth their time. Well, who should pass by minutes later but this kind farmer, and the three of you! Thank you, monsieur."

"De rien," the farmer said, a reminder that all of us were saying too much in front of him.

So we quieted down for the next hour until we were near Dole. All except for Albert, who seemed to enjoy the company of the farmer. I hadn't listened to most of their conversation, but I did hear Albert insist he could repair the farmer's broken tractor.

The farmer perked up at this news. "If you are willing to try the repair . . . and if you will cause us no trouble . . . you are welcome to stay in a guesthouse on our property." Albert hesitated, and the farmer said, "My wife and I are too old to care about who you are, or who you are pretending to be. But we will lose our farm if we can't repair that tractor."

Albert reached over to shake his hand. *"Danke dir."* He should have thanked the farmer in French, but I supposed he no longer cared for pretenses.

The farmer brought us from there to his home, a cozy little cottage that reminded me of my grandmother's farmhouse.

The guesthouse in back was quite small, but it was comfortably decorated and surprisingly modern. A telephone was on a desk beside a chair in one corner.

Albert left to assist the farmer while Jakob built us a fire and Liesel and I prepared a supper with the food I'd bought. We chatted about things neither of us cared about, while my mind was on that telephone. The one in the Jewish home we had stayed in a few nights ago hadn't worked. Maybe this one would.

"Meg." Liesel spoke louder. "Meg, will you put the food on the table?"

"Oh yes, of course."

There wasn't much food, only the cheese and bread, and two eggs that the farmer's wife had brought over to us with a little milk. But we were glad to have it.

Once Albert returned, we sat around the table to make the best of what we had, which gave me an opportunity to ask a question that had been weighing on me.

I said, "The notices on the train say your real names are Albert Tabbert and Liesel Welk. You both admitted that you worked for the Nazis. They must have been very important jobs if the Nazis are trying so hard to find the two of you."

Albert and Liesel looked at each other, and then he began, "You already know a little about me—that I was assigned to one of the Nazis' more ambitious programs. Our project began as peaceful technology, something that would have allowed mass production of electricity. But the Nazis corrupted the idea, as they have corrupted all good things. They wanted to harness the technology for use as a weapon that could concentrate the sun's energy into a beam of light capable of burning an entire city. They called it the Sun Gun. Once I realized the potential of this weapon, I knew I had to leave. Not only that, but I destroyed all my research, a lifetime of work, in hopes it will never be replicated. That will not undo the damage I have done, but at least I will not create any further harm."

"Was it the same for you?" I asked Liesel. "Did you ever think about the people on the other end of your work?"

"Of course," she said. "Based on my reports, the Nazis would conduct air strikes or raids against their enemies. They'd destroy whole camps in a single night."

I shook my head, shocked at her words, horrified at what those words had meant to me over the past two years. "I've lost friends, Liesel, real people who meant a lot to me. So maybe it's—"

"My fault," Liesel finished. "I'm so sorry, Meg."

"Apologies won't bring them back," I mumbled.

"Nor will it save my parents," Jakob said. There was tension in his voice, stronger than before.

Albert only hung his head and frowned. "No, it will not bring them back."

"Albert saved your life." The words burst from my mouth before I had any thought to stop them. Both Jakob and Albert turned toward me, and I didn't know which of them I should look at first, so I lowered my eyes and just spoke to Jakob. "The day that your father was reported, so was mine. Albert couldn't save them both. Your father gave himself up for my father's freedom. So maybe I owe you an apology, but Albert doesn't. The only choice he had was whether to save you, and he did."

Albert turned to Jakob. "Your parents were the best of people. I wish apologies were enough to bring them home again."

"But there is no way; we both know that." Jakob brushed at his eyes. "I'm sorry for the things I said before."

"You said nothing so terrible."

"Yes, I did." Jakob smiled through his sadness, a little. "Just not when you could hear me."

Since it was late and everyone was tired, we agreed to go to bed early. A small loft was upstairs, which Albert and Jakob could use, and Liesel took the small bedroom to the back of the guesthouse while I would sleep on the rug near the fire.

But long after everyone else had turned in for the night, I lay awake, my eyes fixed on the telephone. No matter how hard I had tried telling myself not to call home, the trying had only made it worse.

Finally, when I could stand it no longer, I crept over to the telephone, picked up the handset, and waited for the tone, just as I had before. This time, the dial tone rang. My finger shook as I dialed a zero. A moment later, an operator came on and requested the number and area, which I whispered to her through my cupped hand.

"One moment, please," the operator replied.

Grandmère didn't have a telephone, but her friend next door, Madame LeClair, did. She would be able to help me.

It felt like an eternity passed before the first ring, then a second and third ring passed, and I worried the operator would disconnect us if no one answered.

Then, *"Oui, allo?"*

"Madame LeClair?" I asked. "It's Meg Kenyon. Could you get a message to my mother?"

"Your mother, yes. Meg, where is your mother?"

I paused, tilting my head. "Madame LeClair, my mother is Sylvie Kenyon."

"Yes, I know. But where is she, and your grandmother too?"

I frowned. "Don't you know?"

"Two mornings ago, I went to return a borrowed egg, but nobody was home. I returned later that day, twice yesterday, and again today. We've had fresh snow, but the only footprints around your home are mine. Meg, when you see your family, please tell them I've been worried."

"Yes . . . of course."

I fumbled to hang up the phone, and even when I did, I kept my hand there, as if holding on to the handset might somehow change what I'd just heard.

"Meg?" Liesel walked in, her eyes shifting to that hand. "You didn't call anyone, did you? That wouldn't be safe." I didn't answer, and she said, "Meg?"

"I have to go home," I mumbled. Then with tears in my eyes I glanced up at her. "I'm so sorry, Liesel. You all need to continue without me. I have to go home."

FORTY-THREE

Thursday, March 5, 1942
663 days since I've seen Papa

I delivered the news to Albert and Jakob the following morning. Jakob's head sank lower and lower until he wasn't looking at me at all. Albert nodded only once, then said, "We respect your feelings, of course. Could your mother and grandmother have left France on their own?"

"How? They wouldn't risk using their real identification papers—that would bring up too many questions."

Albert's frown deepened. "I hope you understand that going home will change nothing. Wherever they are—"

"They wouldn't have just left. Maman would have gotten them into hiding, I know she would have. A letter will be there, or some kind of clue."

"Unless they couldn't leave anything." Liesel's tone was gentle. "It's possible that the lieutenant arrested your mother first—"

"Then came to find me." That wasn't just possible; it was the most likely explanation, though I could hardly bear to think about it. "If that's true, then they probably found Captain Stewart too!"

"I'm sorry, Meg. You shouldn't have to think of such things."

"I have to go home; I have to know." My mind was spinning faster than I could hold my thoughts together. "If I can find out what's happened to them—"

"Then what?" Jakob's words snapped into me. "Can you walk up to Becker and apologize for your mother's work with the resistance, your own work with them? Will he accept your apology for hiding a British spy in your home, or for spending the last week helping three German fugitives escape their clutches?" He stood, and now his tone softened. "I lost my parents too. I think about them all the time, every single second that I don't have anything to distract me. I still love them, and I wish more than anything that they were here, but I would not destroy this whole mission to go back to my empty house. What would be the point?"

I glanced away from him, then said, "If you had the smallest chance of rescuing your mother right now, would you go home, Jakob?"

He kicked at the floor for what seemed like a very long time, then replied, "We need you here, Meg."

Albert sighed. "We must make our own plans now.

Perhaps return to Captain Stewart's original idea of crossing the Pyrenees Mountains."

"They're so far away now," Liesel said. "Surely we can find our own way over the Alps."

"We're only here because Meg said she knew these mountains. None of us do." Jakob sounded angry again, and I hardly blamed him. He continued, "Albert can barely see a meter in front of him, and we still need to get inside the Forbidden Zone. How can we possibly do that on our own?"

A beat passed. Then Liesel spoke the words they must have all been thinking. "We can't. It's over."

"Over?" I shook my head. "No, it's not. Listen to me. I'll go home, I'll find my mother and grandmother, and even Captain Stewart, and when I return, we'll do this the right way. I'll bring everyone here with me, and we'll cross the Alps together, all of us. I just need—"

"It's over," Liesel repeated. "You are going back to the Perche, and we send you with every hope of success."

"If hope was enough to bring our families back, I wouldn't be here right now." Jakob's eyes pled with me. "Meg, nothing is left there but empty walls. I know how awful that moment will be, how much it will hurt you. Please don't leave."

"She must do what she feels is right." Albert leaned down and kissed the top of my head. "We will miss you, Meg. You've become like part of our family."

But we weren't a family; *they* weren't a family. They were only part of a mission that I still wanted to complete— that I was still desperate to complete.

But not at the expense of my mother and grandmother.

So I hugged Albert and Liesel, and waved to Jakob, though he only shrugged in response. "I'll come back when I've found them," I whispered, but no one answered this time. With nothing more to say or do, I put on my coat, hoisted Captain Stewart's backpack over my shoulders, and began the very long journey back to the Perche.

FORTY-FOUR

Rule: *Learn to see every possible solution to a problem.*

I avoided the main roads, and with only myself to look out for, it was easy to avoid anyone who happened to pass by. Even when I left the trail, it was a simple thing to keep my direction. The Durands couldn't have known that the little guesthouse wasn't even seven kilometers to the front door of my childhood home. I knew where Papa had stored some money, which I would need for the journey to Grandmere's.

Although I knew this area well, it had changed a great deal since I'd last been here. The usual warmth and openness of the locals seemed to have been replaced with suspicion and silence.

As I walked, I saw a few old friends of my parents, families I had once known, or other children I had played with. But if they recognized me, they showed no sign of it. They only put their heads down and went back to work.

I also passed a few bakeries, and my stomach rumbled at the sweet smells of fruit and sugar and bread, delicacies that only the very wealthy could afford . . . and the Nazis. I glanced inside one shop, hoping to buy something, but the only customers I saw wore Nazi uniforms. With a sigh, I moved on, telling myself I couldn't have afforded anything inside that shop anyway.

Finally, I saw my home in the distance. It had been almost two years since I'd been here, but the familiarity of the place came rushing back at me. Everything was just as I remembered it.

Our home wasn't large, but it had everything we needed. It was made of mostly stone and wood and plaster with two bedrooms upstairs and a sitting room with a fireplace, and kitchen below. A door from the kitchen led to a small garden area out back, and behind that were the woods where I had played all my life.

I continued to stare at my home, only realizing I was crying when I had to brush a tear from my cheek. How I had missed this place!

But I would have to be careful. I approached the front door with caution and even knocked, but there was no answer. Jakob had found plenty of abandoned homes on our way here. This must have been the same. I turned the handle, and the door opened.

It felt strange to walk inside after so long.

My home smelled as it always had, and looked nearly how I remembered it, with only a touch of dust. But even though it had appeared the same from the outside, it felt different inside. I couldn't decide why. Maybe the difference was me. I was older and had seen more of the world, and the effects of war. Maybe I'd seen too much, and this place was now only a memory of a childhood I never had the chance to finish.

But this was home.

We hadn't left any food behind, but I had a few crackers in Captain Stewart's bag. They'd have to do until I could find a market with only Frenchmen inside. Rather than think about food, I curled up on our sofa and began making plans to get back to the Perche.

Or at least, that was what I should have done. Instead, I opened Papa's yellow note and studied it again.

Dearest wife, Daisy, and Mom;
One day I'll return, you'll see.
Nothing can stop me from climbing
to you. Watch perfectly as
the sadness becomes numb.
Remember my smiles, brightened
under tender skies by the sea.
Straighten the spine, Daisy.
Take courage, even when hurting,

have faith until this battle
ends. Until then, be calm.
Regards,
Rosbif

The last time I'd folded the note, I'd been in a hurry and
had used a different seam than before, so instead of only one
lengthwise fold, this time a second seam ran almost next to
it, dividing the first letters of the top three lines, the "D" and
the "O" and the "N."

Don.

Like a person's name. Maybe that was Captain Stewart's
first name.

No, it wasn't. He'd told me his first name was Henry.
But . . .

I drew in a sharp breath. Could Papa have used the first
letters of each line to send me an entirely different message?

Who was Don?

I pulled out a pencil from the backpack and beneath
the note, wrote out the first letter of each line: D O N T T R
U S T H E R R.

The first word wasn't Don. But the three words that rose
from the page were so plain, I should have seen them from
the start.

I drew a slash between each word and read Papa's secret
message.

DONT/TRUST/HERR

Who was Papa talking about?

The only person on this mission that he knew: Herr Durand.

Albert.

My brain began spinning. Albert told me he had helped my father get to a safe house. Was that true? What if Albert had betrayed my father, and now was here as a spy for the Germans?

This must have been the true meaning of Papa's note, to warn us not to trust Albert!

Suddenly, I froze. Outside, an engine was approaching.

Engines meant soldiers, and this engine stopped in front of our door. I scrambled to my feet, stuffed everything that I had taken out back inside Captain Stewart's bag, and shoved my feet into my boots before racing into the kitchen, darting around our large old stove, and heading toward the back door.

I opened it but was yanked backward. I turned, wondering how the solider had caught me so quickly, then saw the strap of my bag had caught on the handle of the stove.

The front door slammed open. "Is someone here?" a German voice demanded from the sitting room.

My mind raced. Had I moved anything in there, even a little? I didn't know. I couldn't remember.

I slipped the strap off the oven handle, but I didn't dare

to run for the open door. Instead, I backed against the wall, keeping myself partially blocked by the stove.

"If anyone is in my home, show yourself now and it will go better for you!" the German shouted.

He had said *if*. He didn't *know* that I was here.

That would change in the next few seconds. Because whether I gave myself up or I was caught, nothing could make this better for me.

And I was about to find out exactly how bad it would be. I saw a gray-green uniform with a red Nazi patch enter the kitchen. All he had to do was turn his head and look.

CHAPTER
FORTY-FIVE

Rule: *Your greatest enemy is often very close to you.*

I was trapped in here. Our stove stood out almost to the middle of the room, and I crouched between it and the wall.

The soldier saw the opened rear door and raced straight through the kitchen. The instant he did, I ran back through the front room, yanked open the door, and raced as quickly as I could to reach the cover of trees. I didn't stop there, continuing to run until I reached hard ground that didn't show my footprints.

I ran and ran until I could barely breathe, until my lungs ached and my legs wobbled beneath my weight. Even then I staggered forward, finally settling somewhere in the middle of a patch of woods where I sank to the ground, sobbing.

He had called our house *his* home, but it wasn't. That was my home, *my* home! Wasn't it enough that they had taken my country, taken my family, and with it, our happy lives? Now one of them had my home too. He probably slept in my parents' room, in their bed. He ate at our kitchen table, sat on the sofa where I had just been, and took from me the last bit of my family and my life.

When those tears dried, new ones formed. This time for Liesel and for Jakob, who were making plans for an escape with a man my father was warning could not be trusted. But he had also been helping in our escape, and I couldn't explain that. He'd helped, even at times when he could have easily betrayed us.

So if it was true that we could not trust Albert, then he had to be involved in a bigger plan than simply turning us in. I just didn't know what.

The only thing I knew for certain was that I now had a decision to make. Either I could go back to the Perche and try to find my mother and grandmother, or I could return to that little guest home near Dole and warn Jakob and Liesel.

I felt I was being torn in half, having to make such a decision. I could not save everyone, and choosing one direction sacrificed the other.

Yet through it all, something that Jakob said to me before I left still echoed in my mind. I could not save my mother and grandmother, even if I returned to the Perche. They were already gone, and I had no way of getting them back.

But I could rescue my father, and Jakob and Liesel, if I hurried.

With my decision made, I lifted Captain Stewart's bag onto my shoulders, realizing for the first time how much lighter it had become. No, I began to realize how much stronger *I* had become—that was the difference.

It was almost dark when I began the long walk back to the guesthouse where the Durands had been staying. I hoped they were still there.

I got my answer late that night as I approached the guesthouse. A thin wisp of smoke trailed up from the chimney, and through the closed curtains, I caught an occasional shadow and some movement.

The door opened and I ducked behind a tree, hoping to see Jakob. Instead, it was Liesel, who called, "I'll set the milk outside for the night."

She closed the door behind her and carefully looked around the area. When she believed she was truly alone, she laid out her red scarf over the wide post railing to protect the wood from moisture, then set the jug of milk over it. I hoped the milk wouldn't ruin the scarf. She couldn't possibly have a third one with her.

Once she had finished, she brushed off her hands, looked around the area again, and returned to the house. The last thing I heard her say before she closed the door was "I hope Meg is safe out there. It's a cold night."

I hadn't noticed the cold at all. Instead, nervousness warmed me as I tried to think of a way to lure Jakob outside. Finally, I gave up on trying to be clever about it and simply tossed a rock against the side of the wall.

I hoped Jakob would be the one to come check on the noise.

Sure enough, seconds later, the door peeked open and Jakob peered through the gap. He said something to Albert and Liesel, then widened the door and cautiously stepped outside, closing the door behind him.

I shook the tree over my head. Snow dusted down on me, but that was all right. I had his attention, though maybe not in the way I'd hoped. He broke off a stick from a tree near him and approached me with the stick over his shoulder, ready to swing if necessary. I really didn't want that.

So as soon as he was within sight, I stood and held out my hands. "Jakob, it's me. It's Meg."

"Meg? You're back?"

A slight pause followed, and Jakob dropped the stick and crossed over to me, pulling me into a hug. It was strange and awkward and not at all what I had expected.

But in a strange and awkward way, I really didn't mind.

FORTY-SIX

Rule: *First determine if it is right. Then ask how it can be done.*

As quickly as possible, I explained to Jakob about my father's code, and about the strange behaviors I'd noticed from Albert.

But Jakob only shook his head. "I don't believe it, not Albert."

"Three days ago you said that if I knew who he really was, I'd get as far away from him as possible."

"I was angry, that's all. I've known him for a long time, Meg. He became disgusted by the Nazis. He would never spy for them."

"It's in my father's note!" I pulled it out and showed him the first letter of each word.

Jakob still frowned. "The note says not to trust *Herr*. That could be anyone. Maybe Captain Stewart—"

"Captain Stewart isn't German. *Herr* is for a German man."

"No, it's a German word that could be any man. Would your father really have written a note that warned about Albert, then given it to Albert?"

"That's why he put it in code! We have to tell Liesel."

"Not until we know for sure." Jakob took a slow breath. "Maybe you're right, but for now, let's both keep a close eye on Albert. If he does anything suspicious, then we can tell Liesel. But until he does, I think we should act as if everything is normal."

Reluctantly, I agreed. I pulled out the silk map, hoping the little light from the moon would be enough for us. "We need to come up with a plan—and a good one, because it won't get any easier from here. If Albert is going to interfere, then our plan needs to be almost perfect."

"An *almost* perfect plan." Jakob grinned. "How hard can that be?"

I knew he was teasing, but this was no time for jokes. I put my finger down on the map and said, "Back in the Perche, Yvonne told me that if I could find someone in Dole named Pierre, he could help us get into the Forbidden Zone."

"Find someone named Pierre in France?" Jakob ran his fingers through his hair and chuckled softly. "Our challenge will be finding only *one* Pierre."

"If we can find the right Pierre and get into the Forbidden Zone, then we can make our way into the Jura Mountains. That will be our route over the Alps."

Jakob let out a low whistle. "Be honest, Meg. Do you really think this plan has any chance of succeeding?"

"Yes." I wasn't sure that I believed it, but I did think it was the only plan that had any chance at all, and that was nearly the same thing. I added, "It will be difficult, though, and that's if everything goes perfectly."

Jakob locked eyes with me, and we both understood the problem with what I'd just said. It wouldn't go perfectly. Nothing ever did.

After a long silence, he said, "It's too bad your father isn't here. If he could put that code together, he could help us plan the rest of this."

I opened the yellow paper once again. I didn't need to— by now I had the entire thing memorized. But it would help to look at the words rather than think them in my head. Because Jakob had probably stumbled onto an idea I should have thought about earlier.

"Maybe Papa did plan all this!"

Jakob leaned forward to look at the paper. "What do you mean?"

"A good code has layers of meaning," I said. "I think my father left me at least one more."

Dearest wife, Daisy, and Mom;
One day I'll return, you'll see.
Nothing can stop me from climbing
to you. Watch perfectly as
the sadness becomes numb.
Remember my smiles, brightened
under tender skies by the sea.
Straighten the spine, Daisy.
Take courage, even when hurting,
have faith until this battle
ends. Until then, be calm.
Regards,
Rosbif

This time, I ran my finger down the letters of each line, letting his other message reveal itself to me: M E G S B D A Y G E M S.

Jakob looked at the letters and shook his head. "I see your name there: Meg. But I don't see how any of the rest can be words."

"The last four letters make the word 'gems.'"

He pointed to the word *ROSBIF*. "No, the last five letters are G E M S F. What is that F supposed to mean?"

"I don't know, maybe nothing. It's just the end of Papa's nickname. The last word is 'gems.'"

Jakob folded his arms. "And the letters in the middle?"

"They'd only make sense if you knew English better. Those letters are short for 'birthday.'" My palms began to sweat with excitement. "Meg's birthday gems!"

On my birthday, shortly before the Nazis invaded France, my grandmother gave me a necklace that she had made from some of her old jewelry. She told me that I was old enough now to have it, but to keep it safe because it was very valuable and that if the Germans ever did come to France, they'd want to steal it. When we had to abandon our home after the invasion, Papa worried the necklace would be taken from us if we traveled with it. So he hid it somewhere he believed it would be safe.

I told Jakob about the necklace, and his excitement seemed to grow, until he asked the question that had already sat like a pit in my stomach.

"So where did he hide the necklace?"

I didn't want to say it, because I knew how awful the answer was. But I forced out the words anyway. "It's in my old home."

His head tilted in disbelief. "In the home where the Nazi officer is currently living?"

"Yes." Now the sweat on my hands turned my fingers cold. "I don't know if the necklace is still there, or why my father might want me to get it. Most of all, I don't know if it's even possible to get back inside again, but we have to try."

Jakob stood and jammed his fingers into his pockets. Maybe his hands were feeling numb too. "You're not going alone. We'll do this part together."

I had secretly hoped he would offer, and not only because the thought of returning there terrified me. But also because there was something else that we absolutely needed for our escape to succeed, and I couldn't get it without him.

FORTY-SEVEN

Rule: *Things are often more than they appear to be.*

Once Jakob and I had finished making our plans, he returned to the guesthouse. We had agreed not to let Albert and Liesel know that I was here, not yet. Not until we had returned from my old home.

Jakob would wait until Albert and Liesel were sleeping, then slip back out and meet me. Until then, I knew I had a long, cold wait ahead. I filled the time by pulling out Captain Stewart's small flashlight so that I could read more of his spy book.

I tried to turn the flashlight on, but it didn't work, which was exactly how my luck seemed to be going lately. I fished around in the bag hoping to find a replacement battery, but instead found a lighter, which I figured would work even better. If I could start a small fire, I could have a little heat as well as some reading light.

Jakob had snuck out my wool blanket, which I threw over the brush behind me to block out any light from the fire, though I doubted Albert or Liesel would look out the window anyway. They were far too cautious for that.

Then I bundled up enough twigs and dry leaves to create a small fire. The lighter worked well enough, but something was odd about it. It was rounder and heavier than other lighters I had held.

I turned it over and over in my hands, looking for a way to open it, if I could. My thumb pressed some sort of button and I heard a small click. The kind of click that might be useful to a spy.

On a hunch, I set down the lighter, then picked up the flashlight again. I unscrewed the back of it where I would've expected to find a used battery, and there instead was a bullet. I couldn't believe it—this was a weapon! I wished Jakob were here. He'd be as excited as I was. I screwed the flashlight back together and carefully laid it beside the lighter, then reached into the bag again.

I pulled out the lump of coal, the turnip that I'd been saving to eat until I became desperately hungry, and the pencil I'd been using to write down pieces of the code. I stared at each object for some time, almost afraid to touch them, now that I knew about the flashlight.

"The spy book!" I hissed. Surely it would tell me what these items were and how to use them. Angling the pages toward the fire, I scoured through a chapter near the end of the book about the tools of an S.O.E. spy. This must have been the reason why Captain Stewart had wanted his bag so carefully guarded.

The camera with the small straps finally made sense. It was intended to be mounted to a trusted pigeon for aerial shots. For several minutes, I tried to figure that out. How exactly did a person obtain a trusted pigeon?

I unscrewed the thermos, and, again on a hunch, pulled out the inner lining for the water. Sure enough, packed between the lining and the thermos were stacks of money from what must have been the currencies of most of the countries in Europe.

And what of the coal, the turnip, and the pencil? Each one of them, when used properly, was an explosive. I was very relieved I hadn't tried eating the turnip.

I practically bounced on my heels for Jakob to return. Not only did we have a plan to get into Switzerland, I was certain that we were going to have some fun getting there too.

About an hour later, I heard footsteps crunching through the crystalized snow. They stopped, and Jakob hissed, "Meg!"

I popped out from behind the blanket, then quickly stamped out the fire. "I have so many exciting things to tell you," I began.

"Good." He kicked at the ground. "That's good, but—"

I stepped toward him. "But what?"

"I've been thinking. We shouldn't go back to your old home."

"Why not?"

"The code said 'Meg's birthday gems.' Not 'your birthday gems.'" He paused a moment. "The note wasn't written to you. He sent it to your mother."

"Yes, because he believed I'd solve the code and then we'd all leave together."

"That's not my point. Do you believe that your father really would want you to return to a home occupied by a German soldier?"

"Why does that matter? I'm the one who is here. He said to get those gems, so I've got to get them."

"Answer my question. Would your father want you to go back to that home?"

I huffed. "No, Jakob, he wouldn't. Nor was Captain Stewart supposed to get injured. I wasn't supposed to solve the code after I'd already left, which means I shouldn't be out here all alone, but I am! Nothing that Papa imagined in his plan has worked the way he thought, but so far, it is still working. If the plan needs the gems on that necklace, then I'm going to get them, with or without your help."

My words hung in the air for a very long time, until Jakob kicked at the ground a second time. Finally, he shook his head. "When I first met you, I thought you were a little stubborn, but I was wrong." Now he looked up. "You are easily the most stubborn person I've ever met."

"That's something we can agree on." I picked up Captain Stewart's bag. "And do I ever have some fun things to tell you!"

FORTY-EIGHT

Rule: *Never abandon a team member.*

While we walked, Jakob and I put together a plan for after we reached my old home. His job was to get into the barn out back and retrieve two sets of skis and poles, which we would absolutely need to cross the snow-packed Jura Mountains. As difficult as his job would be, every thought of what I had to do made my knees feel weak. But I was the only one who could do it. I'd have to get inside.

When talk of war began, Papa built secret compartments into our walls to hide our valuables. In many ways, I supposed my father was thinking like a spy even before working for the S.O.E. Maybe I would work for them one day too.

The compartment that held my gems was in the kitchen behind a loose brick near the stove. I could have kicked myself for not having solved Papa's code earlier, because it was the exact place where I'd stood before escaping. I could have grabbed it then.

"You shouldn't go in there alone," Jakob said as we walked. "If you're caught—"

I shrugged. "Better one of us is caught than both of us."

"Better that neither of us gets caught. I'll wait for you in the woods."

I forced a smile to my face, displaying a confidence I absolutely did not feel. "If I'm fast enough, then I'll be there waiting for you!"

We parted ways at the lane to my home. He would sneak along the fence line toward the barn. I would do the same toward the back door. I'd left Captain Stewart's bag in the woods, all his spy gear except for the explosive turnip. If necessary, I would toss it to keep the Nazi from chasing me. I didn't imagine that a turnip would do much damage, but if necessary, it would give me a chance to escape.

The house was dark. No smoke came from the chimney, and everything was quiet. Too quiet. A barking dog in the distance would have been helpful, or a tree brushing against the house in some wind. But I wouldn't be so lucky tonight.

At least it was so late by now, I was sure the Nazi must be asleep. No, I wasn't at all sure of it—that wasn't the right word. I *hoped* he was asleep.

I tried the doorknob, but this time it was locked. Many

homes didn't even have locking doors, but Papa had insisted on finding locks before we left the home. "Not to keep the Germans out," he had said, "but to give us a way back in once this is over."

For that reason, Papa had left a spare key beneath a rock in the garden, and I worried about the noise the key would make when I inserted it into the lock. The key was easy to find, but my cold fingers still shook when I tried to slip the key into the lock. The key scratched against the metal a few times before I pulled it away.

No, this wouldn't do! Maybe it was a tiny sound, but it wasn't a natural sound either, and surely the Nazi soldier inside was a light sleeper. Everyone slept lightly during war.

I took a slow, deep breath, then lifted my hand again, this time inserting the key straight into the lock. It turned, again with a click that was louder than it ought to have been. I paused there, waiting for a light to come on, or the sound of footsteps on the stairs. When everything remained quiet, I slowly twisted the knob and opened the door, entered, and lightly closed it behind me.

After several tiptoed steps, I had crossed our sitting room and entered the kitchen. Day after day, I'd sat in the corner and played while Maman cooked, or sometimes she let me help her, which was always wonderful. Even in the darkness, I knew this kitchen as well as I knew any other place on this earth. The stove was five steps inside the kitchen, and the wall was four steps to the right. Once there, I'd crouch low. The loose brick was the fifth one above the floor. Slide it out, remove the gem necklace, slide it back. Run.

I'd rehearsed this plan a hundred times in my mind, but now I had to actually do it. I took my first step forward, then the second and third.

The floorboard creaked, and I stopped. I didn't remember these floorboards ever creaking before. Did they used to do that? How had I never noticed?

On my next step forward, I heard another creak. I glanced down, certain that creak had not come from the floor beneath me.

But I had heard something.

That creak had come from the stairs!

As quietly as I could, I darted the rest of the way to the stove, crouched low, and slid out the loose brick.

I heard footsteps now in the front room. I wouldn't have time to get away.

I grabbed the necklace and held it in my fist with one hand while I replaced the brick with my other hand. Then I slid beneath the claw-footed stove. It was filthy under here, and still warm from whatever the Nazi had cooked earlier that evening. But I made myself as small as I could get and tucked in my legs just as the kitchen door swung open.

The Nazi walked into the room in bare feet and stood

there a moment as he looked around. The room was so impossibly quiet, I was certain he could hear my pounding heart, and I held my mouth open in hopes that he would not also hear my breathing.

This was why I had to come alone. Because if I was caught . . .

I stopped there and made myself think differently. At least Jakob would escape.

Or would he?

The Nazi cocked his head, then walked straight out the back door, even in his bare feet, shutting the door behind him. He would have only one reason to go out that way.

He must have seen Jakob!

I scrambled out from beneath the stove and raced through the front door, just as I had escaped earlier. I made it into the woods, though I was far from where Jakob and I had intended to meet, and I was anything but safe. Under the cover of darkness and in the shadows of the trees, I slowly made my way toward the meeting place, pausing with every step to listen for any sound of that Nazi.

He hadn't come this far, I was sure of that.

But nor had Jakob come back.

I was at the meeting spot for nearly ten minutes before I remembered to unclench my fists. There, inside, was the necklace that Papa had given me two birthdays ago. I wished I knew why he'd wanted me to get it.

But I didn't care about that now.

My mind raced with a single thought: Jakob still wasn't here.

Three minutes passed.

And another seven or eight. Or maybe ten. I was losing track by now.

If I stood tall on a nearby rock, I could see the upper floor of my old home. I saw a small light on in my parents' old room. The Nazi was still awake, and possibly out here somewhere.

Possibly, he had found Jakob.

He must have, or Jakob would have returned by now.

I huddled against the side of the rock, wrapping my arms around Captain Stewart's bag.

And waited.

And waited.

And waited.

But still . . . nothing.

FORTY-NINE

Friday, March 6, 1942
664 days since I've seen Papa

I must have fallen asleep at some point, because the next thing I knew, a hand was shaking my shoulder. "Meg."

I awoke with a start, crying out before I remembered where I was. Then I nearly screamed with excitement to see Jakob in front of me. He put a finger to his lips and shook his head in warning.

"Let's head back," he whispered.

I stood and started to lift Captain Stewart's bag onto my shoulders, but he shook his head again. "That's not necessary. Look what I found."

He pointed to my old wooden sled. With it, I'd raced down hills hundreds of times when I was younger. Two pairs of skis and poles were already strapped to the wood. Jakob took the backpack from me and set it on top of everything, then strapped it down too.

"This will make a much easier walk back," he said.

I fell in beside him, but my smile quickly vanished. "Where were you, Jakob? What took so long?"

"Well, in the first place, the skis were not where you said they were. Do you know how hard it is to search an entire barn in the dark without making a noise?" He paused and stared at me. "You are so dirty, by the way. What happened to you?"

"Never mind that," I said. "Did the Nazi come out to the barn?"

"Oh yes. But I was already hiding when he entered. Even after he left, I waited where I was for a very long time because I had heard his footsteps approaching, but there was no sound of footsteps leaving, so I knew he hadn't really left. He still thought someone was inside his barn, so he was determined to wait me out. But I also saw that he had bare feet, so I knew if I was patient, he'd give up before I did." Jakob shrugged. "I have to give that Nazi credit. He probably gave himself frostbite waiting for me, but finally he must have decided that nobody was in his barn after all."

"But then you still had to find the skis and this sled."

Jakob chuckled. "That was the best part! I hid in the very spot where these were placed!"

Our walk back to the farmer's guesthouse was much more relaxed than our walk here had been. But as we talked, we discovered more questions than answers, and we were running out of time.

"Those gems have got to be worth a lot of money," Jakob said. "Why would your father want them?"

"Maybe because we won't be able to return to France until the war is over . . . if it ever will be over. These are an important part of my family's history."

Jakob clicked his tongue. "There's got to be something more, Meg. Your father had to know it could be dangerous to get that necklace—"

"Papa wouldn't have known a Nazi has taken over our house."

"Yeah, maybe. But I still think he wanted you to get them for a reason."

I only shrugged back at him, hoping that if there was a reason, I would figure it out soon. I was tired of solving the clues too late or solving them incorrectly. I couldn't afford to make any more mistakes.

The dark horizon was beginning to warm with light when we stumbled through the door to where Albert and Liesel were staying, completely exhausted. We had left the sled and skis near the side of the house where we hoped they wouldn't be seen, so I only had Captain Stewart's pack with me, but our plan to sneak in unannounced instantly failed.

"Where have you been?" Liesel scolded Jakob. Then, "Meg? You came back?"

"I came back."

"Why are you so filthy?" she asked.

Before I could answer, Albert said, "We've waited up all night, worried sick."

"It was my fault that Jakob left," I said.

"It was nobody's fault," Jakob said. "We did what had to be done. Meg solved her father's code, which required us to get a few things from her old home."

"You solved the code?" Liesel asked. "What did it say?"

Jakob and I exchanged a glance. With Albert in the room, all I said was "We've got two pairs of skis. That's not enough for all of us, but it's a start."

"And I have a way for us to continue," Albert said. "I have sold my pocket watch to the farmer. He should be able to fetch a far better price for it on the market than what he has traded me for."

"What did he give us?" I asked, already suspicious.

But Albert only smiled. "You and Jakob should each clean yourself up, then sleep while you can, because as soon as curfew has ended, we will set off for the Jura Mountains, with one horse and that kind man's wagon."

FIFTY

Rule: *Even the best plan can go wrong.*

While Albert and Liesel rode up front in the wagon, Jakob and I traveled in the back with our supplies all stashed beneath what little hay the farmer had allowed us to bring along. Admittedly, we were both still so tired when we left that it didn't take much to coax either of us to sleep, but when I awoke, the sun was higher in the sky, and it appeared to be a pleasant early spring day.

I sat up. "How much farther to the Forbidden Zone?"

Liesel glanced back at me, and then at Jakob as he slowly sat up. "If our estimates from the map are correct, it's not far now. Do you really think we'll be able to get in?"

"My grandmother listens to the radio from London almost every evening," I said. "A few weeks ago, I remember hearing a broadcast that there are fewer Nazis to guard the border crossings now. They've sent everyone they can spare to eastern Europe, where there is more trouble."

That wasn't the whole truth, but with Albert listening to every word we said, now wasn't the time to tell Liesel about the Pierre I was supposed to contact.

Twenty minutes later, we stopped the wagon on the far side of Dole, within sight of a border crossing. Five heavily armed Nazi soldiers stood watch near a barrier gate—a barricade laid across the road that could be raised to allow someone through. Only, no one was trying to enter. Those who had to pass by the area simply lowered their heads and tried not to be noticed.

"Impossible," Liesel mumbled. "We'll never get past all those guards!"

We drove the wagon on, turning back into town until we found a quiet area. The Jura Mountains could be seen in the distance, but here the old homes were crowded around winding streets with little gardens in front or back, though most were still covered with a thin layer of snow. But one didn't need to look far beyond that simple, peaceful life to sense the heavy hand of the Nazis. Different from other places we'd been, here, official-looking signs posted everywhere warned that no civilian travel was permitted any farther ahead without special papers.

Papers we did not have.

"We passed a market a few streets back," Liesel said. "Meg, will you see if they have anything for purchase? We're nearly out of food otherwise."

I nodded at her, then eyed Jakob. He would have to stay here to watch over Albert. Which meant I would have to go on alone. I took a deep breath, then climbed out of the wagon.

A squadron of Nazi soldiers was marching down the street, so I turned at the nearest corner away from them and walked until I came to the market Liesel had seen. There, I began gathering a few supplies. Not too much, certainly not as much as I knew we would need, but I didn't want to do anything to cause suspicion.

A young mother was in the aisle with me. Very quietly I turned to her and asked, "Do you know Pierre?"

"Pierre who?" Her nose wrinkled in confusion.

"Never mind."

I backed away and turned down a different aisle. A dark-haired boy not much older than me was in this aisle. "Do you know Pierre?" I asked.

He frowned. "That could be one of a hundred people in this town."

I apologized, and would have continued to the final aisle, but a few Germans came in. It was time for me to leave. I paid for my groceries and left the store, but I'd taken no more than three steps toward the street when the same dark-haired boy grabbed my arm and twisted me around to face him.

"How do you know that name?"

I glanced sideways before looking back at him. "Do *you* know him?"

"Were you going to ask everyone in the store about him?"

"No! But I . . ." I closed my eyes and took a deep breath. "My friend Yvonne told me that Pierre could help me and my friends."

He cocked his head. "How many friends?"

"Three others. A family."

"Can you pay?"

"Yvonne never said anything about—"

"Do you want his help or not?"

I reached into Captain Stewart's bag and unscrewed the thermos enough to pull out the money that had been stored in the lining. His eyes widened as I handed him a stack of francs, marks, pounds, schillings, guilders, and bills from other countries.

"Will this be enough?"

"It's never enough." He pocketed the money without counting it. "Please understand, no one is getting rich off this money. It can be very expensive to resist." He began looking all around. "How soon can you be ready to leave?"

My chest fluttered with worry. This was real, then; this was happening. "As soon as possible."

"Good. Ten kilometers south of here is the church of Sainte Claire. Follow the river and you'll get there. If you and your companions are there in one hour, Pierre will help you."

I thanked him and immediately returned to the wagon, parked at the far end of a large stretch of farmland where we shouldn't be noticed or draw much suspicion. "I found someone to help us, but his instructions were very specific." The rest of what I said was a lie. "They want us each to arrive separately. That will be less suspicious."

Liesel clicked her tongue. "Albert would not make it on his own. No, we should go together."

My shoulders fell. I had planned on Albert *not* being able to make it on his own.

Unaware of my plans, Albert said, "I'm glad that's settled. So, where are we meeting?"

"I have the directions in my head," I told them, which was all I intended to say for now. Maybe we still had a chance to lose Albert on our way there.

We drove the wagon south, following the river as Pierre had instructed. As we drove, Jakob and I pulled out the skis to fit the bindings to our feet and check for any damage.

"I hope you know how to ski," I said to him.

He shrugged. "I wouldn't say I'm good, but I can stay on my feet. You?"

I smiled. Because we had lived so close to the Alps, I'd been skiing for most of my life. We still needed another set of skis for Liesel. Neither Jakob nor I was sure what to do about Albert if he did come along. He was half-blind, and I doubted he'd skied a day in his life.

In a little less than one hour, we spotted a tan-brick church with a brown roof. I hoped it was the right place, because otherwise we were lost. And maybe we were very lost, because no one else was here.

Liesel turned to me. "Are you sure this is the right place?"

"I'm sure."

"Then where are they?" Albert asked.

"We're early; someone will come soon."

"Who will come?" she asked. "You met some boy outside a market and gave him all our money, and in return for what? His promise to be here? You were tricked, Meg."

"He will come," I said, closing my eyes and praying that Liesel was wrong. Though from the last several days with her, I'd learned that she almost never was.

FIFTY-ONE

Rule: *Sometimes, trust is the only option you have left.*

The next several minutes dragged by slower and slower, giving me more than enough time to conclude that I had indeed been tricked. I was so convinced of it, in fact, that it startled me when I heard a voice from the shadows say, "Sorry we're late."

I turned to see a blond girl who might've been in her late teens standing with another tall brunette girl near her age, and the boy I'd met in the market.

I stood up straight, surprised at how nervous I felt. "I was supposed to meet Pierre. Is he—"

"Pierre is an idea, not a person," the boy said. "If you need something as we travel, that's the only name to use. One of us will answer."

"Let's go," the blond girl said. She seemed to be the one in charge. "Listen carefully. I'll take the husband and wife and everyone's gear. The rest of you break into pairs. For safety, we'll take separate routes to enter the Forbidden Zone. I see the skis and sled—you're going over the Jura Mountains?"

"Yes," I said.

"We have a safe house at the base of the mountains; we'll meet there. Before we go, each of you must promise to obey every order that is given to you without question. We know these routes, we know the soldiers' routines, and your only chance to survive is total obedience."

Jakob and I looked at Albert before Liesel said, "We agree."

"Then let's go." The girl who'd be escorting Albert and Liesel turned to her left, not looking back once to see if they were following her, which they were, pulling the sled and skis behind them. The brunette waved an arm at Jakob to walk with her, leaving me with the boy, who folded his arms. "You'd better be brave."

"I am." Then I squinted at him. "Why?"

"Come on. Can you manage in very tight places?"

"How tight?" My stomach clenched.

He glared back at me without answering and I closed my mouth, determined to be braver than he thought and stronger than he expected. But I knew I wasn't enough of either one.

Pierre walked me farther down the road until we saw a

warehouse across the street with hundreds of crates out front. Dozens of Frenchmen were loading the crates onto trucks with Nazi markings on them. If my stomach had been tight before, now I felt sick. Whatever Pierre had in mind, I was certain this was a terrible idea.

Pierre pointed to the corner of the warehouse property, to an area thick with trees. "That's where we'll get in. I work here, so you'll have to trust me and do everything I say. Very near the trees will be an empty crate—"

"No." I shook my head. "No, that's an insane idea. I won't."

He frowned back at me. "This war is insane. Attempting to escape France through the Jura Mountains is insane. This is your escape route, or nothing at all."

I closed my eyes, wondering what Jakob was being asked to do, and Albert and Liesel. Were their escapes this risky too? Before I'd opened my eyes, and even before I'd agreed to his plan, he hissed, "Run!"

I followed him across the road, keeping my head down and praying we weren't seen. He slid under the cover of the trees first, and I followed. From there, we crawled onto the warehouse property. Just as he had said, an empty wood crate was nearby. It was square shaped, but I'd have to hunch over to fit inside, and even then I might not fit.

"Will I be able to breathe?" I asked. There wasn't much space between the slats of the crate.

"Of course. Now get in, but don't let anyone see you."

I crept forward, keeping my body low and in line with the crate. I had to crouch my body tightly, holding Captain Stewart's bag between my arms and legs, to fit inside. As soon as I did, Pierre darted out from the trees, grabbed a nearby hammer, and began nailing the crate shut, nailing me inside. The light became completely shut out except for a few tiny lines. I couldn't move at all, and the wood slats of the crate were pressing in uncomfortably around me.

Pierre said to me, "I will be the one to get you out of here. Until then, don't say a word, don't move around, don't do anything or they will find you. If they do, I will not be able to help you, so don't betray me."

Before I could answer, he loaded the crate onto a dolly and wheeled me toward the trucks, asking someone, "Is there room for one more?"

They grunted and lifted my crate into the back of a truck, then another crate went on top of mine. The truck gate shut, and someone said, "This one is ready."

Tears filled my eyes, but I tried my best not to cry. The engine started up, and we began riding away. I didn't know where I was going, or when I would get out, or *if* I would get out. I only knew that there was a very good chance that I had just made the worst mistake of my life.

If I had, then I would pay for it *with* my life.

FIFTY-TWO

Rule: *Everyone has their price.*

The road we were traveling on was bumpy, and each time the truck bounced, I fell to one side of the crate or the other, then regained my balance only in time for yet another bounce. I tried to keep track of how much time had passed, and I guessed it was nearly thirty minutes before the truck finally stopped. The engine turned off, and I heard orders shouted in German. I didn't catch most of what was said, but I did hear a single word that terrified me: *Inspektion*.

Someone wanted to inspect this truck.

The truck gate opened, and a solider climbed into the bed with a flashlight. He began shining it into various crates, starting with the ones below me. I put my head down, remembering again that faces were the most visible, yet I still saw the shadows created when the flashlight shone into my crate. It lingered there, longer than when he had inspected the others. Finally, he moved on, and I felt safe to breathe again.

That was a mistake. I wasn't safe at all.

The soldier climbed out of the truck and gave one more order, to remove my crate from the truck. *Only* my crate.

Pierre and the man who had been driving lifted my crate out of the truck, and it bumped to the ground. The next order was to open it.

"We must deliver this load before five," Pierre said. "All of it."

"Not this crate. Open it."

I held my breath as a crowbar was pushed into the lid. Light poured into the crate, and I squinted against it. As soon as the soldier saw me, he began yelling in German, so fast and so harsh that I couldn't understand any of it.

"*Nimm das!*" I yelled, holding out the birthday necklace I'd pulled from my coat pocket. I was so frightened, I wasn't even sure if my German was correct, but I kept yelling it until he finally turned to look at what I was offering him.

I sat up, keeping my eyes directly on the Nazi. "Take this, please."

"You must be the girl that Lieutenant Becker is looking for," he said. "Where are the traitors and cowards who came with you?"

Slowly, I climbed out of the crate, never once taking my eyes off the soldier, nor the pistol in his hands. "This was my grandmother's necklace. Do you have a wife? A girlfriend?"

His eyes narrowed. "Is that a bribe?"

"It's a gift. I'll walk away to the left, and you can walk to the right. These drivers can finish their delivery. Agreed?" I was so frightened, I barely could form the words to speak.

The soldier wasn't accepting the bribe, but he hadn't yet refused it either. So that I wouldn't startle him, I carefully laid the necklace over his hands as they held his gun. My heart ached to give up Grandmère's most precious gems. They were part of her history, our family's history. But I also wondered if this was why Papa wanted me to have the necklace. Of everything we owned, it could buy our freedom.

The soldier still said nothing, and I genuinely didn't know if this meant I was safe to leave or not, but I figured there was only one way to find out.

Slowly, I lifted Captain Stewart's bag from the crate, nodded at the soldier, and then turned to the left and began walking. The first few steps were the longest, most terrifying walk of my life. But after three steps, I was still alive. At ten steps, I heard truck doors shut and the rumble of an engine. When I turned back at twenty steps, the soldier was gone, and the truck was driving away from me.

I looked up in time to see Pierre watching me from the passenger window of the truck. His face was expressionless, but something in his eyes told me this was not over yet, that I had farther to go.

That was something I understood far too well. I had no idea where I was, though I saw hints of a town up ahead on the road. I would go there and try to figure out what to do next.

But this time, nothing in Papa's code would give me any answers. This was a problem I'd have to figure out on my own.

FIFTY-THREE

Rule: *Accept kindness wherever it is offered.*

I walked toward the town for what seemed like endless kilometers, all the while praying that no one would pass me on the road. I was nearly there when I heard a clopping sound, and a horse and small wagon came around a bend.

The driver was a man with thin white hair and deep-set wrinkles. He wore a wool coat and a beret and seemed to have an easy smile, though he only frowned when he stopped beside me. "Do you need a ride?" he asked.

I lowered my eyes back to the road. "No, thank you."

He let me take a few more steps before he added, "I should have introduced myself. My name is Pierre. A friend of mine in town suggested you might need this ride."

I stopped and turned to him. "What friend?"

Now the man smiled. "As it turns out, his name is also

Pierre. He is much younger than me, but I believe I am handsomer."

I couldn't help but smile too, and with a great feeling of relief, I climbed into the seat of his wagon. Pierre turned the wagon to return in the same direction from which he had just come, but rather than take the road into town, he took us on a side road, toward the Jura Mountains.

When he saw my concern, he gave me a wink, then said, "Officially, I work for the Germans. I am supposed to help protect the Forbidden Zone from people who have no permission to be here: Jews or Gypsies, or anyone looking for a way to escape into Switzerland. Perhaps as we ride, you might help me keep watch for these deserters and cowards."

"Monsieur . . . I might be one of—"

"Because of my work with the Germans, the citizens here call me a collaborator. They believe I am a traitor to France. Likely, that is how history will remember me, which I suppose is better than the alternative—being accused of my actual crimes. Do you think that too?"

I looked over at him, understanding better now. "I will remember you as a hero."

He grunted. "That should be enough."

Our journey continued that way for several more kilometers. I found out he was a grandfather of twelve, though none of them lived in the Forbidden Zone, nor were they allowed to visit him here. He was a widower, too old to have fought during the German invasion, but a patriot who still wanted to do something for his country. He began to say something more, but then his eyes narrowed and he sat up straight. I looked ahead down the road and saw dust rising. Someone was coming our way.

Pierre pulled up on the reins and gestured with his head toward some trees to the side of the road. With a note of alarm in his voice, he hissed, "Go into those trees. Hide!"

I immediately grabbed Captain Stewart's bag and jumped out of the wagon. Pierre called after me, "No matter what happens, stay in hiding until it's safe. Your meeting place is another ten kilometers away. Continue on this road until you see a white home with boarded-up windows. Your friends will be there." He glanced up. "Hurry, go now!"

I bolted toward the trees, crouching low in the barren bushes and hoping that would be enough. Within the same minute, a Tatra drove up—the same kind of high-speed car that Albert had pointed out to me near Paris, the kind of car preferred by Nazi officers. My gut twisted with worry. The Tatra stopped in the center of the road, preventing Pierre from continuing on.

"Greetings, monsieur." Once again, Lieutenant Becker's cold voice filled me with dread.

"Ah, welcome back, Lieutenant," Pierre casually said.

"I am searching for a man, woman, and boy who are traveling under the name of the Durand family, but that is not their true name, nor are they a family. They are in the company of a French girl, about twelve years old."

Pierre let out a low whistle. "May I ask about their crimes?"

"Treason."

My heart pounded. They could execute people for treason. Even children.

"Ah. Serious business indeed." Pierre chuckled. "If there is a reward, I will gladly find them for you."

His offer was met with what sounded like a hard slap. A tear fell from my eye. I hated having to hear this, to be the reason for this.

"This is not something to be taken lightly." Becker continued, "We believe they are in this area, or are trying to get here somehow. Now, you must know this part of France better than anyone. If they did enter the Forbidden Zone, where would they go?"

Pierre's tone had become very serious. "Only fools would think they have any chance to cross these mountains this time of year. Maybe in the heart of winter, or in the summer, but now it is too dangerous. There is too much dirt for skiing and too much snow for walking, and an avalanche could be triggered at the slightest echo against the hills. If they are here, Lieutenant, then they would move south, I believe, toward Italy, where it is warmer."

"Are you certain of that?" Becker asked. "I'm told that we have already caught one escapee tonight, hopefully a member of this family. But I would like to speak more to you about this theory. Please come with me."

"Lieutenant, there is no reason to— *Ooomph!*"

From my angle, I didn't know what had happened, other than Pierre sounded as if he had suddenly been hurt.

"We know who you are, monsieur, the work you are truly involved in. You will come with me, by choice or by force."

"But my horse, and wagon—" Pierre's voice was shaking now.

"Take him," Becker ordered.

I turned in time to see a soldier who had come with Becker grab Pierre by the arm and push him toward the car. I tried to make myself leave, to surrender rather than allow Pierre to be taken, but inside a voice whispered that they would take him anyway. If I left, I would become proof of his crimes. So I stayed where I was while tears silently rolled down my cheeks. Once they were all inside, the car continued on in the same direction it had been headed before, leaving the horse and wagon abandoned on the road. Leaving me abandoned, for the second time that day. But far worse was seeing what had just happened to Pierre, knowing what likely would happen to him next.

I may have given up all our money to get help from the

resistance here, and surrendered Grandmère's necklace, the most precious thing I owned. That was nothing.

Pierre had likely just given up his life.

France would remember him as a hero. One day, I'd make sure of it.

FIFTY-FOUR

Rule: *The right people will always help you.*

Until I was sure it would be safe, I didn't move, or breathe, or even blink. I'd been warned not to make any mistakes, but I now believed trying to cross the Jura Mountains in the first place was the biggest of all mistakes.

Finally, I forced myself to leave the safety of the trees and return to the road. I stared in the direction of the mountains. Pierre had said that I should continue along this road for ten more kilometers. That would take at least two hours by foot. Or . . . I glanced back again in the direction Lieutenant Becker's car had traveled to be sure it was gone . . . or I could take Pierre's wagon.

Once I'd climbed in, I sat there for longer than I should have, picking up the reins, then lowering them again. The guilt I felt for what had just happened to Pierre was almost more than I could stand. If that wasn't awful enough, now I felt like a thief as well.

That was only made worse when I began thinking back on other things Becker had said, namely that they had caught one of the escapees. Who was it?

If it was one of us, I couldn't bear to think of what was happening to them. I didn't even want to think about them capturing Albert. Maybe the Nazis were forcing him to spy on us, and eventually he would tell them what they wanted to know. He would ensure that none of us made it to Switzerland.

Who did they have?

I needed to get to the meeting place and find out who Becker had captured, and then we could make plans for their rescue, or for our escape or . . . I didn't know.

The next ten kilometers passed so slowly, my heart was pounding with desperation by the time I saw the white house with the boarded-up windows. There were no other homes in the area, and no people appeared to be here either. I stopped the wagon out front, grabbed Captain Stewart's bag, and raced to the door. I pounded on it, but no one answered. I pressed my ear to the door, hoping to hear some signs of life inside, but everything was silent.

"Meg, you made it!"

I blinked and saw Jakob coming around from the back of the house. Jakob was here!

"Are you all right?" he asked. "You look upset."

"Was it Albert?" I rushed toward him and began look-ing around the area. Behind the house, the hillside quickly steepened with the Jura Mountains looming high above us, lit up by the sun, now low in the western skies. The girl who had brought Jakob here was leaning against the wall, star-ing at us, but I saw no one else. I turned back to Jakob. "Did they get Albert?"

"Albert? No." Jakob pointed to his left. "There's a resis-tance bunker inside that old shed, but their radio is broken. Albert is repairing it for them. He's fine."

My shoulders fell. "Then they found Liesel?"

"Who found me?"

I turned and saw Liesel walking toward me with a pair of skis in her hands—a different pair than either Jakob or I had.

"What . . . ? I don't understand. I heard that they found someone who is trying to escape."

"Many people try," said the brunette girl who had brought Jakob here. "Whoever they caught is probably no longer alive."

I told her, "There was an older man who drove me here on his wagon—"

"We know." She brushed at one eye with the back of her hand, and I realized she'd been quietly crying since I'd arrived. "He was denounced by someone we thought we could trust. That wasn't your fault. At least you all made it safely this far."

"How did you and Albert get here?" I asked Liesel.

"On a cart, through a secret tunnel." She held up her skis. "But in the greatest moment of luck, right after leaving the tunnel, we happened to pass these leaning on a fence by a house. We were told that the house had been taken over by a rather cruel German, so I felt no guilt when I stole these skis. Now, what to do about Albert?" That question lingered in the air, unanswered.

Jakob leaned toward me. "They brought me here on bicycles. What an adventure that was, cutting through woods and backyards and even two houses. Let me tell you about it . . ."

He had only barely begun to tell his story when the blond girl who had brought the Durands here exited the bunker. Beside her was Albert, holding a square board with what appeared to have various electronics attached to it, and a small sack with wires sticking out of one end. He held them out for us to see. "I fixed their radio, but these are spare parts that I think I can use."

Had he already tested that radio, or sent any signals to Becker? I locked eyes with Jakob. Wasn't this enough evidence yet? Would we also be denounced by someone we trusted? Jakob only shook his head and turned away. I huffed in frustration.

The Nazis had already captured two enemies in this region tonight. What if Albert was about to hand them three more?

"You'd better get moving," the blond girl said. "Go quickly, and you might have a chance to reach Switzerland by dawn, but be careful. These are dangerous mountains in daytime, and they are deadly in moonlight."

The tall brunette who had guided Jakob stepped forward. "Leave everything with us that is not absolutely necessary for your journey. Nothing is more valuable than your lives."

We gave up nearly all our clothing. Jakob kept most of what he had in his pack, but it couldn't have been much, based on the loose way it hung from his shoulders. Albert stared into his pack and frowned.

"Everything I have left in here is too precious."

Jakob peered into his bag. "Physics books?"

"Yes, filled with a lifetime of notes!"

"If you want to keep that lifetime going, leave those books behind," the blond warned. Albert looked like he was at a funeral as he pulled his books from his bag and handed them over to her.

I still had the largest bag, but I wouldn't surrender any of it. I was carrying our best chance to survive.

The first part of our journey was relatively simple: hilly farmland, scattered villages, and small, tidy homes. There was only one narrow road in or out of the towns, but we stayed off it as much as possible—we simply could not risk bumping into Lieutenant Becker, or any of them.

"How far is it to the Swiss border?" Liesel asked.

"Fourteen kilometers, but that's if we keep to the road, and I don't think we should," I answered. Our route would actually be determined by any Nazi posts we might have to avoid. And I had no idea how many of those there would be.

The moon was high in the sky by the time we passed another village nestled up in the foothills. Off the road, the snow was deep and soft, so our feet sank nearly to the ground.

"Do you still have your fishing line?" Albert asked Jakob, who nodded and began digging into his bag.

Meanwhile, Albert turned his attention to a nearby tree. It was an older tree, and the bark had begun to separate from the trunk. He peeled off two pieces, then stepped on them, tying them to his feet with the fishing line.

"Snowshoes!" he exclaimed. "Let me test them; perhaps we can move faster."

"You can't see well enough," Liesel protested, but Albert had already begun walking, almost on top of the snow now, and was getting far ahead of us.

We followed behind the best we could, but I'd already begun looking at other trees to see if I could make my own snowshoes.

"I can't see him in the darkness anymore." Jakob's voice showed the same concern I felt too. "Do you suppose he—"

Jakob stopped speaking as a snowball from up ahead came flying back at us. That could only mean one thing.

"Everyone get down," Jakob ordered.

Each of us flattened ourselves against the snow as the silence of the night was interrupted by the rumble of an engine. It was somewhere ahead of us, but I saw its lights approach, then stop.

A gunshot rang out, its echo lingering in the air, and my heart stopped. Was that shot intended for Albert?

After several tense minutes, the engine began rumbling again and the lights grew brighter. The Nazi vehicle drove slowly, and someone inside had a flashlight that they were waving across one side of the road and then the other.

Now they were looking for the rest of us.

FIFTY-FIVE

Saturday, March 7, 1942
665 days since I've seen Papa

New snow is soft and moves beneath the foot like powder. But snow that has been on the ground for days, or across the long weeks of winter, develops a crust. Every movement across that crust has a scratching sound, like sandpaper over wood.

I broke into a cold sweat when I realized that, because my foot wasn't covered by snow. It was sticking out in full view of the Nazis who had stopped directly in front of us. I needed to pull it in closer to me, but if I did, my knee would crunch deeper into the snow.

Leaving my leg where it was might get us killed. Moving it now certainly would.

I kept my head down and barely breathed for several tense seconds as the flashlight crisscrossed the area. I could have sworn it passed directly over my leg, and I waited for the order for weapons to fire. Finally, a radio squawked, and someone said, "The lieutenant wants us all together to organize a search of the mountains. Let's go."

As soon as the vehicle had driven away, I bolted to my feet and ran up the hill to where Albert would be. With Jakob on my heels, we hadn't gone far before we heard Albert mumble, "I'm here. I've been shot."

Jakob reached him first, and when I got there soon after, I found Albert lying on his side with his hand over his thigh.

I didn't know what to do, and by Jakob's expression, neither did he.

"The bullet passed through the flesh, so we can be grateful for that," Albert said. "But we must wrap the wound."

Jakob untied his scarf from around his neck and began wrapping it around Albert's leg. "Is that too tight?"

Albert shook his head but placed one hand over Jakob's as he worked. It was a tender, loving gesture, and Jakob must have felt that too, because I heard the same affection in his voice as he said, "We can pull you on the sled. We will get you over these mountains."

Albert made a face. "You'll pull me on a child's sled like I'm some invalid?"

"That's exactly what we'll do, old man," Jakob said, then a grin tugged at his mouth. "Because right now, you are an invalid."

Albert considered that a moment. "I suppose that I am."

I watched them together, realizing how much Albert truly cared about Jakob, almost as a father would. Despite his protests, Jakob clearly cared about Albert too. Jakob had insisted that it was impossible for Albert to be working against us, and as I watched them, I believed Jakob was right. I'd been wrong about the code. I didn't know who the man was that my father tried to warn us about in his note, but it was not Herr Durand.

Could he have meant Herr Becker—the lieutenant? I'd never have trusted him. Herr Stewart, perhaps? Could Captain Stewart be a double agent, or was someone still ahead a risk to us?

By then, Liesel had caught up to us, dragging the sled behind her. She took one look at Albert's wound and said, "What now? We cannot go on like this."

"We must." Albert gestured for the sled to be brought to him, and when Jakob dragged it over, he rolled onto it. Jakob and I began to pull the sled while Liesel managed the skis. He said, "This is lucky snow." We looked to him for an explanation and he added, "We have moved high enough that the snow has a firm crust. That is easier for sledding."

Other than the occasional home, we had left the villages behind by now. Ahead of us, the hills grew steeper, and the horizon grew darker. We had a good moon to light our path, but the mountain ahead seemed cold and forbidding, as if it was warning us to turn back.

Walking at Albert's side, Liesel said, "There must be an easier way. Let's return to one of the villages. After curfew ends, we might find a guide to hire."

"We don't need guides," I said. "I know this place."

Not *this place*, exactly. I wasn't even sure I could find our location on a map, but we were moving uphill, and every so often I caught a glance of the main road, so I knew we weren't just wandering in circles.

By Albert's best guess, it was well after midnight when we stopped for our first break. We had been going uphill for some time, which was exhausting, but now the land leveled out enough that we could strap on our skis. Cross-country skiing wouldn't be much easier, especially for Jakob and Liesel, who'd now share the work in pulling Albert's sled, but we'd make better time.

We started forward and were making progress, but we hadn't even gone one kilometer more before Jakob stopped. "This is a Nazi ski route." He crouched down and picked up a bundle of twine, and not much farther from it, a military-issued glove. "If we stay on this road, we'll end up directly at one of their posts."

I scanned the area, looking for a way to leave the trail where it wasn't too visible in the moonlight, nor too dark, which might mean a sudden drop-off of land. Papa used to warn me never to leave the ski trails for that very reason.

And here we were, leaving the trail. I pointed to the left

and offered to go ahead, hoping to spot any dangers before it was too late to avoid them.

The problem was, this new route was forcing us northward, but Switzerland was east. We had to get back on course.

Liesel tossed two snowballs ahead, a signal that I should stop and wait for them. When they caught up to me, she asked for the silk map. We spread it across the snow, using the moonlight to read the map the best we could.

"We should go toward the Risoud Forest," I said, pointing it out on the map. My parents used to call it the Thieves' Forest. The dense hills were a favorite place for thieves and smugglers to hide, and we were both now. My family had picnicked there in the summertime, and I knew the area well. A person who knew their way through that maze could easily escape pursuit.

"Why change course now?" Liesel pointed to a mountain pass even farther north. "This is working well."

It was a logical choice—the slope she had chosen was gentler and had fewer dangers in the landscape. But that was the problem.

I shook my head. "That's where the Nazis will be. We need steep hills and thick woods to hide in."

"All places that could kill us." She huffed. "Why are we taking instruction from a child? Albert, let's go back and ask in the villages about a guide."

"Please wait." Albert had been working on the electronics board almost since his first moments on the sled. He had an earpiece in one ear and wound two wires together, then smiled. "I hear static."

"Static?" Liesel threw out a hand. "How does that matter?"

"It might matter a lot, if we can hear what the soldiers are saying." Jakob nodded toward me. "My vote is with Meg. We should go east."

"Albert?" Liesel huffed again, louder this time.

"Yes, east is fine." Albert pulled another electronics part from his pocket. I wondered if he had become so focused on his radio that he had forgotten the danger we were in.

"This is a mistake, Meg. You will see that I was right." Liesel picked up her ski poles, then went on ahead, leaving me and Jakob with everything else to carry.

This time, I followed at the rear of the group. From my position, one thing was clear. Up in front, Liesel was slowly leading us northward, in the route she wanted. Jakob suggested throwing a snowball to get her attention, but she was too far away now. She'd never see it.

I skied up closer to Jakob. "Let's stay east. See if we can pull her back to us."

Behind him on the sled, Albert was continuing to build his radio. I had no idea how he could work under such strange conditions, but his mind seemed to have gone into another world. I softly called his name a couple of times, and he never looked up.

The slope steepened, and we had to remove our skis. Albert rolled off the sled and lay on his side to push himself uphill with one hand and his good leg, towing his sled behind him with the other hand. We were gaining altitude, but our progress was painfully slow, and Liesel was steadily getting farther away.

"What if she doesn't pull back to us?" Jakob whispered.

I couldn't say. All I knew was that we couldn't let ourselves become separated. Not now.

"Help me to my feet," Albert said. It had been so long since he had spoken, I had forgotten he was listening.

We did as he asked, and once he was standing, he made a snowball and tossed it into the trees behind Liesel, causing the snow in the branches to fall. When she turned to see what had caused the noise, Albert made signals with his hands. Liesel shook her head in protest, but finally gave in and began skiing back toward us.

"What did you do?" I asked.

Albert smiled. "In the Great War, I served in the German army as a signaler, and I know Liesel understands many spoken and unspoken languages. I simply reminded her that we have two children with us, and that your safety is more important than her being right."

Jakob caught my eye, silently informing me that this was yet another reason Albert could not be the one my father had warned me about. That wasn't necessary—I no longer suspected Albert. But somewhere along the way, we had put our trust in another *Herr*, an unknown man my father believed would yet betray us.

FIFTY-SIX

Rule: *Know every road, every field, and every exit.*

In response to Albert's directions, Liesel skied to the bottom of a steep slope and waited for us there. We'd have to get down too . . . somehow. It had been a miserable job to get this high up the mountain, but going downhill with Albert and his sled would be worse.

Albert was considering the same question. "If we calculate the angle—"

Jakob smiled. "I'll just have to ski faster than he sleds."

"That won't work—" Again, Albert was cut off, this time when Jakob simply began skiing down the hill, dragging the sled behind him.

It turned out to be a terrible plan. I watched as Albert's sled went faster and faster. He called to Jakob to "watch out," and a second later, Jakob *oomph*ed and went facedown in the snow. Albert's sled rode over Jakob's leg and overturned. His electronics spilled out everywhere, and one of Jakob's skis slid down the hill and out of sight.

I skied down to them just as Jakob was sitting up, rubbing his leg. Liesel went after Jakob's ski while I began gathering the electronic pieces for Albert. We had made far too much noise just now, left noticeable tracks all over this hill, and cost ourselves valuable time.

"That was reckless, Jakob," Albert scolded.

"We're going too slow," he shot back.

Albert slid down the rest of the hill on his own while the rest of us sidestepped to the bottom. Liesel glared at me, as if that had been my fault. "This would not have happened had we gone north."

"Only because the Nazis would have stopped us already!" I countered.

My teeth clenched in anger. It was true that we weren't in a safe area—the cliffs around us were sudden and unforgiving. There might be fewer Nazis, but there were still a vast number of ways the mountain could kill us. If we could get deeper into the Risoud Forest, with its maze of trees and narrow paths, we had a chance.

"Everyone, stop!" Jakob pointed north, not far from where Liesel had just been. On the opposite side of the slope from where we now stood, a small group of Nazis emerged from a bunker. It was so well blended into the hillside that I wouldn't have noticed it even in full daylight.

If we wanted to live, we needed to blend in too, and fast. They began marching away from us, but if any of them turned around, we'd easily be spotted here. The problem was that I wasn't sure which way to go now. My plan had been for us to continue forward, which would take us on the same route as the Nazis.

We remained in our exact position, trying to become part of the night, until the last of the soldiers had marched away. Once they did, Jakob turned to me. "If we see those Nazis again, maybe you can offer your necklace to them as a bribe."

I frowned over at him. "I already gave it up, just to get to our meeting place."

"Oh." He lowered his eyes, but my words seemed to have caught Albert's attention.

"A bribe, eh? If it's big enough, it just might work."

That was a curious response, but it turned my mind to thinking again about finding the necklace in the first place. Something had bothered me since I'd deciphered that part of Papa's code: MEG'S BDAY GEMS F. The "F" was clearly just an extra, meaningless letter leftover from Papa signing his note as Rosbif. It had to be ignored.

But if I ignored the last letter of Papa's nickname, I'd have to ignore the first letter too, the "R." And if I did, it would change the other phrase I'd deciphered. DON'T TRUST HERR would become—I gasped and placed one hand over my mouth to keep silent—DON'T TRUST *HER*.

There was only one *her* that Papa could have been talking about.

Liesel.

With the Nazis now fully out of sight, she pointed to me, but addressed Jakob and Albert as she asked, "We shouldn't be here. Why are you both still trusting her?"

Trusting me? No, none of us should be trusting Liesel. That was Papa's warning—I understood that now. But I didn't know how to say it, or how to prove my suspicions.

"Meg has steered us wrong at nearly every opportunity," Liesel continued. "We should have gone to the Pyrenees. We should have stayed with the original plan."

Liesel had been angry with me for suggesting that we change the plan. Could a trap have been set for us there?

I had to consider that maybe I was wrong yet again. I needed to talk to Jakob.

I looked over at him, trying to silently warn him of my suspicions, but he was already helping Albert get back onto the sled. Before I could say anything, he had begun lowering Albert ahead of us, and angling into a nest of trees off to our right.

There, we were better positioned to hide, but neither of the choices remaining were much good. We could stay in the trees but travel up a very steep slope off to our right. It would be slow, and some areas would feel like we were climbing a cliff. I didn't know how we'd get Albert up there. Or we could take an easier route to our left, but it would put us within full visibility of that squadron of Nazis.

Or there was a third option, one that made my gut twist just to think about it. Straight ahead was a small pass. The trail through it would be narrow with tall, steep slopes quickly rising on both sides. If we took that way, it would probably be faster and relatively flat, but it also would be very dark, with little moonlight reaching us. And the darkness wasn't even close to the biggest risk.

When we had skied here before, my father had forbidden me to ever take that route in the wintertime. Because of the steep slopes on either side of the trail, Papa said if there were ever an avalanche, it would fill that pass within seconds, and there would be no escape.

I explained this to the group and asked for opinions, but no one offered any. No one but Liesel, of course, who said, "We should have gone north."

"North, to that bunker of Nazis?" Jakob countered. She remained quiet after that.

"Meg, you know these mountains," Albert said. "We must trust you with this decision."

I shook my head. "Not this one. The wrong decision might cost us our lives."

Jakob's expression was tight and grim, but he said, "We trust you, Meg."

I sat on a rock to think and kicked at the snow beneath my feet. When I did, I uncovered a single daisy that, impossibly, must not have known it wasn't springtime here, not yet.

Papa called me Daisy, since that was the meaning of my French name, Marguerite. I missed hearing him use my nickname.

"*Je t'aime*, Daisy."

That's what he'd say to me every night before I went to bed. I'd heard it so often that even after so many nights without him, I could close my eyes and still hear his voice saying the words.

Those words!

With my eyes still closed, the letters of the words lined up in my vision, then began rearranging themselves.

JAIMIE STAYED

That had been the last anagram in Papa's code jar.

MY IDEA IS A JET

All the letters were there, but that wasn't his message. How could I have missed it?

JE T'AIME DAISY

Papa's code was so simple. It was the one message he would have most wanted me to know after he went to war, the one message he would have hoped I would remember, no matter how long it took him to return.

And his return was now in my hands. I still had to rescue him.

I stood and picked up Captain Stewart's bag once again. "We're taking the pass. But if we want to survive it, all of you must do exactly as I say."

FIFTY-SEVEN

Rule: *Sometimes there is no good escape. Escape anyway.*

Traveling through the pass required absolute respect for what we could, and could not, control.

Unfortunately, we had control over almost nothing. The slopes above us were filled with layers of snow that had fallen throughout the wintertime. Some layers were densely packed and wet, others were little more than dry white powder. That was the problem. If one layer began to move, it could carry other layers with it.

And it wouldn't take much to start that movement. Papa told me he'd once seen an avalanche start because a pinecone fell from a tree high on a slope.

We'd have no control over any of that.

Which made it even more important to control what we could from inside the pass.

"There are three rules," I said to the Durands. "First, no

talking. If you must communicate, whisper. But if you can use hand signals, that's better."

"What's the signal for being terrified?" Jakob asked.

"Sound does not usually set off an avalanche," Albert said.

It was the "usually" in his sentence that bothered me, but we had no time to debate that. "Just keep moving," I continued. "That's the second rule. Once we enter the pass, let's get out as soon as possible."

"But what if an avalanche starts?" Liesel asked.

"That's the third rule. If there is any trouble, abandon everything, try to get to the nearest cliff wall, and create an air pocket with your arms."

There was a fourth rule, one I didn't say. It was to prepare themselves for the possibility that we would never leave this pass. A little air pocket wouldn't do much good if there was no one on the surface to dig us out.

I led the way, keeping my eye fixed as much as possible on the slopes on either side above us. From this angle, I couldn't see what concerned me most—cracks in the crust of the snow, windblown areas, places where the slope suddenly steepened. However, I did see several reasons to be nervous.

A storm must have recently passed through this area, creating a fresh layer of snow directly over a packed base. A southern wind had picked up over the last hour. That would warm the snow and create movement. I didn't tell the others—there was no point in worrying them—but we were in far more danger than they might realize.

I gestured that we had to move faster. Much faster.

On the sled behind Jakob, Albert had the earpiece in place again, and he was fiddling with some dial in his hands. "Becker knows—" he hissed.

I turned around and gestured for him to be silent, and he clamped his mouth shut. But I almost wished I had let him finish his sentence. What did Becker know?

I had never been in this pass, so I didn't know how long it was, but it seemed to continue on endlessly. Above us, strange noises seemed to filter down from the snow. The sounds were restless, becoming agitated.

Above us, something must have dropped from a tree, causing a tuft of snow to fall over a ledge, landing directly on my head. I froze in place, listening for the cracks of an avalanche, and the others froze with me. But the night became silent again.

I glanced back, and something about me must have been rather funny, because Jakob was stifling a laugh. Even Albert and Liesel were smiling. I brushed off the snow, then put my finger to my lips and turned forward again. If they knew how bad that could have been, they wouldn't have laughed.

"Meg!"

I had been looking up, but with Jakob's whispered warning, my eyes went forward. We had just rounded a bend in the pass and were near the end, but it was hardly a welcome sight. A Nazi post was directly in front of the pass. Two soldiers stood watch, their weapons in hand.

We retreated back around the bend, exchanging looks of terror. There was no way out to avoid being seen.

"What now?" Albert whispered.

And no one answered.

FIFTY-EIGHT

Rule: *Whenever possible, surprise the enemy.*

All of us had probably been thinking the same idea, but nobody wanted to say it. None of us dared to say it.

Finally, Jakob did. "How fast can we ski?"

"Not faster than their bullets," Liesel said.

"I noticed a slope behind that Nazi post. If we come at them quickly, by the time they take aim, we'll already be halfway down." Jakob turned to me. "How steep is it after the bend?"

I shrugged. "I haven't been this way."

"You said you know this whole mountain!" Liesel hissed. She'd been on edge since the moment we entered the Forbidden Zone, but now I had a better understanding of why. She was supposed to take us to Becker.

"We must decide based on the information we have."

Albert turned to Jakob. "Liesel and Meg might go fast, and you could too, without me."

"We're not leaving you behind," I said. My mind shifted to Captain Stewart's book, to the section I'd read on evading the enemy. One of the strategies it taught was that if the enemy could not be avoided, then they must become distracted.

I had some definite ideas about distraction. I reached into my bag and pulled out the modeling clay. Jakob wrinkled his nose. "That smells like almonds! Are you sure that clay isn't for eating?"

"Definitely not," I said. "Nor is this even modeling clay."

Albert frowned. "If that is true, then I know what you really have there. What is your training to use it?"

"None. I need your help, Albert."

He sighed. "I swore that I would never again create a weapon—that I would have nothing more to do with violence."

Jakob held out his hand, and his tone was solemn. "I'll create it. Just tell me what to do."

Albert's eyes misted, but he blinked the moisture away, then said to me, "Does your bag happen to contain a detonator?"

I reached into my bag and pulled out the pencil. "Will this work?"

"It will, if that is no ordinary pencil."

I handed it to Jakob, who said, "Sounds like everyone knows what that clay really is except me."

I looked at him. "If this works, then the soldiers will run in one direction and we will ski in the other. But we need a way to get this closer to them."

"Look in my bag. I know you've got all these fancy spy gadgets and tricks, but I'm more of an old-fashioned kid. I say if it's been good enough for the last few thousand years, it's good enough now."

After a few seconds of searching, I pulled out his sling-shot. "Perfect!"

Albert told Jakob to stick the pencil deep inside the white clay, then whispered, "Meg, can you explain to Jakob how this particular pencil works?"

I pointed to the part of the pencil sticking out from the clay. "This is a hollow pencil. Inside it is a wire that is keeping the entire thing from exploding. There's a copper tube on one end filled with acid. If we crush it, the acid will erode that wire and—"

"Kaboom." Jakob turned to Albert. "So will that thing blow up inside my slingshot?"

Albert tilted his head. "I don't think so."

"You don't *think*—?"

"Just crush the copper tube and throw it. You'll probably be fine."

Jakob rolled his eyes, but Albert was already limping back to the sled.

"How's your aim?" I asked Jakob.

"I won't win any awards, but I'll get them moving away from us."

"Just do it quickly."

Jakob and I came as close as we dared to the edge of the pass. He readied his slingshot. I broke the copper tube against the rock wall and set the clay into his slingshot. Immediately, he shot it far to the right and high in the air. It hit a tree about thirty meters from the soldiers and instantly exploded.

The ground shook beneath us, jolting the two Nazi guards into action. They raised their weapons and ran in the direction of the explosion. We had to go too, immediately, for I definitely heard cracking sounds in the snow overhead.

Liesel passed the rope towing Albert's sled to Jakob and pushed Albert forward. She followed behind them, and I went last of all.

"Halt!"

The echo of a gunshot rang through the air. I didn't know how close it was. I didn't know if another would follow.

"Faster!" I called to the others. Jakob took Albert around the bend, then neatly spun on his skis to allow

Albert's sled to slide lower on the hill, as we had done before. Liesel flew past them on her skis, and I stayed behind to help Jakob, if necessary.

"Are they following us?" Jakob asked me.

"They will be soon." My eyes flew in all directions, desperate to find an escape, but for now, all we could do was to go downhill and try to put as much distance between ourselves and those two Nazis as possible.

"This way!" Liesel pointed to a nest of trees straight ahead. "We can lose them in there."

Or get ourselves killed. I wished the suggestion had come from anyone else, but it was the only idea we had. Liesel entered first and turned to help Albert on his sled. Jakob followed, and I went in last of all.

"They'll see our tracks," I said.

"There were dozens of ski tracks on that hill," Liesel said. "They won't know which ones are ours."

This was true. We'd seen crisscrossing tracks more than once through these mountains. The Pierre who'd driven me in his wagon had explained this. "Locals spend a lot of time creating false trails in those mountains," he had said. "It keeps the Nazis confused about the real trails."

That was small comfort now. We buried ourselves in the dark shadows of the trees and held our breath at the approaching sounds of two men, arguing loudly. I caught enough of their conversation to know that they were determined to find us before we reached the border. They passed us by on skis, never once looking toward the woods.

"Now what?" I asked.

"A bit of good news," Albert said. We turned to him and he held up a messy system of wires and metal parts attached to his electronics board. "I haven't tested this, but I do believe that I have created a transmitter. We can call in help from the S.O.E., who will take us the rest of the way across the border." He sighed. "There's only one problem with using it."

Because of the secretive work my mother had been doing, I already knew what he'd say, and it was anything but good news.

Jakob answered for all of us. "If we use it to contact the Allies, we'll bring the Nazis directly to us. The best chance to save us will likely get us all killed."

FIFTY-NINE

Rule: *Expect an enemy to betray you.*

The decision of what to do with the transmitter was important enough that Albert suggested we each take the time that we needed to place our vote.

"Take all the time you need." He quickly added, "In the next five or ten minutes. I've made my decision, so while the rest of you think, I'm going to close my eyes and rest."

"Wait," I said. "What does Becker know? When you were listening to the transmitter in the pass, what did you hear?"

"Somehow Becker knows we crossed into the Forbidden Zone," he mumbled.

I eyed Liesel. She must have been leaving behind signs of our trail.

"Meg and Jakob, why don't you both go look around?" Liesel suggested. "That might help us decide what to do."

We looked to Albert for help, but he was already sleeping. "I guess I'll go downhill," Jakob said. "If you go up, we can be back in ten minutes."

"Take your time, be safe," Liesel said.

She wanted us to take our time? If she was spying for the Germans, then I had a guess why.

As soon as I was out of sight, I doubled back to approach Albert and Liesel from a different direction. She hadn't wasted a second. Albert was lightly snoring, and she was already leaning over the transmission machine. From my angle, I couldn't see her exact movements, but then she shifted positions and I saw her tapping on a button.

I charged back into camp. "Stop this right now!"

Albert sat up, startled awake. "Meg, what is this?"

I crossed past him directly over to Liesel, who had backed away from the transmission machine like it was poison. "What were you doing?"

"I was only examining it to see if it would work. Nothing more."

"You were sending a message! I saw you. Was the message for Becker?"

Her eyes narrowed with anger. "How dare you accuse me of that? You have no proof!"

"Dash, dash, dash," Albert began. "Dot, dot, dot. Dash—"

"What are you doing?" Liesel asked, though it would be impossible for her not to already know.

"Before I learned signaling in the first war, I learned Morse code. I doubted my suspicions about you, but you failed my test." Albert frowned at Liesel. "Your message must have been for Lieutenant Becker, since I'd already mentioned that he thought we were in the villages. You told him, 'We are east of . . .' I suspect the rest of your message would have given our location, though you have already achieved that simply by using the machine."

"You weren't asleep?" Liesel turned to me. "He can barely see, and now it appears he cannot hear either."

"What's going on?" Jakob asked, walking back into our area.

Albert gestured for him to hurry forward. "We must leave at once. Liesel will not be joining us."

Liesel backed away. "This is a mistake, and I can prove it. Let me show you something from my bag. It will explain everything."

Her bag had been left at the edge of the trees ahead of us. While she went to get it, Albert looked over his transmitter. "Is there any chance I could have heard wrong? Surely, Liesel wouldn't have done this."

My voice was gentle. "You're not wrong. We need to go." I turned to Jakob. "We've got some uphill climbing to do. You and Albert gather up our things. I'll go check on Liesel."

I wasn't sure what I would say to her, but when I went to the edge of the trees, both she and the bag were gone. I ran ahead, following her tracks, and finally saw her halfway up the hill.

"Liesel is on her way to them," I called back to Jakob. "I'll stop her. You and Albert meet me as soon as you can!"

I didn't bring my skis—they'd only slow me down. Liesel must have decided the same thing, for the prints of her boots were evident. I followed those prints, but learned from her mistakes, avoiding the areas where her weight had sunk her deep into the snow.

Finally, I reached the top of the hill and saw her just ahead of me, still trying to get away. I didn't dare call out to her—the echo of my voice would carry for kilometers around. But I had to stop her from reaching the Nazis. On the chance that they had not monitored the location of her transmission, she could still ruin everything.

Liesel's legs were longer than mine, so in any other circumstance, she might have gotten away. But her long legs were a problem here, as was her adult weight. With each step, she sank deeper into the snow, requiring more time to pull her leg out for the next step.

When I was close enough to safely call out to her, I said, "Don't do this, Liesel!"

She didn't respond but continued moving across the top of the hill. The wind that must have constantly swept over this ridgeline had created a thicker crust over the snow. I saw the cracks here that I had looked for when we were in the pass below. This, indeed, was dangerous snow.

"There's nowhere to go," I said to Liesel.

She looked around. Straight ahead and to the right, the slope turned downward, but now that I had seen the cracks, it would be far too dangerous to go that way. Nor could she go left—a sheer cliff was there. A fall from this height would be deadly.

I tried again with Liesel. "Talk to me. If we can understand why you are doing this, maybe we can help you."

"You are a child with a bag full of tricks." She shook her head. "You cannot help me. No one can." Her eyes became colder than I'd ever seen before. "I'm sorry, but it's all over."

CHAPTER
SIXTY

Rule: *Everyone has reasons for the things they do.*

I wasn't sure whether to run back to Jakob and Albert or to remain here and continue to stall Liesel until they could come and help me.

She was backing away, toward the cliff's edge, and at first I worried that she was going to jump. I even held out my hands to warn her. To my relief, she stopped and faced me.

"How did you know?" she asked. "Just tell me that."

She was stalling too, and I realized now why she had moved to that exact position. It was the one place on this hill that she would be visible on the slope below us. I didn't know how many Nazis had gathered to wait for us, but I had no doubt they were there. She was calling them to come up here.

So now it was only a question of whose side arrived first.

"I should have known earlier," I said. "When Jakob and

I were laying out the spikes for the Nazi tires, you went through Captain Stewart's bag."

"That wasn't because of the Nazis. We didn't know you, or what you were carrying. If you had anything dangerous, you might not have even known it."

"Then when Albert tripped and dropped all those canteens, you offered to pick them up. You left his glasses behind for the Nazis to find."

She threw out one arm, becoming angrier. "Blame him for that. He was the one who dropped his glasses in the first place!"

"But you also dropped your scarf. It was knotted around your neck. The only way you could have lost it is if you untied it. You put your other scarf out on the guesthouse railing, beneath the milk. You were wearing it when we left the guesthouse, but it's gone now—that's how Becker knew we were inside the Forbidden Zone. All along the way, you've left a trail for the Nazis to follow."

She snorted with disgust. "Why would I leave a trail rather than just turn you all in?"

The answer came to me as quickly as she had asked it. I stepped closer. "I think you are helping them test this escape route out of France, to learn the secrets and the contacts. Except you were supposed to test the more common one— the Pyrenees, because that's where they are losing most of their people."

Another thought crashed through me. That must have been why Papa wanted the plan changed to Switzerland. If Liesel was working with the Nazis, the Pyrenees route would be a trap.

Liesel's eyes narrowed as she finally gave in. "Yes, it was supposed to be the Pyrenees escape route. We had an ambush planned that would have closed that border forever, and you ruined it. But the Nazis will still win here. When Albert is arrested—and he will be in the next few minutes—they will execute him in public as a reminder to other German scientists of the danger of trying to leave."

I shook my head. "How could you do this, Liesel? After all that you said to make us trust you?"

"Because they have my daughter. Don't you see, Meg, that I had no choice? I *still* have no choice. Dozens of soldiers are waiting for us just over that ridge, and if they got my transmission, then more will be coming from behind us, including Lieutenant Becker. The three of you are trapped. I didn't want to do this to any of you, but I had to."

"My father warned me about you in his note. I just don't understand how he knew the truth about you."

"That's simple." Liesel cocked her head, then said, "The day I went to the factory to meet Albert, I passed two men speaking English, thinking no one understood them. Your father was one of those men; Jakob's father was the other. I reported them to the Gestapo, but your father must have figured it out and included that information in the code. His note has caused me a great deal of trouble. It's time I use it to cause him some trouble too."

She lifted her hand. Pinched between two of her fingers was my father's yellow note, blowing in the wind. If she released the note, it would carry over the ledge and be gone. I hadn't even realized she'd taken it from me.

"I could have solved this for you a long time ago, if you'd let me see it. I see where your father warns you about me, where he told you to get your gems. I see his instructions to retrieve the false papers he had prepared for you, and that he told you to meet him in Switzerland." Her mouth pinched into a fine line before she continued, "But *where* in Switzerland? I suspect that must be in this code as well. And when I've had time to study it properly, the Nazis will know where he is going. The Gestapo will find him and ensure that he never does anything like this again."

I had to get that note back.

I darted toward her, but she grabbed me by the waist and spun me around, forcing me closer to the cliff's edge.

I tried to struggle away from her grip, but my feet found ice and I slipped, bringing her down with me. She let go of my waist as I began sliding toward the edge.

"No, Meg!" She lunged for me and caught the sleeve of my coat just as my legs went over the cliff.

I stopped there, and her other hand held a branch from a

baby fir tree. She had saved my life . . . for now . . . but she wouldn't be able to hold on for long, not to that branch, and not to me.

"Can you pull yourself up?" she asked.

I shook my head. "It's too icy."

"I can't hold on long. I've got to scream—that will call the Nazis to us."

"Don't you dare!" I said. "Liesel, if you do that, you will be the reason that Jakob and Albert are killed."

"And if I don't, I will be the reason that you fall," she said. "Sorry, Meg."

SIXTY-ONE

Rule: *Love is a stronger weapon than hate can ever be.*

Liesel opened her mouth to scream, when we heard a voice behind us.

"There they are!"

Jakob and Albert had just reached the top of the hill. Jakob left Albert where he was and began hurrying toward us.

"Where's Meg?" he asked.

"She's with me, but don't come too close," Liesel said. "It's icy."

Jakob nodded, then ran back to Albert, who had begun digging through his bag. He pulled out the twine we had found earlier that night and passed it to Jakob. He tied one end around a tree near us, then uncoiled it and threw it down to Liesel.

"I'll bring Meg up first," Jakob said.

Liesel gave me the rope and I began wrapping it around my wrist. While I did, Liesel said, "I saved you. Promise that you won't let me fall."

I nodded at her, then tugged on the rope. Liesel released me so that Jakob could begin sliding me up toward him.

Once I was up high enough to be safe, I threw my end of rope back down to Liesel and helped Jakob pull her up.

Liesel reached my side, then frowned at me. "I'm sorry. Your father's note blew away. It's gone."

My heart sank to hear it, but nothing could be done about that now.

She began gathering the extra rope into her hands. "I have an idea. Tie me to one of those trees up by Albert. When I'm discovered, I'll tell the Nazis that I tried to stop you from escaping. If I can make them believe me, I still may have a chance of saving my daughter."

I nodded back at her, and together we hiked up to Jakob, and then to Albert. I explained to them my agreement with Liesel. Jakob helped me tie her, though we kept the rope loose and showed her how to free herself, if that became necessary.

Liesel said, "Please understand, there are no good choices in war. Albert swore an oath to serve the Führer, but he betrayed that oath and now will work for the enemy of his country. He has disgraced his family name and left behind coworkers who will now be under even stricter observation and rules. But he will be called a hero in the end, and I will be the villain." She looked at me with pleading in her eyes. "If I did not have a daughter back in Germany, I would do the very same thing. I know their mission is evil. I know that what they are doing in these prison camps cannot end in any way other than tragedy and despair. So I must return to Germany for my daughter, but I will hold a spark of hope deep within my heart that this war will end soon for the cause of freedom. I will give you as long as I can to escape, and if Becker comes this way, I will try to stall him. Go quickly."

Albert nodded at her, and Jakob only shook his head before picking up his skis and returning to our path. I finished strapping on my skis, dug my poles into the snow, and said to her, "Perhaps one day, when this war is over—"

"I hope I will be able to introduce you to my daughter." She smiled through her tears. "Farewell, Meg. Keep them safe. Now go find your father."

I returned the smile, then threw my weight forward. Our mission still had a chance to succeed, but it would require our boldest move yet.

SIXTY-TWO

Rule: *Big problems require big solutions.*

It was a hard thing to leave Liesel behind, wondering what might happen to her now. But time was not on our side. A wide plateau lay ahead of us, and we had to cross it as quickly as possible.

Jakob was pulling Albert in the sled again and looked exhausted, but Albert glanced back at Liesel, looking even sadder than I already felt. "I cannot believe she lied to us all this time," he mumbled.

"There's a bigger problem now." Jakob gestured with his head toward the ridge. "I can see the Nazis down below, maybe twenty or more. We won't outrun them."

"Leave me here," Albert offered. "That is our only choice now."

No, it wasn't.

I pointed in the direction away from the Nazis, far to our right. "Go that way. Stay as high on the ridge as you can, and ski as fast as you can."

"I don't think they'll shoot," Jakob said. "It's too dangerous an area." He glanced over at me, and I caught the hint of a smile. "But I think you already know that."

"What about you?" Albert asked.

"I won't be far behind." I pointed again. "This is a hill that I know. Keep going until you see a very large rock that splits the trail. Go around it to the left. That will lead us toward Switzerland. But for these next few minutes, don't stop, don't look back for me." I paused. "Don't look back at all. I will catch up to you."

"No, Meg," Albert said. "I insist that you explain what you . . ."

But Jakob was already pulling him away. I was glad that we'd had experience with downhill sledding earlier tonight because Jakob would know what to do now, when it was critical that he not make any mistakes.

Just as I had feared, though, once they appeared on this open ridge, I heard orders echoing through the valley for them to stop.

My skis were strapped to my feet, and I'd already begun unwrapping Captain Stewart's bag. I pulled out the lump of coal. There wasn't much wood around us, and it was too wet to burn anyway, so I had to use the only burnable thing

I had with me: Captain Stewart's spy manual. I hoped he'd forgive me.

Behind me, lights dotted the hillside around where Liesel was tied up. That could only mean one thing: Becker and even more Nazis had come. To have arrived so quickly, they must have been closer than we believed.

I had to focus. I had to hurry.

Crouching as low as possible, I pulled out the lighter, flicked it to create a flame, and lit the spy manual. At first, the wind threatened to put it out, but instead, the flame fanned out wider.

"There she is, the girl!" That was Becker shouting. "Get her!"

I wanted to go, I needed to go, but I couldn't leave until I was sure that the flame had taken hold of the coal. Behind me, the Nazis were coming closer, far too quickly.

The instant the coal lit, I stood and began racing away, following Jakob's trail.

The Nazis already below were following Jakob too. They were lower on the ridge than me and not far behind where I was. I prayed that the coal was more than it had appeared to be.

Within seconds, I had my answer. The coal was exactly what I thought.

When the clay had exploded, I'd thought that was bad, but this was so much worse. The initial blast of the coal toppled a tree high above me, which set off loud cracking sounds, and then an enormous *boom* echoed through the entire area.

I kept skiing, but Becker's group of Nazis were forced to stop as several feet of wet springtime snow separated and began to slide. Becker shouted at them not to use their weapons or they'd only make it worse, but I doubted this could get any worse. I increased my speed, but I was far from being out of danger.

The snow beneath my feet was sliding now, carrying me faster than I could have gone on my own—too fast. If I fell, I would immediately be buried in snow. I heard Papa's voice in my head, of what to do in moments like this: continue skiing sideways as much as possible, away from the danger.

Away from the avalanche.

It rumbled down the slope, gaining speed and size and picking up whole trees as it flowed downward. The Nazis below me who could turn back did so. Others turned directly downhill, which was the worst possible choice to escape.

Gradually, I skied past the avalanche, but to my dismay, so did at least six Nazis. And in my hurry, I'd had to leave the backpack behind. It would be lost now in all this snow. Which meant I had no tricks left for my own escape.

SIXTY-THREE

Rule: *Every problem will come to an end.*

I raced along the bend, dismayed to find Jakob standing at the side of the trail. "Go!" I yelled. Jakob only motioned for me to ski toward him, but the area behind where he stood was so thick with trees, a crash into any of them would kill me. He continued gesturing so desperately that I turned my skis toward the trees, twisting them from one angle to another until I came to a stop not five meters from where Albert was still on his sled.

Jakob had followed me in, and I asked him, "What was that for?"

"Maybe you have the spy gear, and I'll grant you, that was an incredible avalanche." Jakob grinned. "But I told you before, I'm more old-fashioned."

"Argghhh!"

I glanced toward the trail in time to see one of the

Germans who'd been chasing us lying on the ground with one lost ski and the other ski aimed straight up. Another soldier behind him tried to slow down, but hit something invisible in the air. His body actually flipped head over heels, and he landed in a tangle in the snow.

"The fishing line?" I asked.

Jakob winked at me, then picked up his poles. "Let's cut through the trees."

The fishing line definitely slowed the soldiers down, but it did not stop all of them, and as soon as we emerged from the trees, we found ourselves back on an open ridge, once again far more exposed than I wished we were.

"Build up speed," I called to Jakob. "We'll go uphill soon."

"We can't let them catch up to us now," Albert said.

Or get close enough to shoot.

"What's that ahead?" Jakob asked. "At the top of the hill."

I squinted and shook my head, but Albert said, "Describe it for me."

"Remember those chocolate candy bars, shaped like a row of triangles? It looks like that."

I squinted and understood what he meant. There was indeed a row of triangles, but they were very large and made of concrete. They created some sort of barrier.

A barrier to keep us in France.

Albert shook his head. "We might have come all this way for nothing."

"Why?" I asked.

By then, we were at the low point in the ridge, and in trying to figure out what Jakob had spotted on the hill above us, we had lost our momentum. The only way up this hill was to sidestep. It would be incredibly slow.

Too slow. The Nazis weren't far behind.

We left the sled and skis behind to begin the steps by foot, helping Albert, who had to sit on his side and scoot uphill. When I asked again about what Jakob had seen, Albert said, "We saw a bunker earlier. This must be another one, and it must be very large to have all those concrete barricades. You can guess there'll be a hundred or more soldiers in there, all of them armed, and they absolutely will have seen us. They may already be waiting until we literally walk into their hands."

Jakob looked at me. "Meg, you must know a way around this."

I didn't. I knew if we went farther to our right, the mountain became treacherously steep. And if we went left, we'd just meet up with the Nazis who were still chasing us.

"Halt, halt!"

Two Nazis were below us, but they weren't bringing out their guns, perhaps for fear of triggering another avalanche.

We climbed faster, but a third Nazi had just arrived at the base of the hill.

"They shouldn't have stopped," Jakob said.

He was right. If they had simply continued skiing, their momentum would have carried them almost as high as where we were now. They could have caught us.

But they only watched as we scurried up the hill, probably because they knew what was waiting for us at the top. I angled us away from the triangle barriers, but I didn't know if it was possible to get far enough away.

We finally reached the top of the ridge, and I realized something that should have been obvious before: It was becoming lighter outside. I didn't know the time, but morning had come.

"Mademoiselle, stop. It's all over."

A man in a white uniform stepped out from behind a tree. He was armed, though he had not yet raised his weapon. Behind me, Jakob and Albert stopped too.

"Arrest me and let them go." Albert lifted his arms and stood up, balancing unevenly on his one good leg. "I'm the one you want. The children do not matter."

"On the contrary, we are very interested in all three of you."

My head tilted, curious. This soldier spoke in French, but with a different accent than mine or even Jakob's.

"None of us should mean anything to you," I said, sounding as tired as I felt. "We're not soldiers; we pose no threat to anyone."

"That cannot possibly be true," the soldier said. "We saw the avalanche. Which one of you created it?"

"Which avalanche are you referring to?" Albert asked.

I sighed. That was hardly helpful.

"We're just trying to get to Switzerland," Jakob said. "Please, let us pass."

"Let you pass?" The soldier smiled. "Didn't you see the stone wall?" He chuckled to himself. "Probably not, since your avalanche likely covered it. My friends, you are in Switzerland now."

He pointed behind him and on the bunkers, a few Swiss flags were hung, the white cross against the red background waving in the breeze. We had come through so quickly, I had not noticed them.

I looked back at the soldier, unable to believe what I'd heard. "Say that again. Are you sure?"

His smile widened. "Welcome to Switzerland."

I breathed out an enormous sigh of relief, and almost collapsed into the snow.

"I must urge you all to keep going for a little longer if you can," the Swiss soldier added. "The Germans can still make a claim on you unless you are fifteen kilometers inside our borders. Get to a village ahead named Campe. Ask around and you'll meet a family who I know will take you in."

Albert limped forward. "Will they have a telephone? It is urgent that I make a phone call as soon as possible."

SIXTY-FOUR

Rule: *Remember that the world is a beautiful place.*

Campe wasn't really a village. It was more like a collection of small shops and homes, one of them belonging to a kind family who brought us in for a warm bowl of stew and the promise of a bed, even if we'd be a little crowded there. We ate beside another dozen people who must have also recently escaped: Jews and resistance fighters, and others who kept to themselves but who clearly were here for their own reasons.

Albert refused the stew until he could first make the phone call to London. I was there at his side as he informed them of his and Jakob's safe escape into Switzerland. Then the person on the other end must have asked about Liesel, because Albert lowered his head and replied, "We were deceived by her, though we bear her no ill will."

Was I still angry with her? I wondered. I'd been so eager

to escape, so terrified in those final moments, that I hadn't considered my own answer to that question. But I didn't need to think about it. No, I felt extremely sorry for her, and for her daughter, but I wasn't angry.

"Oh yes?" Albert said, his voice perking up to whoever was on the other end of the receiver. "I will share that news at once, thank you. And now to fulfill my half of the bargain. Herr Kenyon has been hiding in Frankfurt. He will require the help of agents there to get him out. He will most likely have a very specific request as to where he wishes to go next."

While Albert continued giving instructions, I ran the words of Papa's note through my mind. Liesel had asked a question that had been poking at me since the moment she said the words: *Where* in Switzerland?

The silk map had been stuffed in my pocket, and I laid it out in front of me. Only the border areas between France and Switzerland had been printed on this map, but I studied it anyway, running the various lines of his note through my mind.

"Nothing can stop me from climbing to you."

Papa would come to the mountains of Switzerland.

"What are you doing?" Jakob sat beside me.

More excited than ever, I glanced sideways at him. "Papa's code must have told me where in Switzerland to meet him. I still have to figure it out."

"There was that part of his note that said, 'Remember my smiles . . .'"

"Yes, that was his book." Then a light flicked on in my mind. "But that was only the first part of his sentence. He wrote, 'Remember my smiles, brightened under tender skies by the sea.'"

Jakob began studying the map. "What sea?"

"If we're meeting in the mountains, 'sea' might mean any area of water—probably a large lake."

Jakob pointed out a few of them on the map, all of them in the mountains. "That's still a lot of places to look."

I agreed, but my mind had shifted to the phrase in between, "under tender skies."

That was an odd way to describe the sky. He might have said, "blue" or "beautiful" or "bright," but he used a word I'd never once heard to describe the sky: tender.

Why?

I searched the map, running my finger over the various small towns and landmarks. And suddenly I looked up at Jakob and grinned. "I know where he'll be."

Albert hung up the phone and paused only a beat before he said, "I just spoke to an S.O.E. agent in London. He is radioing his contact in Germany at this very moment. They will get your father out of Germany as quickly as possible."

"Are you sure you can trust the agent that you spoke to?" I asked. "Why would they risk their people on the ground just to save my father?"

"Because your father is one of their people on the

ground," Albert said. "At least, that's what Captain Stewart just told me."

I stopped there, confused. Had he spoken to Captain Stewart just now?

I stood and faced Albert, whose mouth was forming into a wide smile. "If you spoke to him, then . . . did he mention my mother?"

"Of course. And your grandmother. They were anxious for any news about you."

I didn't understand. "How—"

"Your mother was able to rebuild her radio enough to send an emergency message to London. They got your mother and grandmother and Captain Stewart safely to London, where they are eager to see you again. Once we find your father, Captain Stewart will bring us back to London as well. He said to tell you specifically that 'My idea is a jet.' I wonder what that means."

I went to answer him, but he had already turned his back to make another telephone call. The only words of the call I heard from him were "Yes, you may take everything."

Now it was my turn to wonder what he could have meant.

SIXTY-FIVE

Monday, March 16, 1942
674 days since I've seen Papa

Papa wanted me to meet him near the Lac de Joux, a long, narrow lake at the base of Mount Tendre, in Switzerland. The Tender Mountain.

A widow there named Madame Lebas offered to let us stay with her until my father came. At first, Albert refused. He stood in her doorway and said, "We can do chores, and if you have any need for physics, I'm at your service. But I am a penniless man. I cannot pay for our stay here."

Madame Lebas merely opened her doors to us and had been nothing but kind. That first week wasn't finished before I began to think maybe Albert had thoughts of remaining there permanently. At least, he smiled at Madame Lebas a lot.

I wondered if it would be hard to start a new life having been forced to leave his wealth behind in Germany when he fled.

I also wondered about Jakob. Every day we were here, I had spoken to him endlessly about my father, about how I imagined it might be when he returned. And every day his smile came on slower and faded faster. So I didn't speak to him about Papa anymore. I believed it made him too sad for his own parents.

"What will you do now?" I asked him one morning as we were out gathering firewood.

He shrugged. "Albert says I can stay with him as long as I want. He's a good man, but . . ." Jakob's sentence fell away from there. I didn't ask him to continue.

Minutes later, we heard the rumble of an engine and ran to see a silver car driving up the lane. A man and a woman got out of the car and began looking around. There was nothing notable about their appearance, other than their clothes were a little dirty and worn.

"Should we be worried?" I asked Jakob.

He didn't answer me. I wasn't even sure that he had heard me. He only mumbled, "How . . ." then dropped the sticks in his arms and began racing down the hill.

The couple had been facing the house, so they didn't see him until he was right behind them. When they turned, the man dropped to his knees, and with a happy cry, the woman pulled him into her arms.

I didn't know how either, but Jakob's parents were here.

They hugged and looked at one another and hugged

again, and in their joy, failed to notice Albert in the doorway of the home, smiling through the tears in his eyes.

And in that moment, I remembered his words after he had heard about the soldier I had bribed with my necklace, that "if it's big enough, it just might work." After telephoning Captain Stewart, Albert had made a second phone call, and had told the person on the other end of the line to "take everything." Albert truly was penniless.

Because he had given up everything he had left in the world to buy freedom for Jakob's parents.

I started forward, to explain that to Jakob, and maybe to be part of their reunion, their happiness. Just to borrow a bit of it for myself.

But this was their time, not mine. Papa would come here one day, and in the meantime, I still had chores to do.

So I picked up the sticks that Jakob had dropped and started up the hill to gather more.

"Daisy!"

At first, I thought Albert must have been calling me, but only one person ever called me by that name. Slowly I turned and realized another man had left the car.

He was too thin to be my father, and maybe not as tall as I remembered him. His hair had gray in it, and my father's never did.

But . . . maybe . . .

The man seemed to have fixed his eyes directly on me.

He began climbing up the hill, running as much as the snow allowed.

"Nothing can stop me from climbing to you." I mumbled the words from Papa's letter.

I began to run too, and with every step closer, the hundreds of days that I had been without my father melted away. Papa was here, in front of me, his arms wide open. I ran into them and squeezed him as tight as I had always planned to do.

"Daisy, it is you!" he said, and I knew he was crying.

I was crying too, more than I ever thought I could in all the times that I'd imagined this moment. I kept a tight hold on him even as I whispered into his ear, "I knew you would come."

"I would have come sooner, but Albert had one more escape to arrange first."

We looked over at Jakob just as he looked back at me. For all the times I'd seen him smile over the past few weeks, nothing came close to the joy I saw in him now.

"Your mother and grandmother will meet us in London," Papa said. "Gather your things. The driver will bring us all to where a jet is waiting."

Captain Stewart's idea was a jet.

I took Papa by the hand, and as we began to walk back down the hill, I mumbled, "The rescue is complete."

"Just rescue? I rather expected you'd have given this mission a code."

"I did." Papa looked confused, so I said, "RESCUE. Each letter stands for something."

Run

Escape

Ski

Climb . . .

Until the

End

I smiled up at him. "See? This is the end."

Papa squeezed my hand. "No, Daisy. For our family, this is only the beginning."

Tuesday, March 17, 1942
 Days since I've seen Papa: 0

SECRET CODES

Meg proved she had a talent for solving codes. Maybe you do too!

ANAGRAMS are created by scrambling the letters of a word or phrase. Although it can take time both for encoding and decoding, a simple anagram can almost always be solved, so this is considered low-level security.

So, if someone said they were expecting a RECORD RAIN WEEK*, what are they really saying to you?

(Hint: Sometimes it helps to find new words if you put the letters together.)

RECORDRAINWEEK

Any guesses? _ _ _ _ _ _ _ _, _ _ _ _ _ _!

SUBSTITUTION CIPHERS are created when one letter in a word is substituted for any other letter, number, or symbol. The more randomly each letter is assigned, the more difficult the message is to decode.

A basic substitution cipher simply shifts letters into a different position, like this one, where each letter of the English alphabet was moved three spaces ahead.

A B C D E F G H I J K L M N O P Q R S T U V W X Y Z
D E F G H I J K L M N O P Q R S T U V W X Y Z A B C

Based on the letters above, can you decode this message?**

L V L W W K H Z H H N H Q G B H W?

That may have been a little challenging, but if you want something harder . . . can you decode a new message without a code sheet? This one will be difficult, because this time, the alphabet has not just been shifted. Each letter is replaced by a different, randomly chosen letter.***

HJAM FUM U IAEEAZXQH ZRIV—TRX IAI AH!

Here are a few hints (though not all will apply to this code):
In English, the five most commonly used letters, in order, are: "E," "T," "A," "O," and "I."
The five most common words are: "the," "of," "and," "to," and "in."
If a single letter is used, the word is either "a" or "I."
The most common letter to begin a word is "T." The most

common second letter in an English word is either an "H," "E," or "O." And "E" is the most common letter to be the third, fourth, or fifth letter in a word.

The code that Meg's father wrote on the yellow paper was an **ACROSTIC**. This is where the first letter, syllable, or word of each line of a poem spells out a message separate from the poem. Could you create an acrostic if the message you want to send is: HELP IS COMING.

Sample:

Hello friends, is everyone

Excited for a day of

Laughter and a fun

Picnic?

Now you try finishing the message!

I

S

C

O

M

I

N

G

The science of codes and ciphers is called **CRYPTOGRAPHY**. **CODES** are when one word or sentence is substituted for another.

CIPHERS are when the letters of a word are mixed up. Both have been used by spies and secret agents throughout history and are still used today—though thanks to computers, they can be far more complex now.

And there are still many old codes that have never been solved. One of the most famous comes from World War II France. Several years ago, the remains of a messenger pigeon were discovered inside an old chimney. The note attached to it was dated June 6, 1944, which was no ordinary day in history. This was D-Day, when the Allies stormed the beaches of Normandy to restore freedom to France. The events of that day may be very important to solving the code.

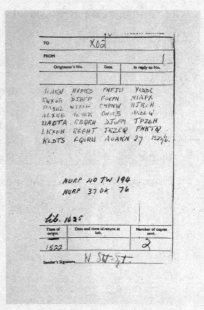

Nobody has solved it yet. Can you figure it out?

* Nice work, Reader!

** Is it the weekend yet?

*** This was a difficult code—you did it!

THE SPECIAL
OPERATIONS
EXECUTIVE

On July 22, 1940, the British formed the Special Operations
Executive (S.O.E.) to conduct secret missions the government
could not officially recognize during the war. These secret missions would include sabotage, information-gathering, spying,
and helping resistance groups organize. Winston Churchill nick-
named them the Ministry of Ungentlemanly Warfare.

Since the government could hardly put out a Help Wanted
sign for spies, they would instead target an individual they
believed had the necessary personality traits and invite them in
for a job interview. If the recruit passed, they were told to report for
a second interview to an address that would be nearly impossible
to reach. Those who made it were officially invited to begin
training. They would learn combat, parachuting, code making,
sabotage, escape work, and how to create and maintain a believable cover while in foreign territories.

Once released for fieldwork, the S.O.E. officer would have a variety of secret weapons and tools at their disposal. In addition to the tools Meg discovers in the book, they might also have a canoe that could travel underwater, a radio disguised as a tree trunk, or fake animal droppings that were really explosives.

Working for the S.O.E. was very dangerous, and both male and female agents did their part to carry out their missions. Not all missions were successful, but a few had major impacts on the war. Some of them include:

THE SAINT-NAZAIRE RAID. Although the S.O.E. suffered heavy losses, their courage and determination resulted in the destruction of a strategic dock, which grounded a German warship that would have been powerful enough to sink the British navy.

OPERATION GUNNERSIDE, in which Norwegian commandos trained by the S.O.E. destroyed a hydroelectric plant that was seeking to develop an atomic bomb for the Germans.

OPERATION FORTITUDE SOUTH, in which inflatable tanks, painted wooden airplanes, and special sound effects convinced the Germans that an army was approaching. No such army existed there, but the ruse was believable enough that the Germans changed their defensive strategy, clearing the way for a successful Allied invasion of Normandy on D-Day.

The Special Operations Executive officially ended on January 15, 1946. No doubt the efforts of these brave men and women made a significant difference in the outcome of World War II.

A TIP FOR DETECTING A SPY

If someone claims to have come from your country, and you suspect they are a foreign spy, a common trick is to ask them questions that anyone from your country would know. But there is a problem with this technique: Spies expect you to use this trick!

Because of that, they will prepare for every possible question. They will know your country's history, its national flower, the geography of a certain area, and bits of trivia that most people who actually are from your country won't know.

That is where you can be extra clever.

Don't ask the suspected spy for information that anyone from your country will know. Ask them for information that most people in your country *wouldn't* know. If they can answer that unusual question, then you might be right to be suspicious.

What questions do you think might trick even the best of spies in your country?

ACKNOWLEDGMENTS

When I was younger, the Sunday paper had a section where they printed a few different codes each week. I always looked forward to them, though it probably frustrated my mom to see half that page torn out before she'd had a chance to read it. Thanks for letting me take that page, Mom.

World War II is a perennial favorite for historical novels, and I think for me, part of the fascination is because it instills in us questions of the choices we would have made had we been thrust into the challenges and horrors of that war, as millions of people were. What an honor it was to be able to write this book and explore some of those choices.

So here's a round of thanks to my seriously amazing editor, Lisa Sandell, for the opportunity of writing this story, and for her endless support and enthusiasm. Because she is my editor, I am a better writer. Because she is my friend, I am a better person.

I also won the agent lottery with Ammi-Joan Paquette,

whose intelligence, encouragement, and wisdom benefit me in every possible way.

Ongoing thanks to my family for staying on this ride with me, allowing me to run ideas past them, and enduring my history fun facts and scattered notes, books, and paper drafts. I stand in awe of each one of them, watching the accomplishments of their lives.

Most of all, thanks to my husband, Jeff, the person I always want at my side to laugh, talk, and continue to build our dreams together. Jeff, you are, now and forever, my best friend. You are the one I choose, every single day.

And I cannot wait for tomorrow!

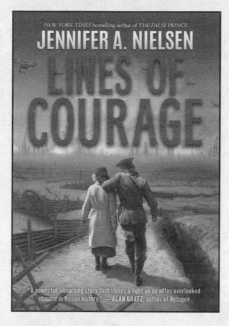

World War I stretches its cruel fingers across Europe, where five young people face the terror of battle, the deprivations of hunger, and all the awful challenges of war.

Felix, from Austria-Hungary, longs for the bravery to resist Jewish deportations.

Kara, from Britain, dreams of earning her Red Cross pin and working as a nurse—or even a doctor.

Juliette, of France, hopes her family can remain knitted together as the war's longest battle stretches on and on.

Elsa, from Germany, hopes her homing pigeon might one day bring her a friend.

And Dimitri, of Russia, wants only to survive the battlefront.

Together, they will discover that friendship and courage can light the way through the most frightening of nights.

In this remarkable exploration of World War I, award-winning author Jennifer A. Nielsen weaves together the extraordinary stories of five children, each of whom holds the key to the others' futures . . . if they are lucky—and brave—enough to find each other.

Read these thrilling stories
from *New York Times* bestselling author
JENNIFER A. NIELSEN

When the Berlin Wall divides her family, Gerta finds herself in a race against time to escape to the West.

When the Nazis occupy Poland, Jewish teenager Chaya decides to fight back…to resist.

When the Russian Cossack soldiers occupying Lithuania arrest Audra's parents, she becomes caught up in the deadly struggle to save her nation.

When one girl fights to save her father from the Nazis, she works with the French resistance and finds herself racing against the clock to crack a crucial code.

When World War I stretches its cruel fingers across Europe, five young people hold the key to one another's futures.